ENTRY WOUNDS

ALSO BY BRANDON MCNULTY

BAD PARTS

ENTRY WOUNDS

A SUPERNATURAL THRILLER

BRANDON MCNULTY

Heather,

Enjoy the book! Best wishes
from a fellow Redeemer grad!

Brandon McNulty

—Ⓜ—
**MIDNIGHT
POINT
PRESS**

ENTRY WOUNDS

Published in the United States by Midnight Point Press.

Cover Design by Damonza.

Hardcover ISBN-13: 978-1-952703-04-1

Paperback ISBN-13: 978-1-952703-05-8

eBook ISBN-13: 978-1-952703-06-5

For My Cioci Sheryl & Uncle Joe

CHAPTER 1

*T*HREE DOWN, *three to go.*

Michelle Saito lifted the barrel of her half-empty snubnose and knocked on the delivery door. The metal-on-metal clang echoed down the alley, all the way to the sidewalk, where a few bums took notice. *Great.* Last thing she needed was witnesses—or, worse yet, company—so she stuffed the revolver in her jacket pocket. The drifters wandered closer, and Michelle glared them down, hoping they'd take the hint. She didn't want to pull the gun on anyone. Not yet.

Deep breaths, deep breaths. Her heart jittered while she sucked in the nighttime fumes of downtown Los Angeles. After spending all her twenty-four years in the city, she yearned to ditch the place, if only for a while. Depending on how tonight's unannounced visit went, she might hit the road within the hour.

The bums finally got the message and wandered off. With the alley to herself again, Michelle knocked and waited.

Peeling yellow decals were pasted to the door. The top one read *Ramen Emperor: Conquering Downtown LA since 1967!* The one beneath read, *Employee/Delivery Entrance ONLY – Customers please use entrance via Central Ave.*

Michelle had considered doing so, but tonight she wasn't a customer. Tonight she was a woman holding a gun—or perhaps it was more accurate to say the gun was holding her. Either way, there was no letting go, not until her sixth kill. Soon she'd get Number Four, but not before garnering info on her final targets.

Growing impatient, she slammed the revolver's butt against the door. It was a humid late-September night, and sweat greased her armpits and lower back. She wanted to remove her jacket, but its deep pocket was the only reasonable hiding place for her gunhand.

Yes, *gunhand*. All one word. That was how she'd come to think of it. Not as a gun in her hand but a complete fusion of flesh and steel. Since she first grabbed it yesterday, she'd been unable to let go.

After more knocking, a metallic pop sounded. The door creaked open. A teenager in an apron and fishnet cap poked his head out.

Michelle tucked her hair behind her ear and cleared her throat.

"I'm here to see your manager," she said. "The Emperor."

"He's not in."

"Then call him. I'm with the health department."

The kid's eyes widened. "Oh. Come on in."

"That's more like it," she said, satisfied that he'd bought the health department routine. It had also worked at her previous stop. She hadn't acted onstage in months, but her skills remained sharp. She wondered if the buyer who wanted the gun could get her a job in Hollywood. She'd prefer that over the money.

In the kitchen, she glanced around and pretended to give a shit. Stacks of pots and pans littered countertops. The sink overflowed with soap suds. The nauseating stench of spoiled shrimp and fish oil suffocated the place. She paced beneath a rickety ventilation system, but the air wasn't any more breathable.

The kid got on the phone and yapped to his boss in Japanese. Michelle couldn't make out a word. She wished she'd learned her parents' native language, but losing Mom and Dad at an early age left her monolingual.

"He'll be here," the dishwasher said. "He said have a seat in the dining area."

"How about joining us?" Michelle said, flicking her head toward the dining area. "Bet you could use a break."

The dishwasher grinned. "Nah, I'm good."

"Join us." She glared at him. "I want company while I wait."

With a nervous chuckle, the dishwasher toweled his hands and followed her.

The main dining area was half-lit at this hour. More than a dozen tables glowed beneath dim lighting. The room reeked of sanitizer, which a college-age waitress was spraying liberally across the tables. She looked up, spotted Michelle, and said, "Oh, excuse me. We're closed."

"I'm with the health department," Michelle said. Glancing across the bar area, she spotted a door marked Celebration Room. Not only did tonight warrant a celebration, but she imagined that such a room would suppress the noise she planned on making. "Your boss is on his way. How about fetching some nice warm sake for the four of us? Let's indulge tonight."

The girl hesitated. "Um, we're not supposed to serve alcohol after closing. Besides, I'm not twenty-one. Neither is he," she said, gesturing at the dishwasher.

"So what?" Michelle said, entering the Celebration Room. "Let's break some rules tonight."

She flicked the lights on. The Celebration Room burst to life. A mural covered the walls, vivid colors leaping from hand-painted artwork depicting scenes from samurai armies to metropolitan Tokyo to Mount Fuji. The sight of Mount Fuji sent a strange tremor through her gunhand. Michelle sat at the oval table in the middle of the room, making sure she faced the doorway. She stared at the impressionistic mural until the tremor faded.

Then she texted her sister two words: *Almost time.*

The waitress and dishwasher entered the room, both holding steaming ceramic cups. Michelle invited them to sit beside her. They set three cups down near her and one across the table for the Emperor. The waitress sat, pushed her sake cup away, and gave a sheepish grin.

"Relax," Michelle said, raising her drink. "I won't bust you."

The dishwasher sat and took a cautious sip.

The waitress frowned. "Don't you have to bust us? You're with the government."

"Underage drinking isn't my concern."

"But still..."

"I'm here for a health-related issue," Michelle said. "Your boss hasn't always made people's health his top priority."

The waitress's eyes went big and wide. "Is it the shrimp?"

Michelle reassured her with a smile. "No, not the shrimp."

A squeal sounded from the main dining area, followed by the metallic slap of a door against its frame. Then footsteps. Michelle straightened in her seat and took a sweet, warm gulp of sake. An old man appeared in the doorway.

The Emperor.

With his droopy face and pale green polo, the Emperor looked more like a retired accountant than the supreme ruler of a ramen shop. The old man wore a fedora, which he reverently removed as he tiptoed into the room. His scalp shined beneath thinning, receding hair. For a moment he glanced at the sake cups with confusion. Then he locked eyes with Michelle.

He cleared his throat. "You're with the health department?"

"Have a seat," Michelle said, her palm burning around the gun in her pocket. As the man lowered himself into the chair, his scalp lined up with the volcanic opening atop Mount Fuji. She slid her finger inside the trigger guard. "Care to guess why I'm here?"

He frowned. "The shrimp?"

She laughed. "What is it with you people and the shrimp? No, I'm here regarding two men who fled the area twenty years ago. They probably changed their names, but you know who I'm talking about."

The old man shook his head.

"Sure you do," she said, her leg jimmying. "One of your ex-yakuza buddies said you mail those two a check each month. Monetary gratitude for what went down twenty years ago."

"Not sure what you're talking about."

"Then get sure." She leaned forward, her eyes hot and moist. "I was there when it happened. I've heard those gunshots every day since. Heard my mother scream. Heard my father hit the pavement. Heard—"

"I should probably leave," the waitress blurted.

"Stay," Michelle said.

Instead of listening, the waitress slid her chair back.

Michelle pulled her hand free and brandished her weapon. The others gasped. Before they could react, she thrust the gun toward the waitress' throat, jamming it hard against her trachea.

The girl shrieked.

"Stop!" the old man said. "Let her go."

"Everybody shut up." Michelle eyed the dishwasher, who sat with both fists clutching his apron. "Go shut the door. Slowly. If you try to run or play hero, she gets a hole in her throat."

The door met its frame and the dishwasher returned to his seat. Tonight's celebration was off to a fine start. Across the table, the old man adopted a stoic demeanor. Amazing how a health inspection ripped his balls off but a live revolver hardened him back into his yakuza self.

"Give me names," Michelle said, stirring the barrel into the girl's neck, forcing a whimper. "Names and addresses. Be smart now. Don't let her blood ruin these gorgeous murals."

The old man stared back. "Do it."

"Wh-what?" the waitress said.

"Go on," he said. "Shoot her."

"I will if you don't tell me," Michelle said.

"Go on. Shoot her. I have no loyalty to her. At least not compared to the level of the two men you seek."

Michelle felt her stomach condense into a hot, solid ball. She squeezed the girl's wrist until she sobbed. "Don't do this to her."

"You're the one doing it." He took out his phone. With a tired sigh he tapped the screen. "Perhaps the LAPD can resolve this."

"Call them and your daughter dies."

The old man snorted. "The waitress you're threatening is of no relation to me."

"I know," Michelle said. She set her own phone on the table and initiated a video call. A college girl appeared on the screen with a blindfold drawn tight across her face. The tip of a knife itched her cheek. Her nervous panting hissed through the phone speakers as Michelle turned the screen toward the old man. "This is your daughter, right?"

He cracked like ice in hot water. Both hands shot across the table. He bumped his cup, spilling sake, as he made a fruitless grab for her phone.

"Guess we found the right girl," Michelle said, raising her voice so her sister Hannah could hear on the other line. "Hey, Slicer, you listening? You're on with the Ramen Emperor. Remember to act dignified."

"No chance of that," Hannah said.

"Unhand her!" the old man said, lunging for the phone. "She's done nothing to you. She's a college student, nothing more."

"Give me names. Now. Or she'll be a college corpse, nothing more."

The old man pursed his lips. Behind his sweaty forehead, his thoughts seemed to spin like flaming wheels. His cheeks twitched as if his face were preparing to rip apart in two directions. Loyalties will do that to people.

"You won't."

"Slicer," Michelle said, "make the Emperor a believer."

On screen, the knife wavered beside the girl's cheek. Michelle held her breath, hoping her sister would deliver. Hannah had planned this whole vendetta, but she tended to hesitate when it came to getting her hands dirty. Across the table, the Emperor looked shaken, helpless. One slice would be enough.

"Cut her. Now."

Nobody moved. Not Hannah, not the Emperor, not the restaurant staffers. Everyone suppressed an urge to act. Finally, the old man broke the tension.

"Your partner is wise," he said, his voice shaky. "Your fight isn't with my daughter but with me."

"Now!" Michelle yelled. "Cut her!"

"Stop this," he said.

"Do it!"

"Think about what you're—"

A staticky scream cut him off. The knife punctured the girl's cheek, forming a bloody dimple around its tip.

Then it happened. From cheek to chin the blade slid, creating a jagged crimson line. The footage on the screen grew pixelated as the girl thrashed wildly, blood leaking from the wound and painting a smeared red wing over her cheek. The thrashing intensified until she toppled from view.

"Enough!" The old man launched to his feet. So did Michelle, who lifted the barrel from the waitress's neck and pointed it across the table. If the old man noticed the gun was aimed at him, he didn't show it. His eyes were fixed on the screen. "Enough. I'll tell you the names."

For a moment, nobody moved. There was no sound but the patter of sake dripping onto the floor. The two staffers shook in their seats, their breaths shuddering. The old man glanced at them, acknowledging them for the first time in minutes. Then he looked toward Michelle.

"Benjiro Orochi and Goro Fujima."

"I need more than their names," Michelle said.

"In the main dining room, check the locked drawer beneath the cash register. You'll find two envelopes with money inside. They're stamped and addressed. I was planning to mail them tomorrow."

"If the drawer's locked, where's the key?"

"My front pocket."

"Slowly place it on the table."

The old man fished out a jingling set of keys.

Michelle ordered the waitress to fetch the envelopes. She gave the waitress thirty seconds. The girl ran out and raced back within twenty. Michelle checked the addresses. One in Texas, the other in Pennsylvania. It appeared she had a long road trip ahead.

No sense sticking around.

"Twenty years ago," Michelle said, eyeing the Emperor, "my parents were murdered in front of me. The bullet that killed my mother caught her in the chest. The one that killed my father tunneled through the right side of his head." She let that sink in a second. "Which would you prefer?"

The old man frowned. "Is there no other way?"

Michelle lined up the barrel with his head. "Look to your left. For your daughter's sake."

Glaring, the old man turned his head.

The gunshot roared.

Four down, two to go.

CHAPTER 2

KEN FUJIMA STOOD outside his classroom on what he hoped would be his final day as a substitute.

The hallways of D. Morgan High School rumbled as his students rushed to beat the third-period bell. Maybe it was his imagination, but everything had a friendly shine today—the students' faces, the pea-soup-colored lockers, even the floors, which hadn't been waxed in ages. Though the school always smelled of wax, the floors never got their share, much like how Ken never got his full-time position. Today, however, things would change. He could feel it.

Today would mark a much-needed fresh start.

The bell rang, and he shook hands with every student on their way in. It was a technique he'd learned from a mentor in college. Shaking hands set the tone and earned kids' respect. Not that it earned him their total respect.

"Yo, Mr. Fuj!" a jock yelled during roll call. "We can't have the test tomorrow."

"Why not?" Ken asked.

"Cause I can't tell the difference between William James and LeBron James."

The other jocks snickered.

"William James and LeBron have more in common than you'd think," Ken said, raising his voice above the piercing squeal of the construction underway outside. "Last night I put together a handout that should make your lives easier."

"Pushing back the test would make our lives easier."

"Don't sell yourselves short." Ken smiled. Around ten years ago he'd been sitting in the same chairs and suffering from the same jitters. He knew how intimidating the first test of the year could be. "I may not know all your names yet, but I know you're all capable of passing. Stay positive."

"Um, Mr. Fujima," a girl up front said. "I think we, like, need to start over."

"Yeah," the jock said. "Let's hit the reset button. No test tomorrow." He slapped his desk. "No. Test. Tomorrow. No! Test! Tomorrow!"

Others picked up the chant.

Ken's smile faded. He could feel himself losing the room. He adjusted his glasses and powered through roll call. Everyone was here except Pete Chang, who routinely slumped in late. Pete wanted nothing to do with this class, which made him Ken's top priority. Once his full-time position kicked in, Ken would sit Pete down to discuss learning strategies and study habits. For now, however, he needed to wrangle in the others.

"William James founded pragmatism," he said, grabbing a piece of chalk off the ledge. "Pragmatism means dealing with your problems in a practical way, as opposed to an idealistic one. So when LeBron gets triple-teamed by a defense—"

"Mr. Fujima," another girl said, waving her hand like she was directing air traffic. "Think you'll be our permanent teacher?"

Heat rushed to his cheeks. Sweat puddled along his back. He wished he'd worn a t-shirt beneath his short-sleeve button-down. "We'll know soon enough."

"Hope you get the position, Mr. Fuj," someone said. "You're nicer than the other subs."

"Thanks. Now, before we get off track—"

The door to the classroom swung open. In trudged Pete Chang. He wore a black hoodie and hung his head as if an anvil were attached to his nose. He took his seat at the front corner of the room without glancing up.

"Morning, Mr. Chang," Ken said, marking his roll sheet. "Any hall passes or late slips?"

Pete took out a notebook and a blue sketch pencil. He flipped to a clean page and started scribbling.

"Mr. Chang?"

The boy kept scribbling.

"Since we're all here now," Ken said, turning his attention to the class, "let's be pragmatic and turn to page sixty."

A goth girl raised her hand.

"Yes?"

"I know we're not supposed to be on our phones," she said, lifting her iPhone above her desk, "but the school website announced the new full-time teacher."

Ken's mouth went dry. The chalk between his fingers dropped to the floor with a click. To steady himself, he planted both hands on his desk. The room seemed to narrow, posters of long-deceased psychologists and philosophers squeezing in on him like they wanted him to join them in that great mystery called death. Outside, the construction machinery grumbled with an ear-wrecking screech.

"Who?" He coughed his words. "Who is it?"

"Hang on," she said. "It's loading. It says...oh."

Oh. Clearly an "Oh" of disappointment. But was she disappointed that he was or wasn't her full-time teacher?

"Oh no." She blushed under heavy makeup. "It's somebody named Trevor Tyson."

Ken stared at the back of her phone. Trevor Tyson? He'd never worked with anyone named Trevor Tyson. Never even heard of him. The guy was probably some outsider they reeled in from Philly or western Pennsylvania. Wherever he came from, it didn't matter.

The job was taken.

Gone.

For Ken, there would be no big turnaround. Not this time, at least. So much for quitting his weekend job and getting his life in order.

The students buzzed with curiosity. Girls wondered out loud whether Tyson was hot. Guys asked if he was related to Mike Tyson. Phones came out. Thumbs patted screens. Somebody found Tyson's Facebook. Girls saw it and squealed. Many hearts throbbed—including Ken's, which flubbed in defeat.

"The website," Ken said. "Does it say when Tyson starts?"

"Monday."

"Well then." He sank into his chair. "Guess you can have a study hall."

Cheers erupted throughout the classroom. The only one who didn't roar with excitement was Pete Chang, who continued sketching in his notebook. Ken wandered over and noticed Pete had scribbled a series of jagged lines. Earlier this week Ken had confiscated an impressive sketch of a crystal cavern, but today it seemed Pete was more interested in grinding his pencil against the paper.

"Everything okay, Mr. Chang?"

Scribble. Scribble.

"You don't seem yourself. Something wrong?"

Scribble.

"We can talk out in the hall if you want."

Scribble.

Out of nowhere a girl by the window exclaimed, "Holy shit, Mr. Fujima!"

Ken should've chided her for the profanity, but he didn't care anymore. "What?"

The girl raised her phone. "This Tyson guy—I creeped on his Facebook and found his relationship status."

"You should ignore that." He shook his head disapprovingly. "Don't get any romantic ideas. Not with a teacher."

"It's not that," she said, blushing. "Tyson's listed as in a relationship—with the principal's daughter."

The news couldn't have struck him any harder if it were strapped to a nuclear missile. "You're kidding."

"For reals," she said. "He's dating Principal Soward's daughter, the one who coaches JV field hockey. Doesn't that make this, uh, what's it called? Neptunism?"

"Nepotism."

When he checked her phone, he almost gagged. Tyson was dating the eldest daughter of the lady who'd hired him. Unreal. One profile picture even depicted the two kissing atop a Ferris wheel.

"What're you gonna do, Mr. Fuj?" someone asked.

"Nothing." Ken tucked his hands in his pockets. It felt like broken glass was stuck in his throat. "I'm sure he's...qualified."

"No way!" a jock said. "Stick it to the principal. Burn her to the ground."

"At least tell someone," a nerdy boy said. "Like the superintendent."

Ken frowned and returned to his desk. "Phones away, please. It's study hall."

"You're not gonna rip Soward a new one?"

Ken had to laugh. "I need to stay professional. Other teaching positions will open up. If not here, then elsewhere."

Chatter spread across the room. Before long, a chant started in the back and rolled forward like a mounting wave.

"Stick. It. To. Soward."

"Stick! It! To! Soward!"

Their support warmed him. No denying that. But the decision had been made and fighting it would hurt him in the long run. The next open position might be his.

Then again, he'd said that last month. And last year. When he returned to teaching after his messy hiatus, he never expected to be subbing this long. Nearly a dozen teachers had retired or left the area, yet he hadn't replaced any of them.

"STICK. IT. TO. SOWARD."

Ken certainly wanted to. The principal had roadblocked him many times, despite his qualifications. Now she was pulling strings at his expense. When would it end?

"STICK. IT. TO. SOWARD."

Perhaps the students were right—he should confront her. Well, maybe not *confront* her, but ask why she turned down his application.

"STICK! IT! TO! SOWARD!"

Yes. He should.

Might be worth the risk.

If he were man enough.

"STICK! IT! TO—"

"Everyone quiet!" Ken straightened his skinny tie. "Behave while I step out."

The class let out a cheer. He was no dummy—he knew they wanted him gone so they could goof off, but the cheer invigorated him nonetheless.

He marched out the door.

CHAPTER 3

THE CLOSER KEN got to Soward's office, the weaker his stride became. With every step, cannon fire boomed inside his chest. How his sternum could absorb such impact was beyond him. He charged onward, rubbing his sweaty hands against his khakis and sucking deep breaths of unusually warm air. Was it just him or had a student started a fire in one of the lockers? The heat seemed excessive for late September in Pennsylvania.

The moment he turned the corner and saw the office's mahogany door, his knees hardened to concrete. Something about this hallway always suffocated him, as if a colorless, odorless poison were seeping through the vent. Now that he thought of it, maybe he should turn back and order an oxygen tank off eBay. Try another time. Play smart. Live to teach another day.

But he'd thought the same thing before and look where it got him. Nowhere. Today he had hard evidence. Something that indisputably exposed her corrupt hiring practices. If he backed down, he didn't deserve the job. Period.

With a wheezy breath, he approached the gates of administrative hell. He gripped the doorknob, remembered to stand tall with his shoulders back, and entered the reception area. An administrator nibbling on a powdered doughnut glanced up. "Principal Soward's on the phone. Mind waiting?"

"N-no." Ken's shoulders slumped. "I'll wait."

There were three seats along the wall. He sat in the one closest to the principal's door. He fidgeted and focused intently on the muffled voice inside. Though he couldn't make out a word, the conversation seemed upbeat. In all the time he'd known Soward, she'd never sounded so pleasant. She even laughed at one point before Ken heard her hang up.

"You can go in," the admin said around a mouthful of doughnut. "Have fun in the lion's den."

Ken forced a smile.

This is it. Stay positive, he reminded himself, *and positive things will happen.*

As he wobbled to his feet, he adjusted his tie, his glasses, his hair. He'd gelled it back this morning for extra confidence, but now it felt oozy, as though his brains were leaking through his scalp.

With a sweaty hand he opened the door.

What the admin referred to as the lion's den, Ken thought of as the torture chamber. Not only did the office sit at the westernmost point of the building, avoiding the morning sun, it contained an absurd number of metal objects. A steel desk stood dead center, topped with a chrome adjustable lamp. The bulb shined over a dented pencil jar containing several pairs of scissors, their blades hiding like sharks beneath the surface. Computer printouts swamped her workspace, some anchored down by tin paperweights. Along the walls ran file cabinets, sealing the room like a cold steel tomb.

The back of Principal Helen Soward's executive leather chair faced him. She pecked at computer keys at the rear desk, coughing before she made a primal, mucus-clearing noise. She reached for a Kleenex, spat into it, and dropped the soiled tissue into her wastebasket before swiveling around.

"Mr. Fujima. Hello." Soward stared him down like a pest she couldn't figure out how to exterminate. She tucked her mustard-colored hair behind her ears, exposing wrinkled cheeks. Many students referred to her as the Mummy, and while Ken wasn't one for name-calling, he found it hard to disagree. The combination of shriveled skin, spray-on tan, and her trademark scowl left her looking like something exhumed from Old Hollywood. "If this is about the pizza party in the teacher's lounge, you're too late to request additional toppings. We already ordered."

"No, it's not that."

"Then whatever it is, make it quick. I'm doing a fire drill in five minutes."

His legs wobbled. "Can I have a seat?"

When he'd left his classroom, he pictured himself charging in here and slapping his hands on her desk like a TV lawyer. Now, however, he trembled as he lowered himself into the chair facing her desk. At eye level was a brass photo frame containing a picture of Soward with her husband and three kids. Each held a hunting rifle and stood behind a deer carcass at their feet. Soward's eldest daughter grinned nearly as wide as in her boyfriend's profile picture.

"I'd like to talk about the open position."

"It's not open anymore. Didn't you get the memo?"

"I did." He clutched his phone. On his screen was the profile picture. He took a shaky breath and tried to make eye contact. "Did you..."

"Speak up, Mr. Fujima."

"Did you..." He cleared his throat. His voice came out a whisper. "Did you congratulate your daughter's boyfriend?"

"Excuse me?" she said. "Speak up."

"I, uh..." He flipped his phone around. "Look."

Soward glanced down, her bony hands folded atop her paperwork. She said nothing, only stared.

It was over. He'd won.

"This isn't fair to me and the other applicants," he said. "What you did was—"

"Hold on." Soward lifted a hand. She grabbed his phone and

studied it—not the screen but the entire device, as if she'd never seen a cell phone before. Her eyes pierced his with a frigid blue gaze. "What's this doing in my office?"

The Mummy lives, he thought.

"Your newest hire," he said. "I looked him up and—"

"Again," she said, shaking his phone. "What's this doing in my office?"

"I'm trying to explain."

"I'll ask one last time. What's this *thing* doing in my office? Because it appears this device"—she slapped the phone down beside her photo frame—"is meant to pressure me into giving you something you want. Are you trying to extort a promotion, Mr. Fujima?"

"No—I just want to be taken seriously."

"I took every application seriously." She rose to her feet. "Do you honestly think I would dole out a job without regard for qualifications?"

"No."

"Do I look stupid to you, Mr. Fujima?"

"No, but—"

"Then get out." She stormed past him and opened the door. "In fact, I'll escort you out since I have to pull the fire alarm. By the way, who's covering your class?"

He swallowed hard.

"Nobody?" She fumed past the admin's desk. "Wonderful. You left your class unattended. How professional."

Ken hurried alongside her, trying to match her gait as they headed down the hall. "I want the job, Mrs. Soward. I have experience—years of it. I won awards. My students had the highest test scores in the area. Even now I sacrifice my lunch breaks to help students if they need it. I always put them first. Isn't that the whole point of what we do here?"

"The point?" She stopped at the fire alarm and curled her fingers around the lever. "The point, at least from my perspective, is to hire the appropriate candidate. You may have experience, but there's a good reason your previous school fired you. Or am I wrong?"

A thousand knives poked his stomach. *She just had to go there.* He wanted to tell her off, or at least tell her she was wrong, but he knew she'd never see it that way. The people who controlled his life never saw things his way.

"Can I say one thing?" he asked. "In my defense?"

Soward narrowed her eyes.

The lever dropped, and the bell rang its shrill, machine-gun chime.

CHAPTER 4

THOUGH THE FIRE drill lasted only fifteen minutes, a siren wailed inside Ken's head all morning. Everywhere he went, alarms sounded, his mind urging him to get out of this school, this town, this life. Rather than heeding the warning, however, he oversaw two more study halls before wandering into the cramped second-floor teacher's lounge.

There he was greeted by the tangy scent of fresh hot pizza. Ken took a window seat over by the fridge and lifted a cardboard lid to reveal a steaming pie covered in hot peppers and extra sauce. It was from Gerry's on Carey Ave, and on any other afternoon he would've devoured half the pie before reaching for a napkin. Today, however, the sight of melted cheese left him queasy. He sank into his chair and stared across the table at two brand-new student teachers who would likely obtain full-time positions before him. They tore at mozzarella strings without a care in the world.

Sighing, he glanced out the window. Beyond the faculty parking lot stood a wall of evergreens that stretched toward the distant gray line that was Interstate 81. Tiny cars and trucks flitted by. Some approached the exit near Walmart, where Ken spent his weekends explaining 4K TVs while wishing he were teaching something more valuable.

His thoughts were interrupted as a figure dashed between two parked cars in the middle of the faculty lot. The person ducked behind a sedan, out of sight. Ken slid his chair back against the fridge and craned his neck for a better look. Who was it? A thief? A student? If it were the latter, Ken couldn't blame them for making an early escape.

The lounge door squealed open. In strutted Angela Marconi, the biology teacher. Ken's eyes shot toward her before he could stop himself. She wore a fitted black dress that matched her hair almost perfectly. That hair of hers always left him breathless; when she walked, it swished around her smiling cheeks like a dark, elegant fire. Today her triangular neckline dipped enough to reveal the upper squeeze of her cleavage. He wondered how any boy in her class could concentrate on cell walls and mitochondria.

"Hey, all! Happy Thursday!" Angela said. Her energy brightened the room. As she approached the fridge, Ken realized he was blocking the chrome door. For a moment she studied him; then she grinned. "Do I have to fight you to get my chicken and quinoa?"

"Well, yeah," he said. "No way am I surrendering that quinoa."

Angela burst out laughing. That laugh was part of why he'd been crazy about her ever since he co-chaperoned a field trip with her last year. He didn't consider himself a comedian, but recently he'd been getting a lot of laughs out of her, especially in the past week.

"Tell you what," she said. "Let's call a truce. If you agree to concede, I may let you indulge in a spoonful—just a spoonful, though."

He rubbed his chin, pretending to consider. When she sent him puppy-dog eyes, he caved and slid his chair under the table.

"Thanks." She pulled a container from the top shelf and headed over to the microwave. "You're too good to me, Ken."

Hoping to look casual, he grabbed a pizza slice. He wasn't

hungry, but he took a bite and chewed until he noticed both student teachers smiling at him.

"What?" he said.

"She's looking at you," a guy named Jeff whispered.

Ken waved it off. "She's looking at the pizza. Anything beats quinoa."

"Another sneaky glance," Jeff said. "Corners of her eyes, bro."

Ken glanced sideways and caught Angela in the act. She turned back to the microwave, but not without reaching up to twist a finger through her hair. He felt his stomach float.

"Go for it," Jeff said.

"I can't," Ken said. "Angela's off limits. Remember, her name's *Mrs.* Marconi."

"Not according to that shiny new name plate on her classroom door," Jeff said. "It says *Ms.* Marconi."

"So? It's probably some politically correct thing."

"Maybe. Maybe not. Hell, ask her."

Ken squirmed in his seat, the chair legs squeaking underneath him. There was no denying he was curious about the "Ms." nameplate. And considering how bad his day was going, asking her a private question and looking like a moron wouldn't sink him much lower.

"Angela?" he said. When she turned, he cleared his throat. "I walked past your classroom earlier and noticed your new nameplate. How'd you get it?"

"I asked the custodian," she said, taking the seat beside him. His pulse hiked as she stirred her quinoa, which smelled overdone. "Wait, do you need a nameplate? Oh my God—did you get full-time? That's great!"

Normally he loved her enthusiasm, but now it embarrassed him.

"Not me, no." He shifted uncomfortably.

"Aw, Ken..." She faced him, her lips pouting. "Next time it'll happen for sure."

"Definitely." He pinched his pizza crust. "So what'd you tell the custodian?"

"That I wanted my nameplate updated."

"Updated? Why?"

"Because," she said, "I wanted a letter taken off."

A chill blew through him. Froze him to his seat. He tried to reply, but his jaw wasn't functioning. The student teachers stood, said their goodbyes, and left.

Ken felt the pressure mounting. While Angela stirred her food, he glanced out the window, trying to collect himself, trying to decide how to play this. Whenever he'd spoken with her, she'd never discussed her husband in detail. She'd mentioned the guy a few times, but in the way you'd mention the mailman. Considering that and the fact that she'd been flirty in the past week, Ken liked to believe he had a shot.

Plus, she no longer wore a ring on her finger. That had to be a signal, right? She could be finalizing a divorce for all he knew.

His thoughts were once again interrupted by movement in the faculty lot. That same figure sneaking around. Ken stood for a better look, recognizing his student Pete Chang. The boy crept between cars and SUVs until he reached the chain-link fence separating the parking lot from the forest beyond. He squatted between two vehicles and anxiously shook the fence.

"Any action outside?" Angela asked.

"Yeah, a student's sneaking around."

"Ooo, should be interesting." She stood beside him, their shoulders brushing as she craned her neck for a better look. "Must've snuck out the smoker's door. Oh, wait—that's Pete."

"Yeah, he's in my one class. Was acting strange today."

"How so?"

"He was...mopey, angsty. I asked what was wrong, but he shut me out."

"He's a brilliant artist," she said. "Artistic types usually have their rough stretches."

"My brother was that way." Ken frowned. "That's why I'm worried about Pete. I'd hate for him to—wait, see that?"

The trees twitched behind the fence. Someone wearing a black hoodie emerged. The guy made a "gimme" gesture with his hand, and Pete poked some money through the fence. In return, the hooded man passed him something.

"Great," Ken muttered. "Pete's going down the same path as my brother."

Angela shrugged. "Could just be weed."

"If he wanted weed, he'd wait till after school. Sneaking outside now and risking a week in detention—he's hooked on something else."

"You're probably right."

He pushed his chair in. "I'm gonna talk to him."

"Wait," she said, taking his elbow. "If Pete shut you out this morning, he'll do it again. I have him for a study hall next period. Let me try."

He glanced back outside. Pete snuck back toward school while his dealer vanished into the trees.

Ken balled his hands into fists. This frustrated him like nothing else. On the many occasions he'd witnessed his brother scoring drugs, he always fantasized about breaking the dealer's legs and throwing the asshole down the nearest storm drain. He'd like to do that right now. If only.

"It'll be fine," Angela said, squeezing his elbow. "I'll talk to Pete and figure out how to help. Trust me."

Her smile sent tingling relief through him.

"Thanks," he said, noticing her hand still held his arm. *Now or never.* "Hey, Angela, you know what I hate about our lunches together?"

"What? The smell of quinoa?"

"That too," he said, "but what bothers me is we don't get enough time to talk."

She tilted her head. "Oh?"

"What I'm trying to say is...would you like to get dinner this weekend?"

Her eyes widened. She released his elbow. "Dinner?"

"Yeah." His cheeks burned. "You and me."

"Out in public? I-I don't know about that."

"Oh." He stepped away. "Okay."

"Look, Ken, you're a sweet guy. It's just...things are complicated right now."

"Say no more. Forget I asked." Blood drained from his legs as he stumbled toward the lunchroom door. He bumped into chairs, causing an embarrassing rattle. *Stupid, Ken! Why'd you even think you had a shot?*

"Hey, Ken?"

He stopped short. "Yes?"

"I'm hosting a cookout tomorrow night at six," she said, twirling a finger through her hair. "It's supposed to be the last warm weekend of the year, so there'll be burgers, drinks, swimming, other fun stuff. It'd be great if you could come."

He couldn't tell if she were inviting him out of pity or genuine interest. Maybe it was the latter. He liked to believe so. After all, she hadn't been opposed to dinner, just dinner *in public*. Considering her marital situation, public meals with other men were likely a no-no. This cookout might be the next best thing.

After taking a deep breath he said, "I'll be late. I have to make sure my father gets into bed without any issues. Otherwise, I'll be there."

Her dark eyes smiled. "Is that a promise?"

"Sure," he said. "Can't picture anything stopping me."

CHAPTER 5

DRIVING EAST across the country had a funny way of snuffing the sun below the horizon. Though the clock on the dash read 5:14 pm, that was only true back on the West Coast. Now, out here in the Lone Star State, the two-hour time difference drained life from both the sky and a road-weary Michelle Saito. After driving left-handed for thirteen of the last seventeen hours, she could barely grip the wheel. Fatigue crept beneath her skull. Soreness swallowed her arm. Her fingers cramped in spots she never knew existed.

In the passenger seat, her sister Hannah leaned against the van window, inhaling musty A/C fumes and snoring like a buzzsaw. Eight hours ago Hannah took a snooze pill, and she'd dozed through the entire American Southwest, oblivious to its towering mountains and shaggy desert shrubs.

Now, with the gas needle drooping and Michelle's eyelids doing the same, it was time to refuel their rickety Ford Windstar and swap seats.

"Hey, Hannah," Michelle said. "Wakie wakie."

When Hannah didn't respond, Michelle stretched her gunhand out and knocked the revolver's butt against her sister's shoulder.

"Ow," Hannah muttered. Her voice sounded groggy. "Why you hitting me?"

"Thought you should see Texas."

Grumbling, Hannah pushed her choppy hair from her eyes and stared ahead at the endless highway. "Great. Texas. Woo-hoo."

"Since you're so energized, how about driving the final few hours? There's an exit coming up. It's about time we switched."

At the next gas station Michelle pumped unleaded while Hannah went inside to order hot food. Michelle hadn't eaten since taking the wheel—it was hard to drive and snack with only one hand —and at this point she'd devour anything she could chew. Stomach growling, she whistled along with a country song drawling through the overhead speakers. Some wannabe cowboy bemoaned the death of his dog, the loss of his girl, the misfire of his gun.

Luckily I haven't had that problem yet, she thought. *Two more direct hits and I'll be able to wiggle my fingers again. Yee-fucking-haw.*

Hannah returned with a couple Cokes in one hand and a plastic bag the size of a money sack in the other. When Michelle climbed into the passenger seat, Hannah set the bag on her lap and tucked the sodas into the cupholder. The bag was cozy warm on Michelle's thighs; toasted subs were a road trip favorite. She devoured one, relishing the tangy buffalo flavor until she realized there was no meat in it.

"They forgot the chicken."

"No, they didn't." Hannah buckled herself into the driver seat. "I ordered veggie subs with buffalo sauce."

Michelle groaned. "Hannah, I'm starving. Veggies won't cut it. Go back inside and order one with grilled chicken."

"You go order it."

"I can't. Not with a gun in my pocket."

"Then you're stuck with veggie subs."

Michelle rolled her eyes. "Y'know, I used to think it was cute that you stopped eating meat. Now it's a full-blown pain in the ass."

"So are you."

"Oh, please. I'm pure bliss. That reminds me, I had an amazing idea while I was invading the ramen shop. Picture this—me on a Hollywood set. Cameras, directors, everything. When we take this gun back to our buyer, I'm gonna ask if he has connections. Maybe I can costar in something with Scarlett Johansson. Or Gal Gadot. Or J-Law."

Hannah glared at her.

"What? Can't a girl dream? I've got talent."

"Chelle, you couldn't even convince the Ramen Emperor to give us the names—not until I cut that poor girl's cheek open."

"You're still broken up about that?"

"Yes," Hannah snapped. "I am."

"Well, don't bitch at me. It was your idea."

"Only the old man was supposed to get hurt. Not his daughter."

"Relaaax," Michelle said. "I bet she's fine."

"Oh, sure. She probably loved waking up in the hospital today."

"Depending on what painkillers they gave her, you may be right."

Hannah didn't laugh. She sat there staring at the steering wheel.

"Try inserting the key into the ignition," Michelle said coyly. When her comment earned no reply, she took another bite of her meatless sub and said, "You think too much. Sometimes when you make mistakes, you gotta let things ride."

"I can't stop hearing that girl's screams," Hannah said. "Can't stop feeling the knife cutting through her face. And the blood, Chelle —I didn't know people's cheeks had so much blood in them."

Michelle set her sub back in the wrapper. Gone was her appetite. "Ready to hit the road? Maybe it'll take your mind off things. Either way, I need you to drive. I haven't slept in over thirty hours. Can you do that much for me? For Mom and Dad?"

Hannah frowned at the wheel. She turned the key.

As Michelle drifted in and out of sleep, she grew feverish. Her forehead burned while the rest of her shivered. Then something strange happened. While she dozed against the window, her gunhand, which had been resting in her lap, moved on its own. At first she thought it was nothing. Just a stray twitch, a reflex, or her body overreacting to the greasy meal. But upon opening her eyes, she watched her wrist bend firmly toward her left.

Toward Hannah in the driver seat.

The hell?

With her free hand Michelle clutched the weapon and steered the barrel toward the passenger door. Her heart rate soared as anxiety crept beneath her freezing flesh. To counter her nerves, she drew deep breaths of the stale air, counting to ten several times before her pulse settled.

Exhausted, she leaned her head against the window. The moment she shut her eyes, hideous thoughts cluttered her mind. Red, hateful ones. She recalled when she was a toddler and Hannah gave her an unwanted haircut with a pair of safety scissors. After Michelle saw herself in the mirror, she bawled for hours. The next day she retaliated by firing a squirt gun at Hannah's eye with enough accuracy to warrant a trip to the optometrist. But now as that memory replayed itself, the details changed. Instead of a squirt gun it was the revolver in Michelle's grasp. And when she pulled the trigger, little Hannah's head burst like a watermelon.

Michelle shook awake. She gasped. Found herself staring at the nighttime highway ahead.

It was a dream, nothing more.

But a cold stiffness cuffed her wrist, as if the circulation were cut off. Her gunhand angled itself toward Hannah again, wrist bent sideways to the point of snapping.

Michelle grabbed the revolver. She tried redirecting it away from her sister, but her wrist wouldn't budge. She applied more force, using all her strength, growling through her teeth.

"Chelle?" Hannah glanced over. "What's wrong?"

A nasty urge overtook Michelle. The sensation was fueled by a lifetime of sisterly disappointment, irritation, and betrayal. Like the unwanted haircut. Or when Hannah wrecked Michelle's first car—a blood-red Chevy—on the LA freeway. Or, most prominently, when Hannah put their parents in fatal danger.

Michelle couldn't understand why these memories were bothering her. Normally they didn't. After all, her hair grew back. The Chevy was replaced. And their parents would have been murdered anyway.

Right?

No. Her vicious mind insisted otherwise. Bitter memories swarmed, corrupting the image of her bossy big sister. She hated every offense, every indiscretion. The list of lifetime grievances mounted and mounted until the gun targeted Hannah's face.

Without hesitation, Michelle pulled the trigger.

CHAPTER 6

KEN WHEELED his father into the moonlit bathroom and parked him next to the toilet. They each took a deep, audible breath. Next came the fun part. Ken straightened his back and squatted so he and his father were at eye level. Dad never looked him in the eyes at this stage. Needing help getting onto the toilet crushed the old man. Hell, it crushed him that he needed help, period.

"Ready, Dad?"

"Go ahead, Kenny."

Ken took another deep breath, inhaling the lingering scent of ocean surf body wash. The air was still warm from the shower he'd taken after dinner, and the room had a cozy, sauna-like atmosphere.

"All right," he said, leaning in and wrapping his arms around his father's back. Dad hugged onto him. "On three. One, two, three."

Ken strained as he hoisted Dad out of his wheelchair. With a twist of his waist, he shifted Dad toward the toilet, centering him above the booster seat. Through gritted teeth, he said, "Get your pants."

Dad released his secure hold across Ken's back. One hand grabbed a nearby support bar while the other went to work on the waistband of his pajama pants. A rustling sound followed as he tugged them down. Ken's shoulders and lower back strained until Dad finally signaled him with a pat on the back.

He lowered his father and gasped with relief.

"Whew." Ken rubbed his lower back. "Mission accomplished. I'll leave you to your bowel movement. Give me a yell when you're done."

"Thanks, Kenny." Dad reached up and patted his cheek. "Without you, I wouldn't give a shit."

Ken laughed. "I'm sure you would. We'd just have to do extra laundry."

In the kitchen Ken double-checked Dad's nighttime meds and got a pan ready for omelets in the morning. He had a feeling tomorrow would be a great day, and not just because they had a fresh carton of liquid egg whites. Assuming Dad didn't run into any complications, Ken would visit Angela tomorrow night. Sure, it wasn't a legit date, but his gut told him the future was bright.

Then the doorbell rang. Four times in quick succession. Only one person would bother them at this hour.

Yawning, he answered the door.

Outside stood Robby. While he twitched in place, his shaggy chin-length hair shook across his face. Sometimes Ken thought his brother kept his hair long just to avoid making eye contact during these awkward meetings.

Robby frowned. "Where's Dad?"

"On the throne. Wanna leave a message?"

Robby swiveled his head, glancing at his girlfriend's beat-up Kia parked outside the tavern next door. The Backfield Bar spilled neon light along the sidewalk, turning his girlfriend in the driver seat lizard green. Robby caught her attention and shrugged. In response she lifted her purse, suggesting they wanted money. That was all the evidence Ken needed to shut the door.

"Wait, Ken!" Robby stopped the halfway-shut door. "I gotta see Dad."

"Don't worry. He's doing well."

"C'mon, let me in. For shit's sake, he's my father."

More like your piggy bank, Ken thought. *Would it kill you to help around here? The two of us could lift Dad on and off the toilet without a hitch. Hell, you could even take care of him during the daytime. Then we wouldn't need a nurse.*

"C'mon," Robby said. "Gimme two minutes."

"Best I can do is relay a message."

"Fine. I got a job interview. Office gig in Scranton. It's tomorrow, and I need new clothes."

"New clothes. Right."

"I'll show you." Robby slapped at his pockets until he found his phone. He tapped the screen and showed him a men's dress shirt that was on sale for $19.99. Then a pair of black slacks on sale for $29.99. "Only need fifty bucks. Then I can march into that interview looking like a man with a plan."

"How about you borrow my clothes?"

"They're too big on me," he said, stretching out his narrow arms. "I'll look like a total clown."

"Dad's not coughing up fifty bucks. Not after last time."

"But this is legit."

"Heard that before."

"I don't always mean it. This time I do. I'm sick of feeling useless. Can't you tell? You're supposed to be able to tell. It's like with those kids you teach. You say you can sense when they want to work harder. Can you sense me?"

Ken said nothing.

Robby hung his head. His hair dangled like the legs of a dead spider. After a heavy sigh, he picked himself up. "Tell Dad if he can spare fifty bucks, I need it."

"He said he's not giving you a dime until—"

"Yeah. I know." Robby scratched his scruffy cheek. "See ya around, Ken."

As Robby trudged down the sidewalk, Ken recognized that dejected stride. He too had moped around quite often these past couple years. Neither of them had been able to catch a break, and Robby continuously destroyed himself every chance he got. Seeing his brother trudging away made Ken wonder if he'd added to the destruction.

"Robby," Ken said, reaching into his back pocket. "I'll make you a deal."

Robby spun around. "You'll talk to Dad?"

"Need a favor," Ken said, peeling a few bills from his wallet. Robby's eyes pounced on the money. "Tomorrow evening I'm going to a party. Starts around six. Think you can drop by and babysit Dad?"

"Me?" Robby blinked. "If I set foot in there, Dad'll run me over with his chair."

"I'll talk him into it."

"Okay. Yeah. Hell yeah. I'm in." He reached for the money, but Ken pulled it back.

"Bring me the receipt. Got it? And I want to hear how the interview went."

"You'll hear great things."

Ken handed him the money.

Robby tucked the bills away in his pocket. He then shook Ken's hand, squeezing tight with his slim, reedy fingers. "How about this handshake, huh? Think the interviewer will be impressed?"

Ken squeezed back. "Don't let me down."

CHAPTER 7

PAIN SWALLOWED Michelle in a hot purple blaze. It consumed her entire body, a widespread warning siren that quieted a little, allowing her to recognize specifics. Her collarbone came into sharp, screaming focus. Then her neck. Elbow. Wrist. There was a bloody taste in her mouth and a dull ringing in her ears. Upon opening her eyes, she noticed a smear of blinking light. Her cheek lay on hard plastic—the van's dashboard, she realized—and after picking herself up, she spotted withered brown shrubs crammed against the front headlights.

Did we hit a shrub? she thought groggily. *Wait, they don't plant shrubs in the middle of the highway. And highways are supposed to be paved, not covered in dirt. What's going on here?*

Gingerly, she twisted her neck toward the driver's seat. "Hannah? What the hell's going—Oh *shit!*"

The memories tumbled into place. They'd been driving toward Dallas until Michelle aimed for her sister's head and fired. Then came squealing tires and a chaotic blur. Now Hannah hung draped over the steering wheel, head drooping toward the window.

Her eyes tear-soaked, Michelle leaned forward to give her sister a clumsy sideways hug. Hannah was still warm, and when Michelle rested her chin on her sister's upper back, she sensed movement. The subtle rise and fall of breath.

Michelle peeled her sister off the steering wheel and saw her face was clean. Hair lay smeared across her forehead, stuck there by sweat, not blood.

"Hannah," Michelle said, shaking her. "Wake up."

Hannah coughed. Her eyes opened.

Michelle did a mental backflip in celebration. *She's okay! The gunshot must've missed.*

Hannah blinked several times before turning her head. For a moment she appeared as though she were struggling to register Michelle's presence. Then she hopped in her seat and yelled, "What the fucking fuck! You almost killed me!"

Before Michelle could reply, Hannah grabbed Michelle by the hair.

"Hannah, stop!" Michelle could feel her scalp lifting from her skull. The two sisters wrestled until the motor rumbled and the van crunched over the shrubs. "We're moving—hit the brake!"

Hannah stomped the brake and parked the van. Then she resumed her outburst, shoving Michelle against the passenger window.

A throbbing purple wave overtook Michelle's mind. Ugly, murderous thoughts cropped up again. Oh, how she wanted to stick the barrel between Hannah's teeth and fire. One juicy blast would be enough. Better yet, make it two. Or three. Or—

No, enough. This was her sister. The only person she trusted. What was she thinking? Why had she shot at Hannah like that?

Michelle took her sister's hand. "I didn't hurt you, did I?"

"Came awful fucking close!" Hannah gestured toward her window. In the center was a bullet hole surrounded by spiderweb cracks. Had Michelle been slightly more accurate, the window would be fine and Hannah would be dead. "What were you thinking?"

Michelle pointed her gunhand toward the floor. She was embarrassed to admit the revolver had manipulated her wrist and her thoughts. "I...don't know."

"You almost *shot* me," Hannah said, sounding heartbroken.

"I didn't mean to." Michelle leaned across the armrest and hugged her tight. "I was sleepwalking or something. It won't happen again. I'll shoot myself before I even consider shooting you."

"Don't shoot either of us." Hannah returned the hug with a nervous squeeze. She tied her hair into a messy ponytail and glanced outside. "Where's the highway?"

Michelle thumbed over her shoulder. "That way. But we can't let anyone see that busted window. Can you roll it down?"

Hannah tried. It slid partway down before getting stuck. That would be a problem. They couldn't drive into Dallas without someone noticing the bullet hole.

Michelle climbed out and went around to the driver side. She flung open the door and surveyed the damage before slamming the revolver against the window. A few good hits sent glass spilling in chunks and shards.

She turned to Hannah. "Better hope it doesn't rain."

"If it does, you're driving."

They merged back onto the highway and drove toward Dallas. Michelle grabbed her phone off the floor and reattached it to the windshield. According to the GPS app, they were an hour from their destination. An hour from kill Number Five. She double-checked the name and address on the envelope. Benjiro Orochi was the target, 24 Warm Haven Road the location. Only a matter of time.

Yet she could barely resist her urge to shoot.

If only this damned revolver had a safety. Better yet, she wished she could remove the remaining bullets, but the cylinder wouldn't open. Nor was she able to empty the gun by firing continuously— she'd already tried that on Tuesday. The only way to reduce the ammo supply was by taking a life.

The mere thought caused her wrist to bend toward her sister.

Shit. Michelle grabbed the revolver and stuffed it between the seat and the door. She panted, drawing shaggy breaths.

"What's wrong?" Hannah asked.

"Drive faster."

"I'm already doing fifteen over the limit. You wanna get pulled over?"

"No, but..." Michelle didn't know how to explain, but she figured she should say something rather than be stranded with her thoughts. "Before I shot at you, I had this dream. Remember when we were kids, and I hit your eye with a squirt gun?"

"Hard to forget."

"Well, that memory was in my head. But instead of shooting you with a squirt gun, I shot you with my snubnose." She buried her arm deeper. Sweat soaked her sleeve. "Then I wanted to do it in real life. I wanted it like a trip to the bar after a shitty night's work. Wanted it more than anything."

The van gathered speed. Hannah's knuckles tightened along the wheel. "Did you feel this way back in LA?"

"No. Only now."

"And you still want to kill me?"

Michelle hesitated. Her hand burned while chills slithered through her body. "I think I can hold out if you hurry."

Hannah did just that. They flew off the highway ramp and into the suburbs. The motor growled as they burst through intersections, blew past stop signs, and whipped along the corners of wide suburban streets. They built speed until the GPS announced they'd reached their destination.

Hannah thumped the brake. The sound of squealing rubber compounded Michelle's hatred for her. *How dare she generate such an irritating noise. How dare she park the van. How dare she run outside.*

The farther Hannah ran, however, the less Michelle wanted to kill her.

But the gun was hungry. It hadn't eaten since last night. It could sense a meal nearby. Right up the sidewalk. Behind the door bearing the number 24 waited a meal named Orochi.

Michelle stumbled onto the porch and pounded the door until the front window lit up.

"Help!" she shouted. "Help me!"

Footfalls thumped inside. Along with them came the shriek of a squalling baby.

The door pulled back to reveal a withered, gray-haired man wearing a #1 Grandpa t-shirt. Worry wrinkles spread across his face. He glanced back toward the wooden crib in his living room before facing Michelle.

"What?" he asked, breathless. "What's the emergency?"

She put the emergency right through his forehead.

CHAPTER 8

"GUESS WHO'S COMING OVER TONIGHT," Ken said, sitting across from his father at the breakfast table. The sunlit kitchen smelled of toasted rye and melted cheese. Their egg-white omelets had turned out near perfect—so well that Dad hadn't found any reason to nitpick yet. Ken hoped the A+ meal would put his old man in a receptive mood. Dad wasn't gonna like what he heard next.

"Who's coming?" Dad said, biting into a piece of toast.

"First off," Ken said, poking at his omelet, "I should mention that I got invited to a cookout tonight. It starts at six, and I was hoping to make an evening of it, but obviously I didn't want to leave you here fending for yourself. Then I had a great idea—what if, while I'm at the cookout, you spend time with Robby?"

Dad grumbled and pushed away his breakfast plate. His wheelchair creaked as he wiped a fleck of egg white from his mouth before he threw his napkin down. The last warm weekend of the year had turned aggravatingly chilly.

"Robby isn't welcome here," Dad said, his tone measured despite his obvious disgust. "Not until he gets his act together and returns your mother's jewelry. Those are my terms. And by the way, would it kill him to ask how my legs are doing? He can ask for money—that's for sure—but he never asks about my well-being."

Ken sliced into his omelet. "Tonight you should tell him that face-to-face."

"What's the point? He's got your mother's ears. He won't listen." Dad waved his hand as if sweeping away the conversation topic. "Besides, I can handle myself tonight. You enjoy your party. Long as I'm parked in front of the TV in time for the Dodgers game, I'm happy."

"What about getting into bed?"

"I've got two working arms, Kenny. Besides, you installed that handlebar along the wall near my bed. What was the point of that if I don't use it?"

"How about I move the kitchen TV into your bedroom?" Ken said, pointing his fork at the TV on the counter. A news reporter droned about a local drug bust. "That way, I can get you into bed before I leave tonight."

"That TV's too small for the game. Might as well hand me a radio. Besides, bed is no place to watch TV. Bed is for sleep and sleeping with." He smirked. "Which reminds me, any ladies at this party tonight?"

Ken sprinkled pepper over his omelet. "Some."

"Any of interest?"

Ken shrugged. "Maybe."

"Atta boy!" Dad clapped the tabletop. The noise woke Hopper, their pit bull, who gingerly rose to his feet beside the basement door. Hopper had suffered a leg injury before they rescued him and never fully recovered his stride—not that they loved him any less for it. As he staggered over to the table, Dad reached down to pet his fine gray fur. "Hear that, Hopper? Uncle Kenny's gonna be clinking glasses with a stunning young *onna* tonight." He looked up. "What's her name?"

"Angela. She's hosting the party."

"Let's hope she sends the other guests home early."

"Wouldn't count on that. Not even sure if she's interested. That much is a mystery."

Dad grinned. "You need a little mystery in your life, Kenny. Be a good detective and investigate thoroughly tonight."

"Dad, you're a creep."

"Son, you're a prude. Time you moved on from Olivia. It's not good to dwell on her, especially five years after the fact."

"I know that." Ken scraped at his plate. "Can we not talk about this during breakfast? Or ever?"

"I'll stop mentioning it if you bring home this Angela. It'd be nice to see you happy again, Kenny. We've had nothing but doom and gloom since your mother passed. Speaking of, did you see yesterday's letter from the attorneys? Think we might have that damned negligent doctor on the ropes."

"Nice. I'll read it after school."

"Atta boy. Now tell me about this Angela. Does she—"

The landline rang. Ken popped the corded phone off its hook. "Hello?"

"Goro?" The voice coming through sounded urgent, panicked. "Goro, you may be in danger. Last night in Texas—"

"Whoa, wait," Ken said. "This isn't Goro. This is his son, Ken."

"Put your father on the phone. Tell him it's Takahashi."

Heart racing, Ken cupped a hand over the receiver. "Dad, who's Takahashi?"

Dad's eyes widened. "Give me the phone."

Though Dad spoke to the man in a calm, measured tone, there was no mistaking the stress written across his face; he would've been dominated by a novice poker player. In reply he gave short, clipped answers entirely in Japanese. He mostly sat there, listening. At one point he flinched and said, "A baby?" but little else. Dad concluded the conversation with a thank you.

"What was that about?" Ken asked, hanging up the phone.

"Nothing." Dad dropped a piece of toast into Hopper's mouth. "Just an old friend checking in."

"You mean a yakuza friend." Ken's chest went tight. "Someone after you?"

"Course not."

"Takahashi said you were in danger."

"He exaggerates. That's why he never made lieutenant."

"What'd he say?"

"He said my son should enjoy his party tonight."

"Are you in danger? Be honest. You owe me that much."

"Fine." He sat up straight in his wheelchair. Stared ahead with steely, ageless eyes. "One of my yakuza brothers was murdered last night in Texas. Takahashi worried I might be targeted next, but that's not the case."

"H-how do you know?"

"Because it's my legs that are numb, not my brain. Believe me, I'd recognize danger, and this isn't it. So quit worrying and give your father some space. A dear friend of his died."

Ken had little clue how the yakuza worked. Mom had insisted on never discussing Dad's involvement with the Japanese mob, and now Ken's lack of knowledge left his mind whizzing with nightmarish possibilities, all of which ended with Dad sitting in a bloody wheelchair.

"You sure everything's okay?" Ken asked. "We could book a hotel for a couple nights. Weather out the storm."

"Don't be ridiculous. Get to school." Dad sipped his coffee, then eased back into his chair with a wistful smirk. "Besides, if anybody comes after me, they'll be the ones in danger."

CHAPTER 9

KEN SHOOK hands with each student who shuffled into psych class. Though this would be his last day teaching them, he still wanted their respect. Anyone's respect, really. That particular commodity was hard to come by, especially in this building.

"Mr. Fujima!" a girl yelled after roll call. "Did the principal change her mind? Are you gonna be full-time?"

"Someday." He shifted awkwardly. "Grab your textbooks and—"

"Can we vote?" she asked. "Yesterday before the fire drill, we were saying what a great teacher you are. I mean, we really do know who William James is. We just pretended not to so you'd push back the test."

He chuckled. "Thanks. But sadly, students can't vote on who teaches them."

A jock yelled out, "We can write a petition though!"

"I'll start it," another boy said, tearing off a sheet of paper. "C'mon, everybody sign it."

Bursts of Friday morning approval sounded throughout the classroom. Their kind words brought wet heat to Ken's eyes. He turned to the chalkboard, marking down page numbers while he collected himself. He knew all the petitions in the world wouldn't change Soward's mind, but the gesture moved him.

"Once you're done signing my death warrant," he said, garnering laughs, "turn to the chapter on LeBron's cousin William James."

The petition traveled up and down the aisles until it reached Pete Chang in the front row. Pete had showed up on time today but brought the same gloomy attitude as yesterday. He stared transfixed at the petition as though it carried hidden meaning.

Ken approached him. "Mr. Chang, you need a pen?"

He stared.

"Something wrong with the list?"

He stared.

"If you don't want to sign it, I won't take offense."

He lifted the sheet and tore it in two.

Nearby students flinched. One boy called out, "Yo, what the hell!"

Pete ripped it several more times, gathered the confetti together, and carried it to the wastebasket. Without a word, he dumped the scraps and left the room.

"Everyone, begin reading the chapter," Ken said, hurrying out the door. "Underline anything that doesn't make sense."

He spotted Pete halfway down the hall. The boy's shoes squeaked as he ran past the corner classroom, knocking against a locker with an echoing metal bang. Ken gave chase. When he turned the same corner, he found the hallway empty. No trace of Pete.

The only nearby door led to the custodian's office, which was off limits to both teachers and students. Ken tried the door and found it unlocked. Inside was a converted restroom with tool cabinets stacked beside a lone toilet stall. The place stank of lemon floor cleaner. He held his breath and noticed a pair of sneakers beneath the stall.

Standing by the sink, he said, "Mr. Chang, you forgot the hall pass."

The boy didn't respond. With teenagers, you could rarely tell what was going on in their heads. Sometimes they clued you in, but Pete wasn't surrendering a word.

Sighing, Ken leaned his forehead against the chilly metal stall door. "Did I say something that upset you?"

Silence again.

"Something giving you trouble?" he asked, searching for a grappling point. He didn't want to bring up yesterday's drug deal. That would upset the boy even more. "I saw your sketch yesterday, the one with jagged lines. It seemed...uninspired. You've drawn better."

Pete didn't bite.

"Any students giving you a hard time? You don't have to name names. But if something's up, maybe I can coach you through it."

More silence. The lemon odor was wearing Ken down.

"Girl trouble? Is that it?"

A shuffling sounded inside the stall.

Must've struck a nerve. Either the kid got rejected or dumped. Maybe by his first love. Could be using drugs as a coping method.

"Whatever's bugging you, you're stronger than that. You just need to hang in there. Maybe this girl will change her mind about you. I've seen it happen. Women change their minds." He thought of Angela Marconi and the nameplate on her classroom door. "Best thing to do is carry yourself with dignity. Storming out of my class like that won't win anyone's heart."

"Whatever."

Finally a spoken word. Now Ken needed to seize this opportunity.

"Pete, I want to make sure you're okay." He paused before adding, "You remind me of my brother."

"Pfft. Why, cause I'm Asian?"

"Because you're an artist. My brother Robby used to draw nonstop when he was your age. He wanted to work for Marvel, but after high school, he lost focus. Eventually he pieced himself back together, but it didn't last. I'd hate to see you end up that way."

Pete sat silent.

Ken peeled his forehead off the stall door. He took a hall pass from his pocket and slipped it through the door crack. "Here, hang on to this. I don't want you getting a detention."

After a moment's hesitation, Pete took the pass.

"Listen," Ken said, "if you don't trust me, that's fine. But if there's another adult you trust, don't hesitate to—"

His words were cut short as the custodian's door opened behind him.

In stepped Principal Soward with her trademark scowl.

"Mr. Fujima." No part of her face moved except her mouth. "You left your class unattended again. I walked past it and found chaos."

"Mrs. Soward, I—"

"*Principal* Soward," she corrected, peering past him. She noticed Pete's shoes beneath the stall. "This is the janitor's closet. Why are you in here?"

"Came to check on a student," Ken said. "Pete rushed out, and I worried he might be sick."

The stall door creaked inward. Pete emerged, hanging his head as he shouldered past them and fled out into the hall.

"Young man," Soward snapped, reaching after him. "Get back here. Hey—I'm talking to you. That's a detention!"

Pete hurried down the hall.

Soward faced Ken, her penciled eyebrows pinched together so tightly he expected her forehead to rip open. She glared at the stall, then back at him. "Something reeks in here, and it's not the toilet cleaner. I don't like this, Mr. Fujima. A student shouldn't be disappearing along with a beleaguered substitute like yourself. Especially not a substitute with your history."

"My history?" That was the last place he wanted this conversation to go. He held up both palms. "Listen, whatever you might've heard, those rumors aren't true."

"Rumor or not," she said, "I don't want you alone with any student—male or female—for any reason."

"You need to understand. I was worried about Pete. He's been acting strange lately."

"So have you. And I don't tolerate odd behavior from educators. Unless your goal is to get banned from this teaching district, I recommend straightening yourself out." She planted her fists on her hips. "Do I make myself clear?"

His mouth went dry. There were a million points he could've made in his defense, but he knew better: that million would ultimately add up to zero. It didn't matter that he had a student's best interest at heart. All that mattered under this roof was the word of Principal Helen Soward.

"Return to your classroom, Mr. Fujima."

CHAPTER 10

THE DAY ONLY GOT WORSE. When six o'clock arrived, Robby did not.

Ken waited on the front porch, fists clenched as he watched the sun sink toward the horizon. Before long it was past seven, and his brother wasn't answering texts. Chances were, Robby wasn't ignoring him because the job interview went well. More likely, the fifty bucks Ken loaned his brother had gone toward a narcotic nap.

"He's not coming, I take it?" Dad asked when Ken reentered the living room.

"Apparently not."

"Surprise, surprise." Dad muted *Wheel of Fortune*. "Told you, Kenny."

"After all the times I helped him..." Ken gritted his teeth. "It's like I can't trust my own family."

"Not true." Dad patted his arm. "You can trust me and the pooch."

Hopper lifted his head from the couch cushion. His tongue drooped from his mouth in a doggy grin.

"Come on, Hopper," Ken said, rubbing his head. "You've earned a can of Blue Buffalo for dinner."

"What about me?" Dad said. "Have I earned a plate of your mother's curry?"

"I'll start the rice."

Even though Mom had been gone two years and Ken had cooked the curry dozens of times, he still double-checked the recipe. It was in a scrap book containing photos from the '90s, back when they'd lived in LA. In one photo the family sat at the table while Mom scooped a glob of curry onto Dad's plate. Dad looked preoccupied in the photo.

Preoccupied by what? Ken wondered. *An attempt on his life?* Ever since that phone call this morning, he'd been dreading a visit from the West Coast yakuza. Though it probably wouldn't happen, he couldn't stop picturing scenarios where men in black suits drop-kicked through the living room windows, ripped Dad out of his wheelchair, and snapped his neck or shot his brains out or impaled him with a katana like they did in the movies.

Ken shut the scrapbook and started dinner.

By the time the meal reached the table, a rich, spicy aroma had claimed the house. The air tasted of calories, and before Ken sat down his stomach was half-full. Dad ate slowly, savoring every mouthful. As Ken tucked a forkful of short grain rice into his mouth, he closed his eyes and pictured Mom and Robby at the table, everyone alive, healthy, and getting along.

"Excellent, Kenny," Dad said, scraping the plate clean. "Nothing will ever top your mother's cooking, but this comes close. Takes me back in time."

"Yeah." Ken sighed. "Wish she were here."

"You and me both." Dad glared at the stack of mail on the counter. "I'll tell you, I hope that damned doctor gets thrown in jail. You saw what the attorneys said, right? About those kickbacks?"

"Dad, let's not get into it tonight. I'm not in the mood."

"All right." He wiped his lips. "What time you heading out?"

Ken glanced at the kitchen window. Shadows masked the back-yard and the outside world beyond. For all he knew, assassins could be camped in the garden, waiting for him to leave. The thought spread icy tension across his shoulders.

"Soon." He grabbed his plate. "But I won't be gone long. Half hour, tops."

"Hardly enough time to woo a prospect."

"I got a shift at Walmart tomorrow."

"Call off. Enjoy yourself for once."

"I need the money."

"Oh, come on. We can get by."

"Dad..."

"Don't 'Dad' me. Enjoy your party. Have some drinks with a girl. That's what I'd be doing if I were you." He scraped his plate, his expression wistful.

Ken frowned. "To tell you the truth, I'm worried about you."

"I can climb into bed."

"Not that. The phone call this morning."

"Kenny, look at me." When he met his father's eyes, Dad continued, "We've gotten calls like these for years, and yet I'm still here. Besides, when you were growing up in LA, I had run-ins with thugs all the time. Believe me, I'm used to it."

"Back then you had a younger body and working legs. No offense."

"Some taken." Dad narrowed his eyes and wheeled himself back from the table. "Let me show you something."

In the living room Dad parked his chair alongside the fireplace. Though dirty old logs lay beneath the chimney, they never actually used the thing. It had been mere decoration since the day they moved in. Half the time Ken forgot the fireplace was even there.

Dad leaned sideways against his armrest and reached toward the chimney. "Remember ten or fifteen years ago when I yelled at you for trying to start a fire?" he asked, reaching up and patting his hand around the sooty chimney shaft.

"Dad, don't hurt yourself. I'll get it, whatever it is."

Ken's hand whacked something metal against the bricks; he

recognized the rectangular edges of a strongbox. At his father's urging, he lifted it from a hook and reeled it in.

Dad grabbed the crusty old box and set it on his lap.

When he threw open the lid, Ken gave a small gasp.

"See?" Dad said. "I'm prepared. Now go enjoy your party."

CHAPTER 11

KEN PAUSED outside Angela's front door, finger hovering over the doorbell. In his other hand he clutched a bottle of cheap amaretto he bought on the way. Judging by the size of her two-story colonial and the nearby houses, cheap liqueur wouldn't cut it in this neighborhood. If only he hadn't been fool enough to let Robby fleece him out of fifty bucks.

Relax, Kenny boy. Worrying accomplishes nothing. Besides, no beverage offering will win Angela's heart. Either she's into you or she isn't.

He rang the bell.

The night proved warm for late September, so warm he was already sweating underneath his polo and khakis. He thought about untucking the polo, but if he did, the wrinkle line would show and he'd look like a knob. Why had he tucked it in anyway? He was twenty-nine—decades away from dressing like his father.

Relax. Stay positive. She's not Olivia.

The door opened. Before him stood a thick-shouldered man with soap-opera good looks and a square, dimpled chin. He wore a fitted suit, a laptop bag strapped across his sturdy chest. Behind him in the well-lit marble foyer a wheeled suitcase waited.

"Evening, pal," the man said. "You one of Angie's friends?"

"Yeah, I'm Ken." He offered his hand.

"Dom Marconi." The man shook his hand with a strong, practiced pump. "You a teacher?"

"Not exactly. I sub."

"Gotta start somewhere." Dom lifted his chin. "I didn't get to where I am by accident. It's all about working hard, staying hungry, and taking yourself seriously. Sure, I'd love to get drunk in front of the Eagles game every weekend like most guys, but if I did that, I wouldn't be flying out to Hawaii."

"On vacation?"

"No, for business. Big-time pharmaceutical conference. I'm giving the keynote address." He grinned, impressed with himself. A car honked along the sidewalk. "Shit, there's my Uber." He yelled over his shoulder, "Angie, hon, I'm leaving!"

Angela strode into the foyer, draped in a sporty white beach robe. Ken caught a glimpse of the black swimsuit underneath. Judging by her tangled wet hair, she'd already been in the pool and he missed it. He swore, right then and there, that he would kill Robby the next time he saw him.

"Bye, Dom." She pecked his cheek the way a little girl might kiss her uncle. "See you Tuesday."

"Take care of the house while I'm gone." He smirked as he stepped past Ken. "Keep your party animals on a leash."

"You behave out there," she called from the doorway. After Dom loaded his luggage into the car, she faced Ken. "'Bout time you showed up. I see you met my husband."

"Yeah, he seems...accomplished."

She snorted. "That's one way of putting it." Her dark eyes spotted the amaretto. She tapped the label. "Ooo, what have we here?"

"It was the only one they had," he blurted. "At the liquor store, I mean. I would've brought a better one but—"

"Amaretto!" She yanked it from his grasp. "You remembered! I see you were listening when I mentioned my favorite drinks. You have a fine pair of ears, Mr. Fujima."

He smiled. "Yours aren't too bad either."

"Hm? What?" She tucked a wave of dark hair behind an ear. "You say something?"

They laughed. When the laughter settled, she swayed in place, her hips tugging the fabric of her robe in torturous ways. "Party's in the backyard. But let's get you a drink first."

At her insistence, Ken stepped inside and marveled at the two-story vestibule. A chandelier dangled overhead, casting rainbows along the marble floor. The nearby wall was burdened with a massive oil painting of Angela and Dom on their wedding day. The sight of the man in his James Bond tuxedo put a crimp in Ken's gut. Her hubby was handsome enough to turn half the NFL gay.

Angela guided Ken down the hall to a kitchen the size of his house. A counter curved along the side wall, covered in more liquor and beer containers than his brain could process. Bourbon brushed up against twelve-packs of Guinness; empty wine glasses sat atop stacks of Shock Top and Budweiser. Various labels he didn't recognize stretched from one end of the counter to the other.

She went to the fridge along the far wall. She stuck the amaretto inside, then spun around with a six-pack of Easy Street—Ken's favorite brew.

He gawked, stunned that she remembered. Last April they'd discussed citrus wheat beers while chaperoning a field trip. "Wow. I don't know what to say."

"A thank you would work." She set the six-pack in his trembling palms. It felt heavy. "By the way, you can't leave until you finish all six. House rule."

He lifted a bottle. "Want to help me out?"

"I'm not drinking tonight."

"Really?" He couldn't tell if she was joking. "You seem loosened up."

She shrugged. "I'm drunk on good company. Come on, I'll introduce you to the tribe."

Ken twisted open a beer and sipped nervously, letting the smooth, spicy flavor relax him.

They headed outside into a patio area where a group of women in their mid-twenties were playing *Cards Against Humanity* and bellowing with laughter. About two-dozen other ladies and gents yammered in the backyard, some splashing around in the swimming pool while others swigged drinks beside a fire pit. Tiki torches blazed across the lawn, spreading a funky odor that left Ken sick to his stomach. He could barely keep himself together while Angela introduced him to an overwhelming number of unfamiliar faces.

Eventually he settled into a lawn chair near a couple of private school teachers Angela had worked with before being hired at Morgan High. He made conversation, and though they spoke to him at length, neither seemed interested in anything he had to say. He feared they might've heard about his rocky reputation in the school district.

Looking for an excuse to abandon the conversation, he spotted Angela beside the garage. One of her guests was puking between the bushes. He grabbed napkins and rushed over.

"Thanks, Ken." She passed the napkins to her guest. "Some of my friends are enjoying a rare night off from parenting, so they're going all out." She patted the woman's back before stretching tall. It bothered him that he was an inch shorter than her. "How's life on Easy Street?"

It took Ken a moment to realize what she meant. "Oh, the beer. It's great."

"Hey, do you swim?"

He flinched. "N-no. Never."

"Never? What, did you almost drown as a kid?"

"No, nothing like that." His mind wandered back to his wedding day, and he remembered cold water all around him. "Swimming just isn't my thing."

"Bet I can change your mind."

"Good luck with that. Honestly, you'd have to put a gun to my head."

"Well, then." She smirked before cocking her thumb and forefinger into the shape of a gun. She touched her fingernail to his forehead and, in a cheesy Old Western accent, said, "Hop in, pardner."

"That thing loaded?"

She dropped her thumb and said, "Bang!"

He grinned. "Can't swim if I'm dead."

"I fired a blank, you goof. Now hop in."

"Nah, didn't bring my swim trunks. Besides, it's getting chilly."

"The pool's heated."

"Even so, I'm not going swimming in khakis."

"Why not? Oh, come on, Ken. Don't make me throw you in."

"Do that, you'll owe me a new phone."

She crossed her arms. "How bout this then? Let's sit along the edge and get our feet wet. You and me."

Though he hated the thought of being even partially submerged, he couldn't say no to that.

They picked a dry spot several feet down from the diving board. The chlorine odor nipped the air. Ken removed his shoes and socks while she lowered herself to the concrete edge. The way her legs unbent as she dangled her feet over the water hypnotized him. He rolled his pants up to his knees and approached. He wanted to get close enough to brush elbows with her, but his nerves stopped him short. He settled an arm's length away.

She dipped both calves beneath the surface with a satisfied sigh.

He followed suit. The water's warmth soothed him. "Feels nice."

"Told ya." She seized his shoulder. "Now jump in!"

"Whoa, stop!" He leaned back, kicking up splashes. "What's wrong with you?"

"Lots," she said, laughing. "Should I write up a list?"

"That could take all weekend."

"Hey!" She slapped his arm. "Watch it. I've been extra nice to you tonight."

"Didn't ask for special treatment."

"Well, you're getting it. You need something to smile about."

"I do?"

"Definitely." She met his eyes, frowning. "Soward giving the job away to her daughter's boytoy—that's such crap."

He waved it off. "Other positions will open."

"You deserve better." Her hand found his shoulder. "You're one of the best teachers I know—full-time or otherwise. I heard about your students writing a petition for you yesterday. If I'd known, I would've signed my name in massive bubble letters."

His cheeks burned, and he was thankful for the nighttime shade. Between the weight of her hand on his shoulder and the kind words flowing through his ears, he expected to melt into the pool at any moment.

"Speaking of that petition," he said, "Pete acted kinda weird when it was his turn to sign. Did you have any luck talking to him yesterday?"

"Uh, well..." Her hand slid from his shoulder. "Pete's going through some personal issues. He asked me not to tell anyone, so I have to respect that."

"Right, right."

"He'll be okay, though. Give him time. You know how teenagers are."

"Yep. Different every day." An uneasy silence dipped between them. He gulped the last of his beer and set it down. "I should probably head out."

"Already? Don't you want to hop in the pool first?"

"Sorry, can't. Gotta head home and make sure my father's okay."

"Excuses, excuses."

"It's getting late." He withdrew his legs from the water and stood. He gestured across the yard. "Look, even your fire pitters are starting to leave."

"Yeah," she said, climbing out, "but they don't have beers to finish."

He snorted. "Not this again."

"Come on," she said, poking his belly. "That was our deal."

"*Your* deal," he said, wishing he were in the pool with her. Wishing the water didn't make him think of Olivia. "Tell you what. Next summer we'll go swimming."

"You promise?"

"Sure."

"Great! Mark the date on your phone. Third Monday in June. Right after school's out. Deal?"

"Deal." He swiped through his phone's calendar. "What time?"

Rather than replying, she seized his phone and tossed it on the lawn. Before he could react, her hands crashed into his chest and his feet left the concrete. For a moment his mind screamed as weightlessness carried him over the concrete edge. Then he struck the water with a warm, terrifying splash that swallowed him whole and soaked his clothes.

When he surfaced, he spat chlorinated water and glared up at her.

She squatted along the edge of the pool, scrunching her nose. "Whoops. Did I say June? I meant tonight."

"Nice going." He splashed her. "Now my clothes are soaked."

"Easy fix for that," she said with a mischievous grin. "Just take them off."

CHAPTER 12

S*ince* *entering* P*ennsylvania,* Michelle's every thought ended in murder.

Over the past hour she had imagined every conceivable way to put a bullet in her sister, from neck-twisting headshots to spine-shattering blasts. She pictured Hannah bleeding from her eyes and arms and guts and thighs. She pictured Hannah floating in swamps of her own blood. Pictured her skull full of holes. Pictured her dressed in lead. Pictured ammo casings falling by the thousands, burying her beyond sight, beyond memory.

These morbid fantasies whetted the appetite of her gunhand. It ached brutally, the hunger traveling up her elbow, shoulder, and neck, where it settled before snapping onto her brainstem like a pair of snake jaws. The bite clenched tighter by the moment, even when her pain receptors maxed out.

She needed to shoot. To kill.

Yet she couldn't.

Not while lying tied up in the trunk of the van.

Behind her, both wrists were bound by a phone charger cable and a pair of shoelaces. The laces were wrapped directly behind the trigger, blocking its path and rendering her unable to shoot. Earlier she had decided it was the only way to guarantee Hannah's safety until they reached Fujima. So far, the restraints had served their purpose, but now, as Michelle struggled feverishly against her bindings, she wished she'd chosen another target and ended this nightmare sooner.

Over miles and miles, the van thumped along, mercilessly slow, yet fast enough to fling her against the walls on sharp turns. Coupled with the stench of leftover buffalo subs, all the bouncing around made her want to puke her organs out. She couldn't take this anymore.

"Hannah, pull over," she called over the backseat. "Let me out."

"Almost there," Hannah yelled back. "Minutes away."

The minutes dragged like decades. Then—miracle of miracles— the van's momentum dipped. It eased to a complete stop, and Hannah rushed out to lift the hatchback open.

"We're here," Hannah said, panting as if she'd run hundreds of miles instead of driving them. "It's a crowded street. Lot of houses, and there's a bar next door. Once you ice Fujima, we can't linger. We'll have to hightail it, okay?"

Michelle twisted around, her heart rate soaring. Her shoulders strained as she shifted the gun behind her back, trying to aim. She spotted delicious red targets in her sister's eyes.

"Ready?" Hannah said, tugging on Michelle's legs. "Let's move you up to the porch. Then I'll untie you."

Michelle groaned as she pressed her feet to the paved road. Ahead, vehicles were parked along both sides of the street. Neon signs for Rolling Rock and Yuengling reflected off nearby wind-shields. The bar's front door opened, and a Mötley Crüe song wailed as two people in blood-red Phillies shirts exited.

Killkillkill, she thought. *Kill Phillies fans. Kill Hannah. Kill everyone.*

Once the bargoers drove off, Hannah guided Michelle up the sidewalk to Fujima's porch. Upon reaching the front door, her appetite surged. Even with Fujima nearby, she wanted Hannah dead and bloody. She couldn't wait another second.

"Hold still," Hannah said. "Let me undo those knots."

"Wait," Michelle said, her Jekyll overruling her Hyde. "Don't undo them. Just loosen them. I'll do the rest once you're gone."

"Gone? Where am I supposed to go?"

"Drive around the block. Park one street over and wait. Trust me."

Hannah stared back. "Okay. But don't fuck this up. Soon as you drop the gun, pick it up with a towel or something. Then head straight out the door. Don't let anyone stop you. I'd rather die than lose that gun."

"I know, I know," Michelle said, agitated. "Now loosen the goddamned knots."

Michelle steadied her shoulder against the front door. The pressure on her wrists tightened as Hannah tugged at the charging cable and shoelaces. The temptation to shoot worsened as the pressure grew more suffocating. Then a faint coolness trickled through each wrist.

"Loose enough?" Hannah asked.

"Yeah. Now leave."

Hannah kissed her cheek and rushed back to the van.

As Hannah pulled away from the curb, Michelle pried at the slackened cable. What a bitch of a thing. It went tight, loose, tight, loose. Her fingers danced; warm anxiety mounted within her chest. The moment she sensed her bindings slipping free, she pecked her nose against the doorbell like a drunk duck.

Ding-dong.

Behind her, one knot came undone. The rubber cable slid off. Her fingers nipped at the shoelaces. She wrestled with them, gritting her teeth as she yanked back and forth. The laces slid with a satisfying smoothness, then jerked to an agonizing stop. New sweat left her pores as she realized that loosening one knot had tightened the other.

Dead ahead the doorknob jiggled.

No. Not now. Not yet.

The door swung inward. There was no one there. The house greeted her with shadows and silence. A faint odor reached her nostrils, but her sleep-deprived mind failed to identify it. Something like baby powder and cheap soap. Smelled like the elderly.

Then something gleamed in the light coming from the streetlamp.

Something waist high, to the left of the doorway.

It was a pistol.

And a wheelchair-bound man was pointing it at her.

CHAPTER 13

WHILE ANGELA ESCORTED her guests to their vehicles, Ken toweled off as best he could without removing his wet clothes. He stood beside the fire pit, savoring its faint warmth. His shirt and pants clung to him, and his soggy boxers chafed along his crotch. A mucky layer of water that his socks hadn't absorbed squelched inside his shoes. With the night growing chillier and the fire pit dying down, the heated pool was looking tempting.

And so was Angela. Nothing tempted him more than the thought of alone time with her. He could hardly believe the turn of events tonight.

However, excited as he was, this situation made him uneasy. She was attempting to betray her husband mere hours after he'd left for a business trip. Considering what Ken had gone through with his ex-fiancée, he hated the thought of fracturing a serious relationship.

And yet, her marriage seemed meaningless. Her classroom name-plate indicated as much. She never discussed her husband in school, as if he were a sour subject she preferred to avoid. The way she'd kissed his cheek tonight was perfunctory at best; not the kiss of a lover who would miss her departing husband.

The gate squealed. Angela entered the backyard, the night air tossing the hem of her robe. She approached with a relaxed stride.

"Everyone's heading home," she said. In her cartoony Western drawl, she added, "Just you and me, pardner."

He tried to think of a clever reply, but before he could, she spoke again.

"Hey, Ken?"

"Yeah?"

"Tonight somebody referred to you as 'Ken the Eraser.' What's that about?"

His balls hiked up into his crotch. He hadn't heard that awful nickname in years. It reminded him of his failed wedding and the messy aftermath that caused him to get fired from his original teaching job. Not something he wanted to discuss on a first date, or whatever this was.

"It's a long story."

She shrugged. "Okay. I won't pry."

For a moment, neither said anything.

The pressure was on.

He tossed his towel aside. "Think I'll warm up in the pool."

"Great idea." She grabbed his wrist and yanked him toward the water.

At the pool's edge, she released him and began untying her robe. It separated, revealing her black one-piece. The suit hugged tight against her body, clasping her breasts above the smooth slide of her belly. When her robe dropped and she waded into the shallow end, it dawned on him that they were alone together under the moonlight.

Peeling off his wet clothes, he stumbled in place, his mind a cross-fire of excitement and dread. Once his shirt hit the grass, he undid his belt and dropped his pants. Wearing nothing but his boxers, he waded in, the heated water swallowing him from foot to waist.

Ahead, she floated with her arms outstretched and her legs pressed together. Her wet swimsuit glowed under the moon, her breasts two shadowy mounds atop her prone chest. The view and the warm water sent his penis hiking against his boxers.

With a tense breath, he continued into shoulder-high water.

She swung her arms backward and swam away before he could reach her. He followed her into the deep end, where she kicked off the wall and torpedoed back toward the center. When he chased her down this time, he anticipated her escape route and snatched her by the ankle, sending her into laughter.

With his free hand, he made a finger gun. "Caught ya."

"Now we're both outlaws." She twisted around to face him. "Think we should team up?"

He released her ankle, and she stood in the chest-high water, reaching up to push her dark hair behind her shoulders. His heart ached just watching, and when she took his hand and tugged him forward, he almost had a coronary.

They stood face-to-face, her eyes fixed on his. In the shadows she smiled serenely, her head tilted sideways. Her hand hadn't yet released his, and she guided it behind her back. His fingertips brushed her slick suit. The texture sent screeching waves of electricity through him.

"Hold me?"

He embraced her warm, firm body while her arms curled behind his neck. As he stared past her, the two of them cheek-to-cheek, he wondered how any of this was possible. Everything that happened since he fell in the pool was too good to be true. Everything. He was in the arms of a woman he fiercely admired, and they were half-naked. That never happened to Ken Fujima. Not since what should've been his wedding day. The voice in the back of his mind wouldn't stop reminding him either.

He shook a bit loose from her grasp. "Angela?"

"What?" Though he had pulled back, her hands remained around his neck. "Something wrong?"

"Yeah. This is." He glanced around. "It's nice, but—"

"You're worried about my husband?"

"That's part of it, but..." He took a deep breath, inhaling the chlorine-tinged air. "If I'm being honest, this feels like it's coming out of nowhere. Up until recently, I never got the impression you were interested."

"Oh." Her hands slid from his neck. Now that they were gone, he wanted them back. "Sorry, Ken."

"No, it's fine, it just feels rushed." He was breathing fast.

Way to kill the moment, Kenny boy.

"I didn't mean to rush anything," she blurted. "I just...what I wanted...ugh, this is gonna sound so cheesy."

"It's okay." He began to calm down. Hearing her trip over her words made him feel like less of a doofus. "Nothing's cheesy if it's the truth."

She smiled. "Okay. But if you make fun of me, you're a dead man."

"I won't."

"Okay, so..." She bit her lip. It was strangely reassuring to see her nervous in his presence. "Ever feel like you're an actor in a movie you've seen already? Like someone yells 'cut' every night and you have to do another take in the morning and it's the same scene every day?"

"Sometimes. Yeah."

"I keep getting this sinking feeling. When I see the students in my classes, they're always growing. Always working toward new things. They have goals, they have destinations, they have purpose." She hung her head. "But me, I'm the same Angela every day. I wake up, teach, run errands, pretend to care about my husband, fall asleep, and repeat. That's it. No goals, no destinations, no surprises. Just the same movie as yesterday but with some deleted scenes mixed in."

He nodded. "Sounds like my work life. And my family life."

"See, that's what I'm saying. Life's no mystery anymore. It's too safe, too predictable. That's why I invited you here." She pulled at her hair. "I know you said things felt rushed, but we've known each other a while. I don't know about you, but it hasn't been only this week that I've thought about you. When you look at it that way, it's not rushed—it's overdue."

His scalp tingled. "Never thought of it that way."

"Sure you have," she said, grinning. "I've seen it in your eyes. Many times."

His cheeks burned.

"Ken." She took his hands beneath the surface. Her slim, strong fingers squeezed out his fears like juice from a lemon. "Let's stop living in a boring old movie we've seen a thousand times. Let's leave that theater. You and me. Together."

Damn. Her words knocked the wind out of him. He stood there, trying to breathe, trying to think what to say.

Then he realized he didn't need to speak.

Beneath the surface his hands remained cupped under hers. He squeezed tight and pulled her toward him. Their bodies met with a quiet splash, his pulse throbbing in his ear. He felt something warm brush his face and realized their breathing was overlapping. Everything was happening fast. Before he could stop himself, he leaned forward and pressed his lips to hers.

Bombs went off in his brain. Her kiss was strong and soft and exhilarating. It lasted longer than any man deserved. He slid his arms around her back, pulling her body against his, her breasts flattening against his chest. It sent tremors through him and again his penis pushed against his boxers.

She pulled away.

Oh, shit.

He found himself staring back at her. She must've felt his erection against her thigh and got creeped out. Even with the surrounding arborvitae trees shutting out her neighbors, a backyard pool was no place for—

Before he could finish the thought, she reached for the strap on her right shoulder. She pushed it aside and did the same with the left one. Her bare shoulders glowed in the moonlight. His eyes followed her fingers, which curved inside the neckline of her swimsuit. She started to tug it down, then paused, torturing him with suspense.

His mouth went dry.

Instead of finishing the job, she took his hand and guided it toward her, tucking his finger inside her slick cleavage.

A buzzing warmth filled him. He ached for her. There was no hesitation anymore. No fear. Nothing but the desire to keep going.

When she released his hand, she nodded.

With an anxious tug, he freed her breasts from the confines of the one-piece. They spilled out almost comically, but once they settled, he marveled at their fullness, at the white secrecy of her tan lines. He cupped their springy firmness while her hands went searching for secrets of their own.

Beneath the water, her grip closed around his shaft. His mind raced everywhere before stopping at the intersection of "Is this really happening?" and "Don't mess this up." He felt himself ache within her grasp and wondered if they should move indoors. The house seemed miles away, so he hurried her toward the shallow end. He sank down on one of the submerged steps, leaning back against the pool wall, the water line partway up his chest.

Angela climbed over him and slipped, dropping onto his thighs with a splash. She laughed it off; he held his breath. Establishing her footing, she reached between her legs to tug her swimsuit aside.

Meeting his eyes, she nodded breathlessly.

Icy nerves overran his body. The frigid rush turned him half limp, but that changed when her hand found him again beneath the surface. He stiffened as she guided him closer. He felt himself bump her thigh before passing from the pool's warmth into her own.

His life stopped being a boring old movie. It started mattering. Even their clumsy position didn't spoil it. As he and Angela searched for a rhythm, the world around him melted away. It was mesmerizing, losing himself to the sensations—the clutch of her arms around his shoulders, the splash of the water against his chest, the huff of her hot breath against his ear.

Then somewhere a crack sounded, like a snapping tree branch. He hopped to attention, alarmed. His abrupt movement tumbled her off him. While she splashed to her feet, he peeked over the pool's concrete edge, squinting through shadows, trying to locate the source of the noise. It sounded like it came from the rear of the yard.

"Did you hear that?" he said, breathless.

"Who cares," she said. "Probably nothing."

"It was loud." His heart pounded, and not romantically. "You think—"

"Ken, it's probably just a squirrel."

"Or someone watching us." He dipped his shoulders beneath the surface. He felt exposed, as if an audience were watching—an audience that included not only the neighbors but everyone he knew, including his ex-fiancée. In the back of his mind he heard Olivia saying he wasn't man enough for Angela. Not man enough for any woman.

"Relax," Angela said. "I'm sure it was nothing."

Despite the warm pool, he went limp. The water line floated along his collarbones, the same place as on his wedding day. His shoulders exposed to the chilly night air, he shivered brutally.

Angela touched his arm.

He flinched. Backed away with a splash.

"I'm sorry," he said. "I should go."

"You're leaving *now*?" Her voice was half pleading, half insulted. "Right now? In the middle of *this*?"

He climbed out of the pool, grabbed a towel from a lawn chair, and dried himself.

"Ken, please come back."

"It's late." He tossed the towel aside and grabbed his wet clothes. In their condition they were hard to pull on, but he dressed hurriedly. "I'm worried about my father. Usually I help him into bed."

"*Ken!*"

"Sorry." He pulled his soaked polo over his head. "Maybe some other time."

"I'm not leaving this pool until you get back in here." She dropped both fists with a splash. "I mean it. I'll stay here all night. You want me to fall asleep and drown?"

"I'm sorry." He jammed his feet into his soggy shoes and scampered off, taking one last glance over his shoulder at her. She stood there, arms folded across her bare chest. He was already regretting this, but Olivia was right.

He wasn't man enough.

CHAPTER 14

MICHELLE OBEYED the old man and entered the unlit house at gunpoint. It pained her to take orders from Goro Fujima, but if she'd learned one thing this week, it was whoever pointed the gun got their way. Her own weapon remained tangled up behind her, the trigger neutralized by a shoelace. Traveling all this way to get shot by her final target wasn't in the plan. She needed to regain control somehow. She needed justice for her family.

"What you hiding behind your back?" Fujima said. "Turn slowly so I can see."

Michelle stalled, trying to work the bindings. They were too tight. *Fuck, I need to shoot. Never should've told Hannah to leave. What was I thinking?*

"I said turn around."

She followed his order, exposing the revolver to the light coming from the street.

"Hmph. So that's the gun," he murmured, as if familiar with the weapon. "I take it you blocked the trigger to keep from firing?"

She remained silent.

"Foolish move." He lit a nearby lamp. The living room burst into sight, cluttered with cushy furniture and a bright blue dog bed.

Photos of the Fujima family adorned the walls, their smiling faces mocking her. "Step toward the kitchen. Slowly. No sudden movements. If I catch you undoing those laces, I'll shoot."

Michelle glanced over her shoulder and saw he wasn't fucking around. His pistol remained steady and he glared without blinking. As she approached the kitchen, he wheeled himself behind her and shut the front door. A stiff fear tunneled through her chest. Why didn't the bastard just call the cops or shoot her? Why bother marching her through the house like this? She couldn't help feeling like a web were being spun around her, one she wouldn't escape.

"That gun of yours," he said. "Supposedly a former yakuza possessed it. His name was Saito. What's your relation to him?"

She gritted her teeth.

"Answer me."

"He was my father," she spat. "And you killed him."

Fujima's wheelchair creaked as he shifted his weight. "Back in the '90s your father betrayed our clan. In an attempt to gain power, he sold out our captain to the LAPD. Such an act was punishable by death. What I and the man you killed in Dallas did was carry out the punishment."

"Fuck you," she said, unfazed by his 9mm. "My mom—you killed her too."

"She wasn't supposed to be there."

"But she was."

His voice hesitated slightly. "We had orders to kill your father. He knew it was coming. It's possible he kept your mother close to deter us from shooting. Regardless, his crimes warranted immediate punishment."

"That's no excuse for shooting her, you prick. You don't get to make excuses after you pull the trigger."

"What about you?"

"What *about* me?"

"You killed several people."

"Yeah, five assholes responsible for my parents' deaths."

"Your vengeance was sloppy."

"How so?"

"You killed six."

"Not yet. Only five."

"You *shot* five," Fujima said. "But you *killed* six."

Michelle swallowed. "What do you mean?"

"You left two bodies in Dallas. Those of Mr. Orochi and his three-month-old granddaughter. She passed away last night."

"What?" Michelle felt her neck muscles tense. "That's bullshit."

"I'm afraid not. You, daughter of Saito, robbed us of an innocent child."

"But the baby was in a crib—it was crying when I left."

"The exact cause of death hasn't been determined, but we both know that child would be alive if you hadn't dropped by."

"No..." Michelle said. Her fingers, which yearned to pluck at the shoelaces, went agonizingly numb. Her whole body did.

"Why have you stopped moving?" He rolled his chair forward and shook his pistol at her. "Go on into the kitchen."

Nearby a dopey-faced pit bull limped around the kitchen table. It growled, driving her away from the fridge. Ahead lay a washer-dryer and two doors. One opened onto a bedroom. The other was shut.

"I'll get that door for you," Fujima said, rolling ahead and opening it. A shadowy staircase descended below. "Head downstairs."

"Down there? Why?" Before she could protest further, she recognized an opportunity. If she hurried down into the darkness, she could undo her bindings there without being seen. This idiot was giving her an advantage.

But as she approached the top step, he said, "Stop."

"You said to head down."

"Want you to know something," he said. "Two years ago, after my wife died, I had too much to drink one night. When I went downstairs for more beer, I missed one of these steps and took a hard tumble. Ended up whacking my spine, and I lost function in both legs. Since then, I've often wondered if this staircase punished me for my sins. That I'm not certain of, but I know one thing—tonight these stairs will punish you for yours."

Alarms went off in her head. She swung around to face him and found his pistol pointed at her chest.

"You can jump down," he said, "or I can shoot you down. Either way, the stairs will decide your fate."

"Wait!" Her fingers worked frantically at the laces. "I can't jump. My wrists are tied. How am I supposed to break my fall?"

"That's your problem."

"No!" She ripped at the restraints. Laces slid, but not enough. "Don't do this."

He lifted the pistol. "Last chance to jump."

"NO!" Michelle screamed.

That instant the front door burst open.

"Chelle!" Hannah's voice. "Where are you?"

"Stay back," Fujima yelled, pointing the 9mm toward the living room.

With the pistol aimed elsewhere, Michelle seized the opening and charged at Fujima. She headbutted his shoulder, driving his wheelchair back into the washer-dryer with a loud, echoing clang. She fell to her knees but scrambled to her feet and bull-rushed him, this time smashing her skull into his sternum.

The impact left her woozy. The old man groaned when she collapsed against him.

Behind her the dog barked and Hannah shouted.

Michelle twisted her neck and saw the pistol remained in the old man's grasp. She stretched her mouth toward his forearm and snapped her jaws over his soft, hairy flesh. Fujima jerked in his seat. The pistol wobbled in his grasp, and she clenched her jaws, her teeth sinking into muscle. A metallic flavor seeped into her mouth.

Then came a harsh backward tug on her hair. Her scalp burned, and the sudden flash of heat caused her to release her bite. The moment she did, her head was tugged violently in the opposite direction.

Fujima yanked a fistful of her hair forcefully in several directions before shoving her backward toward the basement.

She landed hard on her bound hands. A nasty sting ran up her forearms. When the pain faded, she realized nothing was supporting the back of her head—it dangled over the top step.

She sat up in a panic. Ahead Hannah and Fujima were wrestling over the pistol. Hannah tugged him out of his wheelchair and onto the floor.

Michelle lifted her leg to kick him. She got him once in the shoulder, then drove her heel toward his face.

His hand reached out.

Grabbed her foot.

And shoved her.

Again she landed on her bound hands, but this time her upper body teetered over the edge. Her legs kicked, bicycling wildly as she tried to find her balance. As her head tipped backward, she yelled out, "Hannaaah!"

But it was too late.

For a moment Michelle felt weightless, like she was riding a roller coaster in reverse. The sensation stretched on until her shoulder struck one of the risers. Pain exploded through her back. Then her head. Then her knees. She lost track of what hurt. Each step pummeled her until she struck the concrete floor.

Everything throbbed. The fall had demolished her. In the darkness it was impossible to tell what parts got it worst. At least one shoulder had been ripped from its socket. Her joints were hot, and an eerie numbness covered various areas of her back and limbs. Agony engulfed her every nerve.

Then the pain abruptly faded.

In its place came another sensation. One that acted as a welcome distraction.

Hunger.

The revolver's hunger.

It ate through her pain and allowed her to sit upright. Her neck crunched as she stretched it gently up and down until she was able to look upstairs.

Framed in the doorway, Hannah held the old man in a headlock, her jaw hanging in horror as she stared down at her sister.

"Hannah," Michelle said. "Bring him down here."

CHAPTER 15

THE MOMENT KEN pulled into his driveway, a chill shivered beneath his wet clothes. Something was wrong. He couldn't identify what was off, but he'd lived here long enough to know a normal night from an odd one. When he discovered Hopper pawing at the back door, his worst suspicions were confirmed. Dad never locked their dog outside, which meant someone else had.

Ken's first instinct was to call 911. Trouble was, he'd left his phone at Angela's. He considered borrowing a neighbor's phone, but if an intruder were inside his house, every second counted.

Shivering in the midnight air, he unlocked the back door and rushed into the kitchen, Hopper following behind. First thing Ken noticed was the TV volume was cranked to skull-splitting levels. *SportsCenter* commentary boomed while Hopper gimped toward the basement door. Ken raced there, his waterlogged shoes squelching. He paused when he spotted Dad's empty wheelchair parked in the nearby shadows.

That stopped his heart cold. *Some monster took him out of his chair. What kind of psycho would do that?*

He went to grab the kitchen phone when a shout sounded from the basement.

Dad!

Ken yanked the basement door open.

In his panic, he didn't think, just trotted downstairs. Dim light glowed from the basement's lone bulb, illuminating the concrete walkway between shelving racks and stacked boxes, casting a vaguely human shadow that stretched from the basement's back wall toward Ken at the foot of the stairs.

The shadow belonged to a woman with grungy hair wearing a navy-blue zip hoodie. She was hunched over, her back to him, and appeared to be tying—or untying—someone's wrists. Below her knelt a fidgeting woman dressed in a wrinkled nylon jacket. Bizarrely, the tied-up woman clutched a revolver behind her.

"Hurry up, Hannah, untie me already," the fidgeting woman shouted.

"Shut up and hold still," Hannah said. "Michelle, I can't undo the knot if you keep moving."

When Hannah squatted, Ken saw his father.

Dad sat frozen against the far wall, his useless legs outstretched in front of him. He clutched his right forearm, which was smeared with blood. His face was contorted into a grimace, and someone had stuffed a rag in his mouth. But the worst was his eyes. They reflected the same defeated look Ken had noticed when he had sat beside Mom's deathbed.

Ken's wet clothes became frigid in the chilly basement air. He regretted not dialing 911 in the kitchen. He turned to run upstairs, but Hopper barked.

The intruders turned toward the sound, revealing themselves. They looked Ken's age, maybe younger. Michelle growled and thrashed, as though trying to break free of her own flesh. The other girl, Hannah, drew a gun that Ken recognized as his father's 9mm, the one that had been hidden in the chimney.

"Stay back!" she said, aiming it at him. "Don't make me shoot."

Ken flinched. He'd never faced a live gun before, not even a paintball gun. To think, twenty minutes ago he was safe in Angela's arms. If only he'd stayed with her.

No. He needed to be here. Somehow, he had to rescue Dad.

"Who the hell are you?" Michelle said, twitching. "Why you all wet?"

Ken swallowed. "C-can you please put your guns down?"

She cackled. "If you only knew."

"Please don't kill him," he said, tears rimming his eyes. "He's my dad."

"Yeah?" she said. "Our dad was murdered when we were kids."

"Right," Hannah said. "All thanks to your old man."

Ken was too afraid to ask what they meant. Probably had something to do with Dad's past life. Whatever he'd done, an apology wouldn't fix it. They intended to kill him, and they would succeed unless Ken acted now.

"Cops are on their way," he lied. "You should leave."

"We will." Michelle twisted against a shelving rack, rubbing her bindings against the edge of a metal leg. "Soon as your father pays for what happened to mine."

Her conviction chilled him. On instinct, Ken shifted toward the stairs but bumped into Hopper. Maybe the dog had the right idea. They couldn't run away. Not now.

Instead, Ken leaned forward, his wet clothes dripping. The constant pat-pat-pattering of droplets heightened his anxiety as he gripped Hopper's collar. The only viable plan that came to mind was charging at the armed intruders. A sudden rush might catch them off-guard. Trouble was, they were fifteen feet away—a massive distance under the circumstances. Then again, no distance was too far, not if it meant saving a loved one.

"Stay back," Hannah said, her pistol trembling.

"Relax," he said, "I'm getting my dog under control."

"Move the dog upstairs."

"Okay, okay."

But instead of tugging Hopper backward, Ken let go with a shout.

The moment he did, Hopper bounded forward, his bark echoing through the basement. Ken raced alongside him, wet shoes screeching along the concrete.

Hannah hesitated and aimed somewhere between them.

The gun roared.

Ken would've stopped short if he hadn't already jumped, propelling himself toward her. His shoulder smashed her thigh, and the impact drove her into a nearby shelving rack.

Canned goods tumbled from above. One must've struck Hopper, because he squealed and dodged away. Others struck Ken and Hannah; the rest crashed against the floor, filling the basement with the stench of soggy vegetables.

Ken hit the floor next to Hannah. His elbows struck concrete, but he didn't feel the impact thanks to adrenaline. He pushed himself upright and realized Hannah no longer held the pistol. He searched for it among the pile of fallen cans. Then a subhuman shriek ricocheted through the basement.

Michelle spread her arms wide behind her like a pair of featherless wings. Her eyes dilated as she brought her arms forward, clutching the revolver in front of her chest with both hands. The barrel immediately snapped toward Dad.

No!

Ken met his father's eyes, recognized the unprecedented terror in them. Dad pressed both palms against the floor and pushed, shifting a couple of feet away just as the revolver went off.

The report thundered through the basement, unbearably loud. Ken flinched. A series of faint clicks followed. After he opened his eyes, he wished he'd kept them shut.

Chunks of red pulp dribbled from his father's cheek. Blood dirtied the rag in his mouth and flushed down his neck, spreading a scarlet stain across his white Dodgers t-shirt. Despite all this, Dad's eyes remained open. Lifelessly open.

Ken wondered if his father could survive such a wound. People attempted to shoot their own brains out and failed all the time. This couldn't be much different. A gushing hole in his cheek could be fixed. There had to be a way.

A second blast tore Dad's forehead open.

Dad jerked in place, arm twitching at his side. His liver-spotted hand flopped against the concrete floor, smearing blood in a wild pattern.

Again a series of faint clicks followed.

A third shot exploded in Dad's chest.

His arm stopped twitching.

His eyes drooped open, accepting the blood that trailed from his forehead.

He made no effort to blink.

No effort to move.

Nothing.

Ken crawled forward in a daze. The sight of his lifeless father struck him as ridiculous, impossible. He refused to believe it. This had to be some hidden-camera gag, some morbid comedy experiment that would show up on YouTube. Any second now a cable TV host would run downstairs laughing while Dad sprang to life and told him the blood was corn syrup.

Dad couldn't be dead. Old men in wheelchairs didn't get shot to death. Never.

Michelle shrieked. Her free hand pried at the revolver's grip, as if trying to yank it loose from her hand. While she struggled, a trail of smoke rose from the barrel. Ken had hoped the weapon was a prop, but the chalky, burned odor was too real.

The gun was authentic.

And now it was pointed at him.

Ken gawked at the smoking revolver. The barrel's opening stared back like a blackened, empty eye. It peered at him. Through him. Beyond him. He saw his whole life play out within that shadowy tunnel—twenty-nine years of love and loss, success and mistakes, meaning and insignificance.

He drew a deep breath. Maybe his last.

Then the revolver dropped from her grasp. It struck the concrete with a clack and bounced to a stop right in front of him.

Light gleamed along the sweaty, polished handle.

In his panic he reached for it.

"Stop!" Hannah grabbed his shirt. "Don't—"

Ken picked it up.

CHAPTER 16

FIREARMS HAD INTIMIDATED him from an early age. Never in his life had Ken touched a gun, yet now he found himself appreciating the snugness of the grip against his palm. Though he wouldn't call it comfortable, he welcomed the reassuring feel. A grimy layer of Michelle's sweat mixed with his own and seemed to weld his hand to the weapon. In a surreal way, it was as though he and the snubnose became one.

From the corner of his eye he saw movement. But before he could react, two hands seized his wrist. Hannah growled in his ear as she steered the gun barrel toward the floor. "Michelle, help me pin him down!"

"Fuck that," Michelle said, digging among the fallen cans. "Where's that pistol—I'll just shoot him."

Ken couldn't believe his ringing ears. First these two had executed his father; now they intended to murder *him*. Would they hunt down Robby next? Everything was happening so fast that anything seemed possible. All Ken knew for certain was that Michelle intended to kill him. That left him no choice.

With tears in his eyes, he shoved Hannah aside and lifted his steel companion, lining up the barrel with Michelle's chest.

"No," Hannah cried, tugging on his shirt. "Listen!"

Ken listened, all right. Listened to a private voice that he ignored too often. A voice that insisted it was time he stopped being everyone's doormat.

Michelle raised both palms.

"You don't understand," she said, shuffling backward toward Dad's corpse. "Your old man killed my parents. We grew up orphans because of him."

Ken pulled the trigger.

The recoil hit him like a punch to the hand. Thunder echoed through the basement. His ears rang. His eyes closed. When he opened them, his father's murderer collapsed against the cinderblock wall.

Somewhere—inches away, maybe miles away—Hannah shouted.

He fired again.

And again.

Michelle jerked left and right, blood fountaining from her chest as she struggled to cover the entry wounds. Her hand fell on her stomach as he pulled the trigger a fourth time. He suspected the gun might be empty, but another shot erupted. Ken continued firing, amazed by the ceaseless ammo stream coming from the six-shot revolver. He fired until he lost count, watching his father's murderer bounce in place, absorbing bullet after bullet. Until the revolver clicked.

It only clicked once.

He tugged the trigger for another blast. More reports boomed. Bullet after bullet entered Michelle's corpse. An empty click followed every fifth shot. Then the thunder resumed. He kept shooting despite the hissing heat against his palm, despite the tears stinging his eyes, despite his sore trigger finger. All his grief and pain and love kept him firing.

"Stop!" A pair of navy-blue sleeves wrapped around his neck. Hannah wrestled him to the ground, pressing his cheek to the blood-smeared concrete. He twisted beneath her, throwing elbows until he caught her in the stomach. She coughed, loosening her grip. He jerked his head free and shoved backward, dropping her onto her back.

Before she could recover, he drove the barrel into her cheek, pinning her skull against the floor.

"Ow! It's hot!" she yelled, swatting his arm. "Hot!"

He jammed the barrel harder into her cheek. A distant part of him wanted to pull the trigger, but he restrained himself.

"Hothothot!" She grabbed his forearm. "Get it off!"

He lifted the snubnose.

She shuffled backward on heels and elbows, crashing into a rack loaded with toolboxes and hardware supplies. Against the floor, her legs jerked, kicking a can of veggies into a thudding roll. Panting, she sat up and gingerly touched the ring-shaped burn on her cheek. Then she looked at Michelle's corpse and moaned.

"No...this can't be happening." Hannah sagged sideways. Tears overflowed her eyes. "You idiot. You just...shot my sister."

He blinked, still dazed. Only now did it sink in: he'd unloaded over two dozen rounds into his father's murderer without reloading.

Impossible. Perhaps it was a heat-of-the-moment brain lapse. An illusion conjured by a fractured mind.

His attention drifted toward his father. The sight crushed him.

Oh, Dad. Why?

He wanted to hug his father but couldn't bring himself to try. He worried there might be a speck of life in Dad somewhere. Moving his body might snuff it out permanently.

This can't be real.

Something wet surrounded his knee and he flinched. Michelle's blood. A dark red puddle was spreading across the concrete. Its coppery stench left him queasy, and he staggered to his feet, aiming the revolver around the basement as if phantoms might emerge from the cinderblock walls and strangle him. He didn't know exactly what he was afraid of, but it seemed to be everywhere.

He couldn't stay here.

He needed to head upstairs. Call 911.

Lumbering to his feet, Ken pointed the gun at Hannah. He considered marching her upstairs but thought twice. She could run away or attack him. Better that the cops came down here and got her. But he couldn't just leave her here, not with the missing pistol lying around. Until he found it, he needed her restrained.

On the shelf above her, he spotted a duct tape roll. He gestured toward it.

"Get that tape."

"Tape? Why?"

"Get it. Now."

Wiping her eyes, she stood up. He readied his weapon in case she tried anything, but she grabbed the duct tape and faced him.

"What now?" she asked.

"Tape your left ankle to the leg of that rack."

"Seriously?"

"I need you to stay put while I run upstairs and call the cops."

"Before you do, there's something you should know about that gun."

"All I know is that I'll shoot you with it if you don't listen."

"Okay, fine." Trembling, she peeled off a strip of tape, creating an awful squeaking noise. She bent forward and, with a few wraps of the roll, adhered her ankle in place. After doing the same to her other ankle, she taped her left wrist above her head, her hand raised like a nervous student with a question.

"That gun," she said, her tone urgent. "Try setting it down."

"I'll hang onto it, thanks."

"You don't understand. See if you *can* set it down."

He ignored her odd comment. "Touch your other wrist to the rack and don't move."

Still clutching the gun, he taped her other wrist to the shelving rack. Then he stepped back and surveyed his handiwork. With Hannah secure, he allowed himself a sigh of relief. He turned toward a workbench covered with dust bunnies and wood shavings. He pressed his free hand to the grubby surface and drew several deep breaths.

Settle down, he told himself. *Worst part's over.*

But when he tried to release his grip on the revolver, he understood he was wrong.

CHAPTER 17

THE LAST TIME Ken took his father to the movies, back in 2012, they'd seen *The Amazing Spider-Man*. Neither had wanted to go (Dad hated superheroes and Ken hated that they'd replaced Tobey Maguire), but a July heatwave drove them into the air-conditioned sanctuary of their local RC Theater. Thirty minutes into the movie, they both laughed when Andrew Garfield first discovered his spider powers and found that his hands stuck to everything he touched—toothbrushes, towels, doorknobs, everything.

That scene reverberated through Ken's mind as he attempted to unbend his fingers from the revolver's grip. They remained fixed in place, however, and when he tried ripping the gun loose with his free hand, a flash of sharp heat burst along his palm. Yanking and twisting did nothing. Same with trying to pry his fingers loose with the house key.

Eventually he took a step back.

Closed his eyes.

Breathed.

Chances were, this was adrenaline related. He'd heard stories about people lifting full-size sedans when their adrenaline was rushing, so maybe when he grabbed the revolver his muscles had hardened into place. It was merely a guess, however—he was a substitute teacher, not a physiologist.

Hopper whimpered nearby, brown eyes glossy with fear. Ken was leading him toward the stairs when Hannah spoke.

"There are two ways to drop that gun."

Ken paused on the bottom step. The matter-of-fact way she said it bothered him. She didn't sound like someone crafting a lie. She spoke with unshakable conviction, as if promising the sun would rise.

"How do I drop it?" he asked.

"If you swear not to kill me, I'll tell you."

"Fine. I swear. Now tell me."

"You need to unload all six rounds."

"Pretty sure I unloaded more than six."

"You *fired* more than six. Problem is, each round remains in the cylinder until it kills someone." Frowning, she glanced at her sister. "Remember how the gun clicked after every five shots? That's because a round is missing from the cylinder."

"That's ridiculous." He shook his head, dazed. "There's an explanation for why it's stuck—some sort of glue or something, I don't know."

"Exactly. You don't know. Which is why I'm telling you. There are two ways to drop that gun. Either kill six people or kill yourself."

Ken waited for her to smirk or start laughing. She didn't.

"If you cut me loose, I can help you."

"No thanks." He climbed the basement steps. Upstairs the TV was still blaring, now with a car insurance jingle that promised monster deals. He muted it and grabbed the kitchen phone. He thumbed the number nine, then one, then stopped.

What do I tell them? he thought. *That my father's dead downstairs, that I shot an intruder twenty times in the chest without reloading, that I can't drop this gun? Will they buy that? Will they send a SWAT team? What if the SWAT team charges in here armed with rifles? What if they demand I drop my weapon? What will they do if I can't obey the order?*

Ken returned the phone to its cradle. He went to the sink and turned the water on. He stuck his gunhand—yes, *gunhand*—beneath the stream and squirted dish soap over it. He rubbed it in with his free hand until his fingers were sudsy with green apple fragrance. Both the revolver and his fingers were slick but remained fused together. He rinsed, hoping that might help, but it only sent dirty water swirling around the drain.

Least I removed some soot from the gun, he thought morbidly. *Sure, it's fused to my palm, but no more dirt and dried blood. A clean gun is a happy gun.*

Exhausted, he leaned against the fridge, staring into space. The gun dripped at his side, and Hopper licked the fallen droplets. Ken reached down to pet him, but the pit bull flinched away with a whine. He limped toward the living room and ducked into his doggie bed.

"G'night, Hopper. See you in the morning."

If I make it to morning.

"You'll be fine," he whispered to himself. "Settle down and call the cops. Once they arrest Hannah, they'll figure out how to remove this gun."

There are only two ways, her voice echoed in his mind. *Either kill six people or kill yourself.*

No. Had to be a third way. Maybe he needed some Goo-Gone or another chemical compound. Maybe a drug to relax his muscles, a session with a hypnotist, or a good night's sleep. Anything. He had to think of something.

First, he needed to set his mind straight. He was still in shock over Dad's death. No time to process it or cry.

Do the sane thing, he told himself. *Call 911. Get this sorted out.*

Drawing a deep breath, he popped the phone from its cradle. As he dialed the first two numbers, a dark thought entered his mind. *What if Hannah isn't lying?* What if murder and suicide were the only methods of removing the gun? What would the police say to that? They certainly wouldn't let him trot out into the free world with a gun stuck to his mitt. They'd probably transfer him to a federal agency that would lock him in a bulletproof cell and run tests on him. And that was the sunny scenario. What if the feds killed him so they could have the revolver? They could make it look like a suicide and sweep his corpse under the rug.

Even if they let him live, his life would never be the same. He wouldn't be allowed to attend his father's funeral. There would be no more afternoon walks with Hopper. No more classrooms full of students. No more chances at happiness with someone like Angela. And worst of all, what would happen to Robby? How would he ever kick his heroin habit without family around to support him?

Instead of calling 911, Ken checked the caller ID and dialed Takahashi, who had called to warn Dad during breakfast. Maybe Takahashi knew something about the gun. When the man picked up, Ken found himself unable to speak. Forget the gun—how could he possibly explain his father's death? That would make everything too real.

"Hello?" Takahashi said. "Goro?"

"No, it's Ken."

"Oh. Need something?"

"Yes." Ken wondered how to ask about the revolver without sounding like a lunatic. "When you called my father this morning, why was he in danger?"

Takahashi cleared his throat but said nothing.

"Mr. Takahaski?"

"Your father prefers to keep his past private."

"Please tell me."

"I'm afraid I can't. Good night, Ken."

"Wait," Ken said, his lungs heaving. "Are people coming after my father? Will they break into the house? Threaten him with a knife? A gun? Some strange weapon?"

"Strange weapon? What do you mean?"

"Like something...unusual."

"I don't understand."

"Why's my father in danger? Who's after him?"

Takahashi went quiet. It sounded like two people were whispering in the background. Then he said, "Mind putting your father on the phone?"

"Now?" Panic spread through Ken's chest. "Why?"

"Need to speak with him."

"He's sleeping."

"It's important."

"He needs his rest. I'll have him call you tomorrow."

Ken slapped the phone into its cradle. He trembled all over. Takahashi, his best hope, had proved useless. Ken couldn't think of anyone else to call. His only remaining choice was to dial 911 and hope for mercy.

He picked up the phone and studied the number pad as though it were from another world. The number six caught his attention. He stared at it until the dial tone cut to a beep and startled him.

Then he hung up and ran downstairs.

CHAPTER 18

THE BLOOD PUDDLE WAS SPREADING. Before Ken went upstairs, it hadn't been much larger than a manhole. Now it surrounded Michelle's corpse like a syrupy halo, its outer edge reaching the rear wall. Thin red tendrils trickled between the scattered canned goods. A coppery odor choked the basement; without any ventilation it proved thick enough to taste.

But what unsettled him most was seeing his father's blood-soaked sweatpants. Two years ago, shortly after Mom's death, Dad had gotten drunk and tumbled down the basement steps. He whacked his spine off the risers and never walked again. The first time Ken helped his father into a wheelchair, he promised Dad that someday he would regain his legs, rise from his seat, and leap in triumph.

Promise broken, Ken thought forlornly.

The scarlet mess oozed within inches of the shelving rack Hannah was taped to. She turned her head from the sight of her mutilated sister and sobbed.

"Question," he said, approaching her.

"Cover Michelle up," she said, sniffling. "I can't look anymore."

Under different circumstances, he might've comforted her. Instead, he ripped open a cardboard box and grabbed beach towels.

He carried them toward the bodies, careful to avoid the spill. He dropped one towel along the edge of the puddle to stop its spread. He laid another over Michelle's legs—a challenge with only one hand—and dragged it evenly across her torso. After he hid the ugliest wounds, he leaned forward to cover her face.

The final towel he gently draped over his father's head and chest. A void widened in Ken's stomach as he did. The sight bothered him but hadn't yet broken him. When Mom died, he cried over the railing of her hospital bed for hours. Now he simply felt numb. Confused. *How could Dad possibly be dead?*

He faced Hannah. "It's done."

She sobbed.

He wasn't sure what to say. "You two were close, huh?"

"Well, no shit. She's my sister."

"Right. Sorry."

"Don't."

"Don't *what?*"

"Don't say *sorry*. I hate that word. It's meaningless." She cleared her throat. "You didn't call the cops, did you?"

"Not yet."

"Listen, please don't rat me out. This whole thing was Michelle's idea—she threatened to kill me if I didn't tag along. When she grabbed that gun and realized she had to kill people, she was hellbent on driving across the country. I told her we should stay in LA, but she wanted revenge for our parents' deaths. She insisted."

"Wait, slow down. Where'd she get this gun?"

"The other day we received a security box left by our father. A yakuza delivered it, said we should have it. Inside was cash, a note, and the snubnose. Michelle picked up the gun before she checked the note. Big mistake."

"What'd the note say?"

She scrunched her nose. "Can you move me upstairs? This smell is—"

"What'd the note say?"

"Michelle has it in her phone wallet. Read the thing if you want —assuming you didn't shoot through it."

Ken reached for Michelle's front pocket. He slid his forefinger and thumb inside and plucked the wallet. The outside rubber pouch was moist with blood. He emptied the contents onto the workbench. Credit cards spilled out, along with scratch-off tickets and business cards from acting agencies. He checked the driver's license. Michelle Saito was twenty-four and lived in an apartment in Los Angeles. She was an organ donor.

Pretty sure I shot every organ worth salvaging, he thought. *Since people can't be saved by her liver and whatnot, those should count toward my six kills.*

Between a pair of credit cards, he found a folded piece of yellow legal paper. He unfolded it. Loopy handwriting was scrawled across it.

Hannah and Michelle,

Should I pass away before you receive this, please know two things. First, I love you. Second, everything I do is for your safety and happiness.

In this security box you'll find five grand and a snubnose revolver. DON'T PICK UP THE REVOLVER WITH YOUR BARE HANDS. *Use a t-shirt or rag, but never touch it with your bare hands. It was supposedly cursed by the shamans on Mt. Fuji back in the 1930s. Anyone who wields this weapon can't drop it until they die or murder six people.*

As for how I came to possess the gun, it was given to me by your grandfather. He said he won it gambling, but that's beside the point. What you need to know is this. The weapon has a deep history within the yakuza. If you ever—

The letter ended. There was an uneven rip along the bottom of the sheet, suggesting that a lower portion had been torn off.

He faced Hannah. "Where's the rest?"

"No idea. We found it that way." Her queasy demeanor and downturned eyes made it hard to tell if she was lying.

He reread the note, then studied his gunhand. Aside from the tight tendons, the hand itself looked normal. He considered wedging a knife between his palm and the gun grip, but the thought made his stomach clench. Hell, this whole situation did.

Turning to her, he asked, "Did your sister really kill six people?"

"She had no choice. It was either that or suicide."

"No other options?"

"None we knew of."

He sighed.

She swallowed hard. "What're you gonna do?"

Suicide wasn't a sexy idea, but neither was shooting six people—well, five, since he'd already killed Michelle. But five was still a massive number. Did he even know five people who deserved a bullet? Some people pissed him off—Principal Soward, drug dealers, and many others—but he never wanted to see them die. Especially not by his hand.

He glanced over at Dad, then at Hannah. She'd done far more than piss him off. If anyone deserved—

No. Stop. I'm not a killer. I'm not.

He started toward the stairs.

"Don't leave me here!" she called. "Not with the smell. Remember, I could've shot you earlier, but I didn't. I don't deserve—"

"Shut up!" He stormed toward her, raising the snubnose inches from her tear-streaked face. "You and your homicidal sister came here to kill my father. You could've stopped her, but you didn't. You let it happen, and now I'm stuck with this mess. I'm confused, I'm scared, I can't process my dad's death, and you could've stopped all this."

"You're right," she said, visibly shaken. "I should've stopped it. I wanted to. I really did."

Ken didn't buy it. He thought about the empty wheelchair upstairs. Someone had removed Dad from his seat and dragged him down here. Michelle's hands had been tied, which meant only Hannah could've moved Dad. Ken thought of the times he lifted his father onto the toilet with the utmost care. To think Hannah dragged him downstairs like a sack of potatoes...

He jammed the barrel against her forehead.

"Wait!" she said. "I can help you!"

"I don't want your help. You helped your sister and look what happened. Think of all the suffering you caused."

"We tried not to. We didn't want to hurt innocent people. That's why we went after revenge."

"Revenge?" He gritted his teeth. "Against an old man in a wheelchair?"

"You don't understand!" Her voice was cracking. "My parents were killed by your father. He wasn't a helpless old man to us—he was a monster."

Ken set his jaw. He shoved her, slamming her head against the shelf. The metallic thud echoed through the basement. Her head dropped. She was unconscious, her hair hanging over her face like a black wing.

He touched the barrel to the middle of her scalp. His index finger, the only part of his right hand under his control, stroked the trigger.

He wanted it. Wanted it bad.

So bad that he curled his finger.

Applied pressure.

But at the last second, he backed off.

"Fuck!"

He aimed again but couldn't do it.

"Fuck! Fuuuck..."

He was in trouble.

If he couldn't shoot Hannah, he'd have a hell of time killing anyone else.

CHAPTER 19

KEN SNAPPED AWAKE, the sun in his eyes. He didn't remember falling asleep, but he found himself slumped in Dad's leather recliner in front of the Weather Channel. His head pounded like hell. The recliner creaked as he rocked in place, an empty bottle of vodka tucked between his thighs. Crumpled beer cans surrounded his feet. Sunlight reflected off them and increased the throbbing in his skull. He must've drunk every drop in the house last night. He vaguely remembered grabbing a beer from the fridge after—

Oh, shit.

Ken turned his pounding head and saw his right arm dangling past the armrest. He couldn't see his hand, nor could he feel anything below the elbow. If last night were a dream, his fingers would be empty now. But when he lifted his hand into view, the snubnose appeared, gripped by his unflinching fingers.

He sank back into the recliner, unable to face the day. He sat there until he heard the scrape of the dog bowl along the kitchen floor. The sound was irritating enough to coax him into the kitchen. He filled the bowl at the faucet and patted Hopper's head. Rubbing the smooth fur relaxed him somewhat. Instead of feeling like the entire house was collapsing, it merely felt like the walls were on fire.

Hopper lapped at the water. Ken sat on the floor and welcomed a sloppy lick across the face. He hugged the dog tight, careful where he pointed the gun.

"What're we gonna do?" Ken asked his pit bull. "Can't go around killing people. And Dad's...gone."

A moan echoed from the basement. Apparently Hannah was awake.

Clutching his swollen head, he wandered downstairs. A rotten stench greeted him. It soiled his lungs and greased his stomach. The sensation passed when he noticed Dad, covered with a bloody towel. The sight numbed him. He wondered what to do about Dad and Michelle. What to do about their bodies.

In front of him, Hannah moaned, interrupting his thoughts. She remained upright, taped to the shelving rack. In the dim lighting she looked wan and exhausted.

"What's wrong?" he asked.

"What isn't?" she said. "My arms are on fire, my lower back won't stop throbbing, and I pissed myself at least twice. Either cut my tape or cut my throat, I don't care. My arms... Fuck."

"Quiet down, okay?" He grabbed a retractable knife from the workbench and sliced the tape securing each wrist.

Her arms dropped free, and she groaned. Then she dropped her shoulders and hunched forward. "Ugh, my back. Fuck."

"Quiet," he said, massaging his temple. "I drank myself to sleep last night."

"Lucky you." Clutching her knees, she panted. "Smells so bad here... Can't you clean this shit up?"

He grabbed the mop and bucket from upstairs. Left-handed mopping proved clumsy, but he nonetheless scrubbed both the vomit and the blood, which had partially dried. Despite his efforts, a heavy stench hung in the air. Dad and Michelle were starting to reek of things other than blood.

"Here's the plan," Ken said, eyeing the wooden door at the rear of the basement. "Over there is a root cellar where my mom used to store her garden veggies. I'll move my dad and your sister inside to contain the smell."

After he dragged the bodies inside and shut the door emphatically, he finished mopping.

"Better?" he asked.

Hannah leaned back against the shelves, moaning, arms limp at her sides. "Everything hurts. I want to lie down. Can you free my ankles now? Please?"

"No," he said. "For all I know you'll strangle me once you're free."

"Strangle you? I can't lift my arms. They might be permanently fucked up."

"You're staying here," he said.

The doorbell rang. Or at least he thought it did. He couldn't be sure what he'd heard through the ringing in his ears. His brain was tied in knots. Then the bell chimed again. He pointed the gun barrel at Hannah. "Keep quiet."

He trudged upstairs. In the living room Hopper barked wildly at the front door. Ken nudged him aside and twisted the knob. Then, remembering, he tucked his gunhand behind his back. With a deep breath, he opened the door a crack.

On the porch stood Officer Rick Isaacs, a local cop who lived up the street and patrolled the area five days a week. The sight of his freshly pressed uniform drove stabbing fear through Ken's chest.

"Morning, Fujima." Isaacs' face was puffy today, maybe from lack of sleep, and his gray mustache resembled a roughly used toothbrush. Nonetheless, his eyes were sharp. "Your hair's a mess. Rough night?"

Ken patted his hair down and forced a laugh. "Not really. More like a rough week. Missed out on a full-time teaching position."

"Oh yeah? That sucks. Y'know, my daughter had you for class the other day. Said you're a half-decent teacher."

Ken blinked. It took him a moment to make the connection between Officer Isaacs and Lexi Isaacs, the goth girl who'd announced Trevor Tyson's hiring. "Didn't realize Lexi was your daughter."

"Probably because she hides behind all that sorceress makeup."

"There's nothing wrong with it."

Isaacs waved it off. "Where's your father? Gotta ask him something."

"Right now?" Ken's heart kicked into high gear. "Why? Did we do something wrong?" He cringed, knowing he sounded mega-guilty. "Sorry, I'm a little hungover."

Isaacs narrowed his eyes. "Bring your father out here."

"Can't. He's sleeping. Sleeping in today. Because it's Saturday."

"Not surprised he needed extra sleep after last night. The neighbors complained about loud noises."

"Might've been the bar next door."

"Don't think so. The Carters across the street said the noise came from your place."

Ken swallowed hard. "What'd it sound like?"

"It was loud. Fourth of July loud."

"Probably the fireworks then."

Isaacs scowled.

"I'm kidding." Ken laughed to settle his racing heart. "Guess my jokes don't land when I'm hungover."

"They don't land when you're sober either." The officer rubbed his clean-shaven chin. "What made the noise?"

Ken blinked.

"Answer me, Fujima."

"It was a shelf."

"A shelf?"

"Yeah. A metal rack. It toppled and made a loud bang."

"Hmph." Isaacs peered past Ken's shoulder. "Can I see this shelf?"

Ken shook his head.

"Why not? Running a business in there? One you don't want me knowing about?"

"I don't want you waking my father. Besides, I have to get ready for my shift at Walmart."

"Before you do," Isaacs said, patting the door, "you should know that I looked up local gun registrations."

It took all of Ken's resolve to not flinch.

"Your father doesn't have a gun registered. Neither do you. If the noises were gunshots, your father's gonna have himself a whopper of a problem. And you—if you're covering for him—will get nailed for hindering my investigation."

"There's an investigation?"

"Not officially." Isaacs leaned closer. "But I'll be paying attention."

"Are you th-threatening me?"

"Not at all." Isaacs smiled. "In fact, here's your chance to come clean. Be smart. Take it."

Sweat glided down Ken's back. He could only imagine how red his face was. The longer he stood here, the more suspicious he'd look.

"Well, Fujima?"

"It was a metal rack." Ken forced confidence into his voice. "That's all."

"I see. Next noise complaint will be your last. I won't tolerate that shit. Not six houses down from where my daughter sleeps. You hear me?"

Ken nodded and shut the door, listening to Isaacs's fading footsteps.

It was over. By some miracle Ken's lame excuses and nervous conviction had prevailed. But he knew Isaacs would be back. The man had always been suspicious of Dad because of his yakuza tattoos, which had been on full display years ago when a fire alarm sent Dad running out of the shower and onto the front lawn wearing only a towel. Isaacs was first on the scene, and he inquired more about the tattoos than the cause of the alarm. Ever since, Isaacs had had it out for them.

For now, however, Ken couldn't worry about that. He needed to lay low and figure out his next move.

On shaky legs, he hurried toward the closed basement door.

When he opened it, he found himself staring at the barrel of his father's 9mm.

CHAPTER 20

THE PISTOL STRETCHED to within an inch of his nose. It hovered there, the muzzle wobbling back and forth between his eyes. Though Ken wanted to run away screaming, he remained frozen in position. He hadn't moved since opening the door and couldn't bring himself to do anything but breathe. He should've known that even someone as sore and exhausted as Hannah would seize an opportunity to escape. Now all he knew was the gun—not the one in his hand, but the one in his face.

"Either of us shoots," she said, "and the neighbors will hear."

Fresh sweat leaked along his spine. She was right about the neighbors, but he couldn't let her control the situation. His gunhand rested at his side, pointed at the floor. All he needed to do was bend his wrist and pull the trigger. Though if he made a sudden move, she might shoot. He needed a better way to end this stalemate.

"Here's the deal," he said. "First, you need to head downstairs."

"No thanks," she said. "Now step aside. Let's talk."

"Talk? About what?"

"I'll explain once I'm out of this basement."

"I can't let you up here."

"Why the hell not?"

For starters, she could kill him. She probably didn't intend to shoot—too noisy—but if she grabbed a knife, she could quietly cut his throat and run. Even if she didn't plan to murder him, she might run. While he wouldn't mourn the loss of her company, he couldn't afford to lose the only person who understood this cursed weapon.

"Please go back downstairs."

"'Please' won't work on me today. I'm extra cranky because I slept with my arms in the air." Frowning, she added, "Look, I'm not trying to kill you, okay?"

"Funny. Last I checked, there was a gun pointed at my head."

She set the pistol on the floor. "Happy? Now let's help each other."

"Each other?" Ken stomped the abandoned pistol. "Where the hell do you get off? After everything you put me through, you expect my help?"

"I've got a plan that'll help us both," she said. "Trust me or don't, but you'll need me if you want to get away with shooting people."

"I'm not shooting anyone," he protested.

"You already did," she replied bitterly.

"That was self-defense."

"That was *my sister*."

They stared each other down. This pissing contest was going nowhere. If Hannah expected his help, she might want to rethink that. Despite his hesitation last night, he still considered her his top target. Only if he *had to* kill, of course, but if anyone had to die, let it be his father's co-murderer.

The stare-down concluded when she shook her head. Sighing, she said, "Okay, we're both grieving and on edge right now. Let's try this again. First off, you're right. I should've stopped Michelle. We'd both be happier if I had. But what's done is done, and now you're stuck with the revolver. There's a way out, but we'll need to work together."

"A way out?" Ken glanced at his gun. "So there *is* another way to drop it."

"I didn't say that. In fact, I've got more bad news."

"What now?"

"I'll explain when you let me out of this basement."

That was the last thing he wanted to do. Unfortunately, nobody else could help. He couldn't Google "How to lose an undroppable gun" and expect worthwhile results. Much as it pained him to admit it, he needed her insight. If it could save lives, it was a risk worth taking.

"No sudden movements," he said and stepped aside.

At the kitchen table they sat in opposite chairs. Hannah kept both hands on the table while he poured her a bowl of corn flakes. She ate voraciously, her hair spilling into the bowl. He stayed alert, worried she might try to catch him napping.

"What bad news did you want to tell me?" he said.

"Yeah, about that." Her flakes crunched as she stirred. "See, Michelle picked up the gun on Tuesday. She'd killed four people by late Wednesday night. Then Thursday night I was driving through Texas when she started spazzing in the passenger seat. I thought she was having a nightmare, but she was wide awake. When I asked what was wrong, she aimed at my head and fired."

"She tried to kill you?"

"Yeah."

"Why?"

"Because that revolver has an appetite."

He glanced at his gunhand. "An appetite?"

"Yep. Doesn't like to wait more than a day between meals." She gobbled another spoonful. "Did you notice Michelle's wrists were tied behind her back? After we reached Pennsylvania, she asked me to restrain her. Said she...didn't want to risk hurting me." Hannah sank back into her chair. She looked ready to cry. "Chelle claimed the gun filled her head with angry thoughts, urges to kill anyone in sight. I imagine the same thing'll happen to you."

"We don't know that." But he nonetheless checked the stove clock. It was almost ten o'clock. He'd left Angela's sometime after midnight. If he'd killed Michelle around 12:30 or so, the gun would grow hungry in about fourteen hours. "Was it exactly twenty-four hours before your sister went nuts?"

"No. Nothing was exact. It came on gradually. She became feverish, then nasty thoughts crept in, then she tried to kill me."

"Great." He pinched the bridge of his nose. He didn't want to believe her, but the image of Michelle's secured wrists stuck in his mind. "So, basically, I have to kill five people within five days?"

"Pretty much."

"Well," he said, glaring at her, "if I can't find a peaceful way to drop this thing, I have at least one target in mind."

Hannah flinched. "Wait. Remember—I was dragged along by Michelle. I didn't want to hurt anybody. Hell, I could've shot you last night, but I didn't. You gotta give me a pass here. Otherwise, how are we supposed to help each other?"

"You're not getting *my* help."

"Hey, I'm not thrilled to work with you either, *buddy*. But you have the gun, and I need it back."

"What? Why?"

"Because." She shifted uncomfortably. "In LA there's a buyer who wants it."

"*What?*" He slammed the gun against the tabletop. "You're gonna *sell* this thing? That's your plan? Strike it rich? If you think I want money, think again."

"We can get more than money. If we survive this mess, we'll need new names, new IDs, plenty of other shit. The buyer can make it happen."

"What do I need a new ID for?"

"Think," she said. "Do you honestly expect to resume your daily life after what happened last night?"

Ken shut his eyes. He tried picturing a scenario where he could return to teaching. Nothing came to mind. Even if he found a nonviolent way to drop the gun, he would still need to account for the two bodies in the basement. He could hide them, he supposed, but if anyone confronted him about his father's disappearance, he'd crack.

"Can this buyer be trusted?" he asked.

She nodded. "Michelle and I met with him. He could've killed us and taken the gun, but he didn't. He seemed spooked by it."

"Can't imagine why." He studied the revolver. With his free hand he picked at the grooves in the cylinder, considering the five bullets inside. He hated the thought of taking a life—or, rather, *another* life—but if the hype surrounding this gun was real, his choices boiled down to suicide and murder. Suicide sounded noble compared to quintuple-homicide, but he needed to stay alive. Not for his own sake, but for his brother's. Robby needed Ken, and Ken knew that his suicide would put his brother in a dark, inescapable place.

And he couldn't let that happen.

"Hopefully I'll find a nonviolent way to drop this gun." He slid his chair out, his body thrumming with nervous energy. "If not, I'll do what needs to be done."

"Great. Got five lucky winners in mind?"

Ken hesitated as he rose to his feet. He couldn't name a single person. All he could think about was staying alive for Robby's sake. He refused to lose his brother—his only remaining family—to an overdose. The Fujimas had suffered enough these past couple of years.

"Let's go see my brother," he said, glancing at a sun-faded photo on the fridge. In the photo Robby looked angry. He was always angry at somebody. "I'm sure he can help me brainstorm."

CHAPTER 21

Before heading out, Ken grabbed his father's leather jacket. Though bulky, its large pockets offered the ideal hiding place for his gunhand. The jacket was an obvious choice, but not an easy one. The moment he slid his arms through the sleeves, he caught the scent of his father's soap. It clung to the lining and followed him out the door.

He and Hannah crossed the front yard to his Camry. Even with his gunhand hidden, he felt exposed, as though the sun were a spotlight targeting him. He ducked into the driver's seat and reached around the steering wheel with his left hand to plug the key into the ignition. When he started the car, the dash clock blinked to life: 10:15. On any other Saturday morning, he'd be heading to Walmart, but today he wouldn't be going in. Another part-timer would have to enlighten customers about 4K TVs and iPhone accessories.

Backing out of the driveway left-handed proved awkward; same with reaching across his body to put the car in drive. Once he hit the road, he expected things to get easier. They didn't. His jacket kept reminding him of his father. Dad had received it from Mom as a birthday gift years ago, and when he'd opened up the package, he'd smiled and said, "Good taste, Ellen. Good taste." After she died, Dad wore the jacket whenever he left the house, regardless of the weather.

In the passenger seat, Hannah rubbed her arms. "It's nice not being tied up."

"Don't start."

"Start what?"

"Anything. I've got a lot on my mind."

He stopped at a red light and stared at the passing traffic. Behind every wheel sat a human being with hopes, dreams, problems, and secrets. Unless he somehow found a peaceful alternative, he would have to remove five people from this world. The thought tangled his gut. He slumped in his seat, foot jammed against the brake, even as the light turned green.

Horns honked behind him. Cars drove around.

"Where I'm from, green means go," Hannah said.

"I can't do this," he said. "Hell, I couldn't even kill *you*."

"Probably because you're a good judge of character," she said, massaging a wrist. More horns honked as cars swerved around. "Bet if you found some real scumbags, this would be easier. Ever seen that old movie *Death Wish?* The one with Burt Reynolds?"

"It's Charles Bronson, not Reynolds."

"Well, whatever. The guy runs around Chicago at night shooting criminals. Maybe you can follow suit. Grow a mustache, kill some dirtbags, drop your gun. Think about it—there's gotta be scum around here."

Ken lifted his foot off the brake. He recalled Thursday's lunch, when he and Angela had watched a hooded figure deal drugs to their student. It hadn't been the first time Ken witnessed such a scenario. His brother had been a repeat customer for nearly a decade, and as the image of a loaded syringe crossed his mind, Ken knew exactly who he wanted to eliminate from this world.

He planted his foot on the gas pedal, turned onto North Main, and passed Vesuvio's Pizza, Senunas' Bar, and a stretch of crammed-together houses before making two right turns. Halfway down Wallace Street stood a double-block house that his brother called home.

The front door was unlocked, so Ken and Hannah let themselves in. The hallway swallowed them with unnatural daytime darkness. Only the square outline of a boarded-up window provided any light.

"Fancy place," she said, powering on her phone's flashlight.

The downstairs stank of sweat and dried urine. Scrappy old movie posters adorned the walls, *Pineapple Express* a popular favorite. Soiled mattresses lay scattered, some occupied by passed-out junkies. Whenever Ken took his eyes off the floor, his next step landed with a crunch, usually on a discarded syringe or crumpled fast-food wrappers.

It dawned on him that the previous time he'd entered this den, he'd been ready to wet himself like a frightened boy in a haunted house. Today, however, he felt no apprehension. Sure, someone could leap out and mug him, but he had nothing to lose. Besides, if anyone assaulted him, he could respond with a .38 caliber answer. And it wasn't like they could pry the gun off him.

After searching the ground floor, he ventured upstairs. The wooden steps moaned under his weight. At the top he considered removing the cardboard blocking a window but decided otherwise. He tiptoed down the darkened hall to the first bedroom door. The knob screeched when he turned it, and someone—or something—rustled inside. He slowly pushed the door open. Solid darkness hung within. Hannah shined her light ahead, and a calico cat scurried under a dresser.

"That poor creature," she said.

"Got a soft spot for cats?"

"For most animals. Part of the reason I didn't shoot you last night was because I was afraid to hurt your dog."

"Shooting human beings is fine, though?"

"Well, you're a Fujima," she said, as if that were a valid excuse. "C'mon, let's find this brother of yours."

He turned when something caught his eye.

Hanging from a wall hook was a button-down shirt and a pair of black slacks. Same ones Robby had shown him yesterday. A piece of paper poked from the shirt pocket—a receipt for a total of $49.98. On a nearby dresser were two pennies.

Ken stared ahead, conflicted. On one hand, he felt like dogshit for assuming Robby spent the money on heroin. On the other, he resented his brother for not showing up last night. Had Robby been home, Dad might be alive and Ken never would've picked up this godforsaken revolver.

Exiting the room, Ken heard a distressed voice, a female one, coming from down the hall. It sounded like sobbing. Pained sobbing.

He paused, thinking back to what Hannah said about *Death Wish*. What if this poor woman was being raped? If he walked in on something so horrific, he wouldn't hesitate to shoot. Then he'd have one less bullet and a fresh twenty-four hours to work with.

He hurried down the hall. The weeping faded before it resumed as an agonized, rhythmic moan.

He burst through the door. A moldy stench assaulted his nostrils. Darkness engulfed him; he fumbled for the light switch. As the lights flickered, he spotted a man's arched, sweaty back. Across his shoulders the word HOGWILD was tattooed in gothic script. The guy's spine straightened out before his hips launched toward the woman beneath him with a hungry thrust. She yelped again. Ken noticed pink blotches along her thighs.

"Stop!" Ken raised his weapon. "Get off her!"

Hogwild thrust twice more before making a gurgling noise and collapsing beside her. Neither seemed concerned about Ken's yelling. The woman teasingly picked at the man's clumpy, oily hair. The sex, gross as it was, appeared consensual.

"Hot times," Hannah said. "Remind me later to scrape out my corneas."

Ken pocketed his gun. He backed away but stopped when he recognized the shark tattoo above the woman's ankle.

"You—you're Robby's girlfriend," he said. There was no mistaking her bleached hair and beak nose. Even though she was high as the sky, her eyes gleamed with greed—the same take-take-take attitude that had drained Robby empty. "The hell you doing with this guy?"

"Fuck off," she said in a tired voice. "Go home, Kevin."

"It's Ken, not Kevin. Where's Robby?"

"Down the hall."

Ken tried the other doors. He found Robby passed out on a sulfur-colored couch that crawled with ants. His brother's cheek was propped against the armrest, his hand dangling near the floor where a depressed syringe lay beside a strip of cloth, probably used as a tourniquet.

Though Ken had pictured his brother in situations like this, he'd never actually seen him passed out cold. It was unsettling. Chilling. Without thinking, he shook Robby, who continued to snore. Ken grabbed a half-empty beer bottle and poured the contents over his face.

Robby twitched. And groaned. He reached up to wipe his face without opening his eyes.

"Robby," Ken said. "Wake up."

Robby blinked, his eyes red and glossy. He looked at his wet hand, then at the bottle in Ken's. "That was fucking piss."

"Robby," Ken said with a lump in his throat, "Dad's dead."

CHAPTER 22

ROBBY PEELED his head from the armrest. An unkempt strand of hair clung to his lip and he brushed it away with a scrawny hand. He attempted to push himself upright but quickly surrendered, lying there reeking of sweat and foulness. His eyelids drooped. Ken had to shake him again to keep him from dozing. Sniffling, Robby looked at Ken and said, "Dad...what?"

"Dad's dead," Ken said.

"Dead?" Robby tasted the word. "Don't you mean Mom?"

Ken shook his head, fighting back tears. He hated that Robby was too strung out to grasp the situation. More than anything, Ken wanted to unburden himself of this horrible secret and confide in his brother.

Robby sat up, his head hanging sideways. For a moment he stared ahead before he abruptly leaned forward and expelled stomach acid onto the floor. When he finished vomiting, he dropped back on the couch, his head sinking into the cushioned armrest.

"Robby!" Ken pinched his brother's ear. "Wake up!"

"Ken? Huh? What're you doing here?"

"Focus, Rob. You need to keep this in your head—Dad's dead."

"Head. Dead. Head. Dead."

"Snap out of it. This isn't a joke." Ken grabbed his brother's elbow and yanked him away from the armrest. Instead of sitting up, Robby flopped onto the opposite seat cushion.

"Hannah, get his other arm," Ken said.

Together they propped Robby upright, but the moment they let go, he drooped forward. Ken touched his palm to Robby's bony chest and held him steady while he sat beside him. Hannah ripped the cardboard away from the windows, welcoming hard sunlight into the room. Robby shuddered away from the yellow blaze like a vampire, covering his eyes with a hand.

"Ken," he said. "I bombed the interview. Sorry, man."

"That's okay," Ken said, rubbing his brother's shoulder.

"Did you say...Dad's dead?"

Once Robby's eyes opened, Ken explained what happened. He tore the details out of himself like bits of shrapnel from a festering wound—painful yet necessary. Robby bawled and Ken joined him, weeping for the first time today. Though Ken unashamedly considered himself an emotional person, he'd been numb since last night. His brother rehumanized him.

"Why'd this happen?" Robby sobbed his words. "Dad's just an old geezer. This is bullshit."

A floorboard creaked as Hannah backed into the hall.

Ken gave his brother a clumsy one-armed hug. Robby returned it. They held each other tight, and Ken rested his chin on Robby's shoulder. It felt great to have someone to lean on. Someone to share the burden with.

"First Mom, now Dad," Ken whispered. "Both too soon."

"This blows," Robby said. "Y'know, Dad said I became a disgrace after Mom died. He was right. Totally right. I wanted to prove him wrong though. Get back to my former self. I wanted him to be proud, like he was when I worked in Philly. I wanted him to see me like that again."

Ken knew the feeling. "Same here. Couple days ago, I was up for a full-time teaching position. Thought I'd have good news for Dad, but I got snubbed."

"Sucks to be us." Robby's head sank against Ken's shoulder. "What do we do now? Call a funeral home?"

"We can't," Ken said. "I'm in a tough spot."

"Dad has money. We can use that."

"The problem isn't financial."

Robby pulled back and dabbed his eyes with his sleeve. "What is it then?"

Ken lifted the revolver into view. "This is what killed Dad. It killed his murderer too. And right now it's stuck to my hand."

"Stuck? Are you high or just me?"

After demonstrating how stuck it was, Ken explained his predicament. The one-two punch of news regarding Dad's death and the cursed revolver overwhelmed Robby. He clutched his head, staring at a crushed pizza box on the floor while he mumbled to himself.

"I want you home," Ken said, cupping his brother's elbow. "I need a friend. Can I count on you to keep it together, at least for today?"

Robby sniffled. He lifted his head and noticed Hannah fidgeting in the hall. "Who's she?"

"She—" Ken stopped himself. He'd always known his brother to be volatile, and if Robby found out who Hannah was, he might explode. "It's complicated."

"Oh." Robby frowned. "What're we gonna do about Dad?"

"If you want to see him, we can go there now. Either way, please come home. I need you, Rob." He held up the revolver. "I need your help finding..."

"People to shoot?"

"Yeah." Ken cleared his throat. "Maybe you can name some dealers."

"I can do better than that."

Ken raised an eyebrow. "What do you mean?"

"I know someone who deserves it more." Robby rose to his feet. "You know her too."

CHAPTER 23

KEN DROVE HOME without paying any attention to the road. His mind was on fire. Though he'd planned on shooting heroin dealers until the revolver ran empty, Robby had a point. There was someone out there who deserved it more. Ken was almost ashamed of himself for not considering the target sooner.

Three summers ago, he had taken his mother to the hospital because of back pain. Nothing debilitating, just something that was slowing her down. He hadn't even noticed until one morning when Mom squatted over her strawberry bushes and rubbed her spine with a gloved hand. A week later he found her kneeling beside her pepper plants for an exorbitant amount of time. After helping her up, he scheduled a doctor's appointment for her; she refused to go.

For as long as he could remember, his mother had hated hospitals. She blamed the "dead" vibe they gave off, but he knew it was something deeper, something personal. He never found out the specifics because the secret died with her.

But it didn't have to.

After days of pleading with her and two calls to reschedule, he finally coaxed her to visit the hospital. He'd been out of work at the time, so he drove her to the Internal Medicine building and accompanied her inside. They toured several waiting rooms and finally met with a general practitioner named Dr. Courtney Glinski. The moment Glinski asked about the back pain, Mom attempted to leave. Ken pleaded with her until she finally went through with the exam.

Dr. Glinski seemed equally reluctant to be there. She was a younger physician; her weary face signaled burnout. Ken had seen that look in teachers who soon left the profession, but not in a family doctor. She went through the motions as she examined Mom and hurried her out the door with a prescription for painkillers.

Two months later Mom was feeling worse despite the pills. Ken urged her to meet with another doctor. Next thing they knew, Mom was diagnosed with lung cancer. Worse yet, it had metastasized to her spine. Glinski should've caught it. If she had, the cancer might've been treatable. But by the time they knew, it was too late. Mom didn't last through winter. Never again did she chase rabbits away from her strawberry bushes or lovingly pinch Ken on the cheek during dinner. Instead she became nothing more than a memory and the subject of a medical negligence lawsuit.

Now, as Ken pulled his Camry into the driveway with his brother slumped in the passenger seat and Hannah in the back, he mulled the idea of delivering a bullet to Dr. Glinski. He pictured himself poking the snubnose against her back. He would line it up with her spine, at the spot where X-rays had revealed his mother's tumor.

Boom. Boom. Boom.

He didn't want to do that.

But he had to.

No. Only as a last resort. Need to find a nonviolent way to drop this gun.

As he and Robby entered the front door, Ken felt the house's aura crushing in. For years the house had carried a lonely vibe thanks to his mother's absence. Adopting Hopper had lessened the sting, but now Dad's recliner was empty; there were no baseball highlights on

TV. And maybe it was Ken's imagination, but he could smell the decay rising from the root cellar.

Hannah stepped inside and shut the door. She stood there awkwardly, tucking her hands into her pockets. "I'm gonna use the bathroom."

"No, you're not," Robby said, blocking her path.

She smiled wryly. "Would you rather I go on the floor?"

"I'd rather you explain who you are," Robby said. "Though I think I already know."

She crossed her arms. "Is that right?"

"Ken mentioned two attackers. He shot one dead. Never said what happened to the other." Robby scowled. "It's you, isn't it?"

"I'm helping Ken."

"Bullshit—you killed our father." Robby shoved her into the wall. Photo frames rattled. "And now you want to use his bathroom? What, you think you can just kill him and use his toilet? His sink? His hand soap?"

"Robby, wait." Ken stepped between them. "Let's talk this over."

"Get back here," Robby snapped as Hannah snuck toward the bathroom. When she shut the door, he faced Ken. "Why the hell don't you shoot her?"

"Because her sister forced her into this mess," Ken said, surprised by the conviction in his voice. He didn't trust Hannah, but when she had aimed a pistol at his face this morning, she let him live. That had to count for something. "Hannah could've killed me but she didn't. She's trying to help."

"You're a total sap, you know that?" Robby steered him into the kitchen, his voice a conspiratorial hush. "Wake up, man. She's responsible. Thanks to her..." He rubbed his eyes. "Ken, I let Dad down so many times. Now I'll never get to make up for it. Never. All because of her."

Ken swallowed an emotional lump.

Robby grabbed him by the jacket. "Do it. Blast her skull open. You can't tell me there are five people who wronged us more than her. Come on, you're supposed to be Ken the Eraser. Get us some justice."

"It's not that simple," Ken said. He explained her plan to trade the revolver for new IDs in LA. When he finished, Robby turned his back to him.

"Listen, I have the gun," Ken said. "I get the final say. Like it or not, Hannah's the only one who understands this revolver. If I run into problems, who else can I turn to? Besides, she knows the buyer. I don't."

"What, you think the buyer will only deal with her?" Robby said. "If he wants the revolver, it doesn't matter who delivers it."

"I don't even know how to find the guy."

"Then ask her at gunpoint!" Robby threw his hands up in frustration. "I've had enough of your shit, Ken. You gotta stop being a doormat. If you don't think Hannah deserves a bullet, maybe we should ask Dad for his opinion. What do you say?"

Ken suppressed the urge to smack his brother and watched as Robby darted for the basement door. His brother's energy exceeded anything he'd displayed in years. As he thumped down the steps, Ken recognized shades of his real brother—the man he'd been before Mom died and he lost himself in narcotics. Ken moved across the room to stand at the top of the stairs.

Downstairs the stench was worsening, but Robby seemed unfazed by it. He studied the shelving rack Hannah had spent the night attached to. After ripping off a shredded strip of duct tape, he looked at Ken.

"Did they tape Dad to this?" Robby said, his voice thick with emotion.

"No, I taped Hannah to it last night."

"Should've left her there."

Before the mood could escalate, Ken met him at the bottom of the stairs and patted Robby's back. He steered him toward the root cellar. Though the door was shut, the stench of two cooling corpses leaked out. Ken buried his nose in his sleeve and opened the door. It was a cramped space, so Robby entered alone.

Somehow he stayed inside for ten minutes.

When Robby came out, his eyes were rimmed with red. He leaned toward Ken's ear and said, "You're right. You have the gun. But if you don't start killing the right people, I will."

CHAPTER 24

AROUND 10:30 THAT NIGHT, while Ken was sitting in the kitchen trying to hypnotize himself with a YouTube video, the doorbell rang. It broke his trance and kicked his paranoid mind into overdrive. He pictured Officer Isaacs standing on his doorstep with a warrant and an army of uniformed officers, SWAT team members, foreign mercenaries, you name it.

The bell rang again, and Hopper left his dog bed to bark at the door.

Within seconds Ken flew across the living room, tugging his jacket on before he shoved Hannah into the bathroom where she couldn't be seen.

After the third ring, Robby, who'd spent all evening Googling Dr. Glinski, got off the couch and lumbered over to the door.

"What're you doing?" Ken said in a harsh whisper. "That could be the cops."

"Nah, it's Chrissie." Robby shrugged. "I invited her over."

"You—what? You invited your girlfriend over *now*?"

The bell rang again, and Robby opened the door. Chrissie rushed in and smooched his cheek about a thousand times before kissing him hard on the lips. When she pulled back, she brushed her blonde hair from her face and waved to Ken. "Hey, Kevin. Robby told me about your dad. Bummer, huh?"

Ken's heart skipped multiple beats. "He...told you?"

"Yeah, gave me the cliff notes," she said. "About your dad, the gun—"

"Robby!" Ken stomped the hardwood. "What were you thinking?"

"Chill, Ken," Robby said. "We can trust her. She's basically family."

"Like hell she is." Ken gestured toward the porch. "Go home, Chrissie. Please. Just go home."

Chrissie laughed and spread her arms wide. "But I am home."

Hopper barked at her.

Ken couldn't believe it. The last thing he wanted was another person being privy to his nasty situation—especially someone as devious as Chrissie. Last year she'd visited the house for dinner one night and left with half of Mom's jewelry. Now, for all Ken knew, she might blackmail him into robbing gas stations or carrying out a bank heist. There was no telling what hideous possibilities were slithering through her mind as she eyed his jacket pocket. The way she smiled drove cold, solid fear into his chest.

"So, lemme get this straight," she said. "A gun is...stuck to your hand?"

"For now," Ken said.

"And you gotta kill five people?"

"I'm not killing anyone."

The bathroom door squealed open. Hannah exited and said, "Guess I can come out now. Oh, hey, you're that chick from this morning. Nice to see you with clothes on."

"Excuse me?" Chrissie scrunched her nose. "Who the fuck are you? You must be the bitch who killed Robby's dad. You're gonna look real cute with a bullet in your head, you know that?"

Ken twitched. The image of Hannah dead and bloody sent a sickening warmth through his gunhand. Heat bundled in his knuckles and crept toward his elbow. His throat went dry. The living room turned hazy. Sweat rolled down his face like rain. He untucked his shirt and fanned his chest to cool down.

Soon he was shivering. Along with the chills came a strange tremor in his gunhand. It was like his bones were trying to shake free of the curse. More likely, the curse was shaking his sore fist deeper under its control.

Then his gunhand wobbled. His wrist bent toward Hannah.

Toward Chrissie.

Toward his brother.

"No!" Ken grabbed his gunhand and pointed it to the floor.

He bolted for the kitchen. Hannah rushed over as he drank from the sink, gulping water in hopes of quenching his unbearable thirst. He splashed his burning cheeks, then shoved her aside and headed for the back door. He needed air.

"It's happening, isn't it?" Hannah asked.

"I'm fine."

"I'm telling you, you need to hurry up with those kills."

"I'm *fine*."

Trembling, he flicked on the backyard lights and stepped outside.

The night breeze brought him comfort. The backyard seemed to be the only part of the property exempt from bad vibes. Though the garden plants hung withered and the toolshed showed rot, the lawn itself remained green. He wandered in circles, sucking down the damp night air. A tall wooden fence offered privacy, but nonetheless he buried his revolver in his jacket pocket.

The door creaked open behind him.

"Ken?" Robby asked. "Something wrong?"

"No, everything's perfect."

"My bad. Should've mentioned Chrissie was coming."

"You shouldn't have told her."

"I don't keep secrets from her, man."

They sat side-by-side at a wooden picnic table they'd built together years ago. It had been a surprise Mother's Day gift, where

Mom had sat daily while she sipped her morning coffee. Even after she passed away, Ken maintained the table, giving it a fresh coat of burgundy paint each spring. This year's layer was peeling but still vibrant.

Robby patted the tabletop. "Remember Mom thought we stole this thing from Kirby Park?"

"Even I'm not convinced we built it ourselves."

"Yeah, but c'mon—she made us feel like criminals."

"Yeah..." Ken swallowed hard. "Wonder what she'd say about me now."

"She'd probably say you're doing your best." Robby shrugged. "Then, knowing her, she'd turn you in."

Ken had to laugh. Their mother was notorious for punishing every indiscretion they committed as kids—and as adults. One time in college he called in sick from his busboy job to go shopping with Olivia. When Mom caught him leaving the house without his uniform, she threatened to notify the restaurant. He assumed she was bluffing until twenty minutes later he received a livid voicemail from his manager. At the time Ken had been pissed, but looking back, that incident probably made him a better man. Or at least a more honest one.

If he were being honest with himself now, his wobbling wrist terrified him. He hated to think he was under the same spell as Hannah's sister, but if that were the case, he needed to do something.

But what? The weapon stuck like a magnet, and he'd already spent all evening trying various adhesive removers and relaxation methods. Nothing worked. His options were dwindling, and his murder deadline was approaching fast.

"Ken," Robby said, "maybe it's time to consider using that gun."

"I'm not killing Hannah."

"What about Glinski?"

"No. There has to be a way to drop this thing." He stared at it beneath the moonlight. Its polished grip glimmered under his sweaty fingers.

A wild thought crossed his mind.

Can't hold a gun without fingers. Why not detach a few?

No. Hacking off fingers was too extreme.

More extreme than shooting people?

He imagined two different futures. In one, he ran around blasting people in the streets, dropping bodies along the sidewalk. In the second vision, he saw himself leaving the hospital with a prosthetic hand. He could live with that. Five fake fingers sure beat five genuine tombstones.

He marched toward the toolshed and opened the door. Moonlight slanted across a waist-high cardboard box. On top were garden shears, their eight-inch blades too filthy to reflect light. Quivering, he ran his thumb along the steel edge. There was no guarantee the shears could cut through bone, so he turned his attention to the orange chainsaw sitting atop a nearby cabinet. He pictured the oily chain whirring through his knuckles until his three bottom fingers hit the floor.

The image left him queasy.

Can't chicken out now, he thought. *Whether it costs me three fingers or the entire hand, it's worth it.*

Before he could talk himself out of it, he grabbed the chainsaw's crummy rubber handle and lugged it over to the picnic table. In a small, nervous voice, he explained his plan to Robby.

"No way," Robby said. "I'm not into hurting people."

Ken raised an eyebrow. "Two minutes ago you told me to shoot Hannah."

"That's different."

"Would you rather visit me in prison or the hospital?"

"Neither."

"Listen," Ken said, his chest snug, "while I was in the living room, this sensation overtook me. My wrist started moving on its own. It bent toward you, Rob. Hannah said the same thing happened to her sister. I hate to believe it, but this gun is starting to possess me."

Robby looked ready to faint.

"The chainsaw will be quick," Ken said. "Once it's done, call 911 and request an ambulance. The hospital's not far. They'll be here in minutes." He squeezed his brother's shoulder. "Please. You owe me after all the times I helped you."

"That's not fair, man."

"None of this is. Now start the motor."

After two reluctant pulls on the cord, Robby yanked hard and got the motor chugging. The odor of burning fuel filled the air.

"Wait," he said, cutting the motor. "You'll need a tourniquet."

"Grab my vodka too."

Ken gulped from the plastic bottle while Robby knotted a t-shirt around his elbow, pulling tight until Ken's forearm felt ready to pop. After Robby twisted the knot and taped it in place, Ken set the bottle down and waited for his nerves to settle. He remained hypervigilant even as a veil of numbness descended over his mind.

"Let's get this over with," Ken said.

Robby started the chainsaw again.

Ken swallowed hard. His stomach rumbled in sync with the chainsaw's motor. Sweat poured down his back. He set his arm on the table with his palm facing up, three fingers around the grip, one shaking beside the trigger guard. Robby would first attempt to saw through the weapon's cylinder. If that worked, Ken would empty the bullets. If not, he would flip his hand and Robby would cut through his knuckles.

What the fuck are we doing?

Robby squeezed the throttle. The chainsaw responded with a grinding roar.

Ken winced. His arm stiffened, as if the blood within his veins had solidified. The discomfort spread along his bicep and shoulder.

Robby released the throttle. "We don't have to do this."

"Quit stalling." Ken shut his eyes. Horrible images flooded his mind—Robby taking a wrong angle and lopping off his thumb or index finger or his entire hand. Every scenario ended with geysers of blood. He could barely keep himself together as the whirring noise grew closer.

Closer.

Clo—

Something seized Ken by the throat. Two cold, sturdy hands. They found a grip, the thumbs crushing down on his trachea. When he opened his eyes, nobody was there. But the sensation intensified. It was too firm to be his imagination.

He glanced at his gunhand.

The chainsaw drew nearer.

The pressure on his throat worsened.

Ken struggled to breathe. He tried to muster a scream, but another set of phantom hands clawed through his chest and punctured his lungs. He could feel air escaping into the hollow of his torso.

His head throbbed.

His vision blurred.

This wasn't anxiety. He was suffocating—or rather, *being suffocated.*

As the whirring chain dropped within an inch of the revolver, he pulled his hand away.

Robby released the throttle. The chainsaw quieted to a chug.

"Stop?"

Ken would've nodded, but the pressure around his throat remained. It didn't fade until Robby set the chainsaw on the table. Slowly, the phantom hands released his neck and chest. Breath trickled through his nose, his lungs aching as they received nourishing air.

"Shit," Robby said, "your neck's all red."

Ken sat still, afraid to move.

"Put that chainsaw away," he said once he got his voice back. "We're going after Glinski."

CHAPTER 25

BEFORE ANY MORE UNSEEN hands could suffocate him, Ken marshaled Robby, Chrissie, and Hannah through the front door and into his Camry, which still carried the scent of chlorine from Angela's pool. The Fujima brothers took the front while the girls took the back. Ken, who couldn't stop shaking, failed to insert the key into the ignition. Normally, he wouldn't trust his brother to drive a John Deere through an open meadow, but tonight he trusted himself even less. They swapped seats and hit the road.

"How far is this place?" Hannah asked.

"Far enough for Ken to reconsider shooting you," Robby said.

Ken sighed. "Drive, Rob."

They left Wilkes-Barre and motored toward a small, tucked-away development called Hamilton Acres. It lay behind a sprawling cemetery and a scenic stretch of pines. For a moment they drove through wilderness before luxury homes sprouted up. Glinski lived in a gaudy two-story McMansion toward the rear of the development. Wide stretches of shadowy grass surrounded her home, along with a sturdy steel fence. A streetlamp cast a milky orange glow across the lawn.

They parked in darkness along the curb. Ken moved to open his door but instead his revolver bumped the handle. The gunhand was getting in the way of everything—his lifestyle, his morals, even basic tasks like exiting a parked car.

"Want me to keep the car running?" Chrissie asked.

"No," Ken said. "You're coming with us."

Outside, the night air held a nervous cool. It brushed his tender throat like an unseen blade. He shivered in place, unwilling to approach the house.

"Rob, are we even sure she's home?"

"Positive," Robby said. "She just tweeted a photo of pistachio ice cream on her nightstand."

Pistachio. That was Ken's favorite flavor. Knowing that he and Glinski shared a sweet tooth didn't make things any easier. "I don't think I can do this."

Robby shrugged. "How about I call my guy and get you some Xanax?"

"Do it," Chrissie said. "If he doesn't want the shit, I'll take it."

Ken groaned. "I want this to stop."

"It won't stop," Hannah said. "You can end it, but you can't stop it."

Ken breathed deeply, until his lungs could expand no farther. He approached Glinski's house from the side lawn. The driveway gate was shut so he climbed the fence—a difficult task for a one-handed high school teacher—and nearly tore his arm from his socket before he dropped hard on his hip.

Chrissie cackled. She, Robby, and Hannah climbed the fence with ease.

Ahead floodlights shined across the front porch, highlighting its two-story entry arch and the Corinthian columns that supported the front gable. Ken considered ringing the doorbell until he spotted a security camera above the door.

Great. Honestly, Ken wasn't surprised. Fancy houses always came equipped with security. No telling how many surveillance cams adorned the place, but it was likely that a break-in would trigger alarms and send the cops flying. Instead, he and the others snuck along the bushes beside the house, hunching low, checking for cameras. His gaze bounced around but stopped when a clinking sound startled him.

Ahead, a chain rattled in the pitch-dark backyard. As he crept closer, the rattling gave way to barking.

"Got ourselves a pooch," Ken said.

"What breed?" Hannah asked.

"Who cares," Robby said. "We're not here to adopt."

"I'm good with dogs," Hannah said, powering on her phone light. The beam bobbed ahead but failed to reach the dog. "Depending on the breed, maybe I can calm it down."

"Give me your phone," Ken said impatiently. He grabbed it and approached the pissed-off animal. A thrashing silhouette lunged toward him, each bark harsher than the last. A growling brown snout poked into view. Light gleamed off a set of fangs.

Ken retreated in a hurry.

"What kind?" Hannah asked.

"Rottweiler," he said, pressing a hand over his pounding heart. "Thing's on a long leash. Be careful when you go near it."

"Wait, I didn't say I was going near a rottweiler."

"Then what good are you?" Robby snapped.

For once, Ken agreed with his brother. He agreed so much that he considered executing Hannah on the spot. One quick blast to the forehead was what she deserved. Her hair was already a mess, so her face might as well match. He'd be doing them both a favor, and as he angled the revolver toward her, he—

"Shit." Ken clutched his wrist. "It's happening."

Hannah backed off. "Maybe I should head back to the car."

"You're not going anywhere," Robby said. "Ken needs our help."

"With what exactly? We don't even have a plan."

"Let's just ring the doorbell," Chrissie said. "You can carry me onto the porch and pretend I OD'd. Maybe this doctor lady will buy it."

"If she doesn't, she'll have our faces on camera," Ken said.

"Not if we keep our heads down," Robby said.

The barking went on.

Ken knelt beside the bushes, gathering his thoughts. He considered Chrissie's plan, but the security camera spooked him. They could try entering through a smashed window, but that would likely trigger an alarm. Besides, there was no telling how prepared Glinski was for a home invasion. She might have a panic room or—worse—something to shoot *him* with.

There had to be a wiser option.

C'mon, think!

Frustrated, he stabbed his gun at the dirt. His thoughts crossed and collided. Every time he tried concentrating on a plan, Robby and Hannah's bickering interrupted him. When he told them to shut up, the rottweiler started barking again.

That gave him an idea.

"You guys, head back to the car. I won't be long if this works."

"If what works?" Robby asked.

"Just keep the car running."

They vanished into the darkness.

Ken crept forward. At the edge of the backyard, he crawled inside a corner shrub, concealing himself between the branches. The rottweiler approached. Fear climbed within Ken's chest as the leash rattled. The animal pounced, landing within two feet of his hiding place before the chain reeled back. The barking resumed.

Louder and louder.

Exactly what he'd hoped for.

Ken shook the bush, antagonizing the dog until an upstairs window opened.

Glinski called out, "Sunshine, quiet down!"

Sunshine did not. The rottweiler thrashed against its leash.

Ken held his breath.

Moments later a light above the deck flickered on. The backdoor squealed open. Out stepped Glinski, feet thumping across wooden boards. Through the shrub branches, Ken spotted a navy-blue bathrobe covered in Penn State logos. She leaned over the wooden rail and whistled. She was thirty feet away—so close, yet much too far. From what Ken had learned about snubnose .38s, they were only effective at extremely close range.

"What's wrong, baby?" Glinski asked. "Another squirrel?"

Sunshine barked in reply.

"Oh, you want to come inside? Is that it?"

Another bark.

"All right, you talked me into it," she said, descending the wooden steps. "But no more peeing on the carpet. Got it?"

With her every step, Ken's heart boomed in his chest. This was it. Couldn't ask for a better scenario. The rottweiler was mere feet away. If Glinski came near enough to undo the leash, he'd have an easy shot. The only caveat was that he would have to shoot her before she released the dog. Last thing he wanted was to be mauled during his escape.

Humming a placating tune, she sauntered across the lawn.

He slowly raised his gunhand, restraining his movements. He tucked his arm between two branches and angled the barrel toward the dog. Now he needed Glinski to enter the line of fire.

His next inhale stuck in his throat. Sweat waterfalled down his cheeks while his pulse hammered his eardrums. His shooting arm, already poised awkwardly beside his cheek, shivered beyond control.

Through the gaps in the shrub, he watched Glinski squat beside Sunshine. The animal lunged toward Ken, and Glinski turned in his direction.

"What's with you tonight?" she asked, unknowingly meeting Ken's eyes.

Ice blocked his veins. He re-aimed the barrel, now steady, even while the rest of him trembled. He noticed impatience written across her face—the same expression she'd worn while diagnosing Mom years ago. That infuriated him, but he took solace in knowing that she soon wouldn't have a face.

He slid his finger through the trigger guard.

Touched the cold steel fang that was the trigger.

Applied pressure.

More.

More.

More.

The trigger reached its tipping point. Another nudge was all it needed. Then she'd fall flat and never get up.

Trouble was, Ken's desire to preserve life raged against his need to take it. Staring down the woman responsible for his mother's death forced him to process many emotions. Though most were dark and resentful, there were others. Warm wisps of forgiveness stirred within him. While Glinski was responsible for his mother's death, Ken never wanted vengeance—at least not until he'd unwittingly picked up this godforsaken weapon.

He knew better. It was the snubnose that wanted the kill; not him. And though the temptations were intensifying, he still had a choice.

Quietly, he pulled his arm back and made the right one.

CHAPTER 26

"WANT TO TALK ABOUT IT?" Robby asked, braking for a red light. Once they stopped, he glanced back at the girls before he leaned in and whispered, "I get that you already killed one shitbag last night, but this time was different, right?"

Different for sure. This time Ken hadn't killed anyone. And though he was satisfied with his decision to spare Glinski's life, the fever had spiked into a hot resurgence and multiplied his homicidal urges. Worse yet, he couldn't confide in anyone because they were under the impression that he'd shot Glinski. If they learned the truth, panic would spread. Ken needed everyone calm; a relaxed atmosphere would make it easier to resist the revolver's dark hunger. If he held out long enough, perhaps the gun would surrender and drop from his grasp, hoping to find a new wielder.

Ken liked that idea. But until it manifested, he would consider himself a safety hazard.

The Camry's forward motion shook him from his musings. As they rounded Public Square, he noticed college kids barhopping between Rodano's and Franklin's. He wanted to stick his revolver out the window and shoot, but he restrained himself, opting to shut his eyes and inhale cool nighttime air. Beside him, Robby rambled on about how people should talk about their problems. Ken thought that was the most hypocritical thing he'd heard all year.

When they pulled into the driveway, the Backfield Bar next door was rocking, the jukebox blasting Van Halen's "Hot for Teacher." He normally cringed at sleazy '80s rock, but the lyrics made him think of Angela floating in the middle of her pool. If only he'd stayed with her.

Morbid vibes smothered him as he reentered the house. The place felt abandoned without Dad sitting there grumbling about the Dodgers. At the kitchen sink Ken splashed cold water on his face. It did nothing for his fever, which approached the melting point with each passing minute. He wondered if Hannah knew more than she let on. If she was holding out, now was the time to spill everything.

When Ken reentered the living room, he spotted Robby and Chrissie whispering together on the couch. Hannah leaned against the front door with her arms crossed. She glanced in Ken's direction and said, "None of us heard a gunshot. You didn't shoot Glinski, did you?"

Robby and Chrissie turned to face Ken with wide-eyed, expectant looks.

Ken pocketed his revolver and approached Hannah, the hardwood floor squeaking under his weight. "Here's the more urgent question. Is there anything else you know about the gun? Anything?"

"No." She hesitated before shaking her head. "Nothing."

"I teach for a living," he said, pacing back and forth as if in class. "I know when my students are hiding things from me."

"I'm not your student."

"Yes, but I know you're lying."

"I already told you everything. Try recalibrating your bullshit detector."

Ken gritted his teeth. The nerve of her. Not only was she mouthing off like an unruly student, but she was hiding info he desperately needed. If she wouldn't give him answers, he'd force them out.

He leveled the gun at her forehead.

"Whoa." She leaned back, blinking rapidly. "Please don't."

"Where's the rest of that note from your sister's wallet?"

"I don't know," Hannah said. "I told you, we found it ripped like that."

"Then how'd you know where to find the buyer?"

"I...Michelle found him. I don't know how, but she did." Hannah swallowed hard. Her shoulders bounced with each shuddering breath. "Please. Put the gun down. Thought we had a deal."

"The deal was you would help me."

"That's what I'm doing."

"Tell me the buyer's name and address."

"I don't remember," she said, her back pressing against the door. "It's written down at my apartment in LA, I swear."

"Bullshit," Robby said, rising from the couch. "Tell us." He glared and rushed toward her.

She shook her head. "I legit don't remember."

"Here, let me jog your memory." Robby seized her throat and slammed her head against the door.

"Ow!" She kicked Robby's shin. "Asshole!"

Robby groaned and rubbed the insulted bone.

"Hey, don't hit my boyfriend," Chrissie yelled from the couch.

"Everybody, shut up," Ken said. Straining, he tucked the gunhand in his pocket. His mind juggled images of blasting Hannah, Chrissie, and Robby, but he closed his eyes and breathed deep, trying to suppress the urges. When he exhaled, he didn't feel any better. "Hannah, look at me."

She glanced up, her neck again in Robby's grasp.

"I'm losing control," Ken said.

"Told you," she said. "You're lucky you lasted this long."

"Goddammit, Ken," Robby said. "Why didn't you shoot Glinski?"

Ken ignored him and leaned closer to Hannah. "That note from earlier... What did the ripped-off portion say?"

"Yeah, quit holding out, you twat," Chrissie said. "Spill it before he kills you."

Hannah gleamed with sweat. Stank of it too. Her face muscles flexed with strain as she tried to dislodge Robby's hand. Her mortified expression resembled that of a student who'd failed her way into summer school. Normally it pained Ken to see that look, but now it enraged him. He wanted that look gone. He wanted answers so they could all pass this nightmare exam with an A+.

She swallowed hard. "Already told you everything."

He clenched his teeth. The barrel wanted her, and his finger wanted the trigger. He reached across his body, clutching his forearm, wrestling to keep the gun inside his pocket.

"What did the note say?" he asked.

"No idea."

"Tell me."

"I can't."

"Hannah, I'm at the breaking point. What happened to your sister is happening to me. I can't hang on. Either tell me what you know, or you'll never get the chance to." Tears stung his eyelids. He gripped his forearm tighter. "Please. I don't want to kill anyone. Not even you."

Wincing, she said, "I know you don't."

"Then help me."

"I can't. Please, kill somebody else."

"You're not listening!" he snapped, leaning in till they were nose to nose. "I said I don't want to kill *anyone!*"

But the moment he said it, he knew it wasn't true.

This time when his finger brushed the trigger, he didn't hesitate.

CHAPTER 27

THE MOMENT KEN pulled the trigger, he felt relief. A smooth coolness flooded his brain and spilled through the rest of his body. He
enjoyed it for a split instant before registering the heat of the blast,
the punch of the recoil, and the ear-pounding bang reverberating
through the house.

After the noise faded, he heard Hannah wailing.

Holy shit, I shot her.

Ken backed away from her and realized Robby now had both
hands fixed around her throat. Robby looked petrified, but what
looked even worse was the side of Hannah's gray t-shirt, now soggy
and dark. The stain spread downward, and her screams devolved into
a series of agonized moans, each weaker than the last.

"Robby, let go of her!"

But Robby remained awestruck.

Ken swiveled his head, looking for something to stop the bleeding. On the couch, Chrissie clutched a pillow to her chest, her eyes
and mouth wide with terror. He ripped the pillow from her hands
and rushed to Hannah. Before he pressed it against her wound, he
paused.

A dark realization seized his mind. He could try saving her life, yes, but at this point was it worth it? Someone had to die, and the damage was already done. Besides, part of him wanted to shoot her again.

Do it. Finish this.

He ignored the temptation and jammed the pillow into her side.

Hannah wailed. Her head thrashed sideways, smearing her hair against the door. Robby finally let go when Ken wedged himself between them. He held Hannah in a clumsy embrace as he guided her knees to the floor. The urge to shoot flooded him, but he slid his arm around Hannah's back to keep from targeting her.

"Help me stop the bleeding!" he yelled. "We gotta patch her wound."

"Fuck that!" Chrissie said. "Better her than me."

"It's over, man," Robby said. "She's done."

"Hang on, Hannah," Ken said as her chin fell to his shoulder. "You'll be okay."

"Floor," she whispered.

"Floor?" he asked. "You want to lie down?"

"Floor mat."

"Floor mat?" There were no floor mats nearby. "Hannah, what're you saying?"

"The note." Her free hand pushed at Ken's chest with all the energy of a drooping sunflower. "In my...van. Under the...floor mat."

She tumbled forward, her weight spilling against him. Ken had to reset his blood-slick knees to keep her upright. In the process, he lost the pressure on her wound.

"Robby, I'm losing my grip."

"What do you expect me to do?"

"Help me out!" Warm blood poured across his thigh. He looked for somewhere to set her down, but floorspace was limited and she was already shivering. Last thing he wanted was to set her on a chilly floor. "Robby, grab one of Mom's quilts and spread it across the kitchen floor."

"Man, she's not gonna make it."

"She will if you listen to me."

"It's over, Ken. Besides, you heard what she said about the floor mat. That's the info we needed."

"Get the quilt." Ken twisted around and poked the gun at his brother. "Now, Rob! After all the times I've helped you, you owe me."

"Fine, whatever!"

"Chrissie," Ken snapped, "get over here and help me move Hannah—now!"

In the kitchen they shooed Hopper away and set Hannah on the quilt beside the dinner table. Ken then grabbed a clump of paper towels and pressed it hard against Hannah's wound.

The pressure shocked her back to life. She blinked rapidly.

Ken asked Robby for more paper towels and some duct tape. He crafted a makeshift bandage and taped it tight around her belly. Though he had once worked at a hospital, he'd never learned much about gunshot wounds. All he knew was the obvious—stop the bleeding and call an ambulance. After wiping his bloody hand on the quilt, he pulled Hannah's phone from her pocket.

"You're calling for help?" Robby said. "That's insane. You'll have to explain the gun, Dad's body, everything."

Ken hated to admit it, but his brother was right. If the EMTs showed up, Hannah might be saved, but everyone would face life-destroying legal trouble.

Still, he refused to let her die. He probably should've—especially after the role she played in Dad's murder—but Hannah was different from her sister. The fact that she could've killed Ken this morning but didn't—that convinced him. And since she spared his life, he needed to return the favor.

Ken took her hand and guided it to the bandage. "Hannah, keep pressure on it." He pushed down and she moaned. "I know it hurts, but you need to hang on for about thirty minutes."

"Thirty minutes?" Robby said. "What, we dropping her off at the ER?"

"No," Ken said, "we're bringing the ER to her."

CHAPTER 28

THEY REACHED Glinski's house at two minutes to midnight. The ride over had been hell. Ken had endured homicidal cravings as well as the complaints of Robby and Chrissie, who insisted on letting Hannah bleed out. What swayed them was the revolver. The lethal threat not only quieted them but convinced them to pay close attention as he'd explained the plan to kidnap Glinski. Now it was time to act.

"Pull your hoods up," Ken said, his heart slamming. "Gotta do this quick."

They left the engine running and dashed across the front lawn. The moment they reached the porch, Chrissie played dead under the camera's sightline. Robby squatted over her, pretending to pump her chest while Ken thumbed the doorbell repeatedly.

The ringing echoed inside. Ken checked the nearby windows, hoping for a flicker of light. Each second he didn't see one, a dark weight sank within his chest. He worried about Hannah. When they left her behind, her face had been pale and sweaty, and she barely had enough strength to keep pressure on her wound. She might die any moment now. If she did, would his fever go away? Would the nasty thoughts subside? Honestly, he didn't want to find out.

Behind him Robby continued to pretend to perform CPR on Chrissie. She complained about him being too rough, and every gripe made Ken more eager to go postal.

Before his rage could escalate, he grabbed his forearm and dug his nails into the flesh above his wrist. The sharp pain distracted him. He applied more pressure until, finally, lights flashed inside the house.

"Glinski's coming. Get ready."

Through the stained-glass border along the door, he spotted a robed figure sauntering downstairs. In her hand was a phone that cast light across her face. Her expression was confused. Though he couldn't see her screen, he guessed she was eyeing the camera feed.

The front door opened slightly before catching on a chain lock. She peeked through the gap. "Who're you?"

"My buddy's girl OD'd," Ken said. "Can you help us?"

"If she overdosed, rush her to the ER. They'll take her, no questions asked."

He stuck the gun in her face.

"Oh, God!" Glinski jumped. Her phone struck the hardwood floor.

He slid his foot through the gap. "Unlock the chain."

With shaky arms, she reached for it. A scraping sounded as it extended in length. "I can't unlock it without shutting the door. You have to move your foot."

Instead, he slammed the revolver through the stained-glass panel along the door. She shrieked as shards pattered the floor. Jagged bits nipped the back of his hand, but he set his jaw and ordered her to unlock the chain. The moment he slid his foot away, the door closed. He heard a metallic scrape, followed by a satisfying pop. The door creaked open.

Ken shoved it aside and aimed for her chest. "Step outside."

Panting, she shook her head. Her robe fluttered as she backed away, into the brightly lit foyer. Nearby was the sweeping staircase she had descended moments ago. She shifted toward it, but Ken dashed inside, blocking her escape.

"I said step outside." He gestured toward the porch. "Move it."

Instead she backed farther into the foyer. Her hip struck a French cabinet, sending an adorning crystal lamp into a wobble. She grabbed the lamp and swung it in front of her. The thing was still plugged in, and the cord cut short her swing. She whimpered as she tried ripping it free of the wall.

"Please go away," she whispered.

"Put the lamp down and step outside. Not telling you again."

"Be reasonable," she said. "If you shoot me, I can't help your buddy's girl."

"Who said she needed help?" Robby said, storming inside.

Chrissie ran in after him. "Yeah, Dr. Bitch. Don't I look fine to you?"

Glinski gawked as the three of them surrounded her.

"Drop that fucking lamp," Robby said. "It's time you paid for what you did to Ellen Fujima."

"Who?" Glinski's mouth widened with terror. "I-I don't know what you're talking about."

Her bullshit denial drove Ken's finger to the trigger. He was losing patience. It became harder to restrain himself, especially when he envisioned her forehead covered in juicy entry wounds. He felt himself teetering. If he spared her, he could save Hannah. But if he executed Glinski, both she and Hannah would die, and he'd only have three rounds left. The temptation shook the tightrope beneath his trembling mind.

Robby lunged for the lampshade.

Glinski hopped away but tripped, landing on her side with a hard double thud. Before she could push herself up, Robby ripped the lamp from her grasp and slammed it against the hardwood floor. The crystal base shattered.

"*H-e-l-l-p-p!*" Glinski screamed.

A thumping sounded along the staircase. For a moment Ken worried someone might be home with her. Then a fearsome bark cracked the air. Her rottweiler leaped onto the floor. It snarled as it reset its feet and made a beeline for him.

Ken aimed at the floor and fired twice.

Reports thundered through the high-ceilinged foyer.

The shots sent the rottweiler retreating upstairs.

Glinski, meanwhile, shuffled backward on her elbows. Her robe came apart, revealing a nightgown with a wet stain down the front. She frantically crawled toward the rear room, but Robby held her by the shoulders and pinned her to the hardwood. His face burned red with vengeance.

"Move her to the trunk," Ken said. "We gotta hurry."

Instead Robby barred his forearm across her throat.

"I said move her!" Ken snapped, steadying the gun. Hideous thoughts flashed in, surrounding his moral high ground like rising lava. "Now—I'm losing it again."

But Robby wasn't listening. He growled in her face. His free hand grabbed a dagger-like shard from the floor.

"No, Rob—what're you doing?"

As Ken reached for his brother, something yanked him backward. He turned and saw Chrissie squeezing a fistful of his jacket. Before he could shake free, she wrapped her arms around him, hugging him from behind like a monkey.

"Get off me!" Ken slammed his elbow against her side. After a couple clumsy hits, her grip loosened. He twisted free in time to see Robby clutching Glinski in a headlock. With a trembling hand, Robby angled the shard toward her neck.

"Your call, Ken," Robby said. The jagged crystal gleamed in the light from the chandelier. "Either you ice this bitch or I do."

"Help!" Glinski shrieked.

"Let her go, Rob."

"Not happening." The sharp tip sank toward her windpipe. "Once I slice her open, you can finish the job."

Ken broke free from Chrissie and leveled the revolver. The moment he did, Robby fumbled the shard. Glinski gasped with relief, and Ken felt an overwhelming urge to shoot her. He wanted to shoot Robby too. Shoot everyone. *Shoot, shoot, shoot.* His better self withered beneath his mounting bloodthirst.

He steadied the weapon.

Curled his finger through the trigger guard.

Robby released Glinski and ducked.

Ken pulled the trigger a moment later.

Right after he aimed at Chrissie's head.

CHAPTER 29

KEN CLOSED his eyes and welcomed smooth, easy air into his lungs. When he exhaled, out went the strain that had smothered his mind. Gone were the urges, the needs, the hostility. His brain tingled numbly, sweetly, as though he'd toked a joint and settled back into his favorite college bean bag chair. His muscles softened. His body became a relaxed puddle of flesh on the hardwood floor.

Relief blanketed him.

Soothed him.

Mesmerized him.

Then he heard sobbing. At first, he thought he himself was crying. Then the wailing intensified. It came from somewhere nearby, above him.

When he opened his eyes, he saw Robby hugging Chrissie. She wasn't hugging back. Her head dangled sideways like a flower too heavy for its stem. A syrupy trail of blood leaked from an exit wound above her ear. The blood slicked through her hair and dripped onto the floor. One drop landed on the back of Ken's hand.

He flinched. That single drop splashed him back to reality. No longer was everything sweet and cozy. All illusions of comfort were torn aside, leaving him with only horrid sobriety.

Chrissie's dead, he realized. *Because of me. I killed her. I killed a defenseless human being. She's dead and gone and missing part of her skull. This wasn't supposed to happen. How the hell did it happen? Nobody was supposed to die. Not because of me.*

A frantic tapping diverted his attention. Against the wall sat Dr. Glinski, her legs jimmying against the floor. Her mouth hung open, soundless, as if she'd forgotten how to scream.

For a moment he wondered why she was here. Then he realized he'd invaded her home to kidnap her. The plan had been to coerce her into saving Hannah, who might die any minute. He could mourn Chrissie later; if he didn't hurry, Hannah would join her.

He lumbered to his feet and approached Glinski. In a small voice he said, "I need you to treat a gunshot wound."

Glinski blinked. "But...she's dead."

"Not Chrissie," he said. "Another woman. You need to come with me."

He led her toward the door at gunpoint and then stopped short.

The sight of Chrissie lying dead in Robby's arms struck him like a sledgehammer to the chest. Last night Ken, engulfed in grief, confusion, and panic, had killed his father's murderer. Tonight, however, he knew what he was up against: a cursed weapon that thrust his ugliest desires to the forefront of his mind. Rather than selecting a worthy target while he still had control, he'd waited and waited. His indecisiveness cost Chrissie her life. And though she'd spent the past two years ruining his brother, she didn't deserve that. Not when Ken could've shot anyone else—backstreet criminals, people on the verge of death, even the doctor who'd misdiagnosed his mother.

"Robby," Ken whispered. "I'm so sorry."

Robby sobbed into the unbloody half of Chrissie's head. When Ken reached for his shoulder, Robby shrugged him off—not with anger but with grief.

"Rob, we need to go. The noise woke the neighbors. Cops'll be here soon."

"I don't care."

"You should."

"Leave me alone."

"But—"

"Leave me the fuck alone!" Robby snapped. "Go save Hannah since she's so goddamn important."

The comment burned his ears. Ken backed away, unsure what to say. He wanted to point out that Hannah had spared his life back at the house. That she'd never killed anyone. That she was someone they needed to work with. But out of all the things Ken wanted to say to his brother, he said the one that mattered most.

"Don't get caught, Robby."

Then he steered Glinski out the door and tried to do the same.

CHAPTER 30

THEY MANAGED TO SAVE HANNAH.

Her kitchen-floor surgery hadn't been pretty. It had required alcohol wipes, betadine wipes, scissors, a needle, some thread, and the expert care of a physician with a gun to her skull. Strangely, there was no bullet to remove; by some dark miracle, it seemed to have vanished. That worked in their favor, but without any topical anesthetics, Hannah had to endure the suturing process with clenched teeth and constant thrashing. Watching her suffer was no fun, and Ken spent the entire surgery berating himself for putting her in this position.

Once Dr. Glinski had sealed the wound and wrapped it with gauze, she insisted on moving Hannah to a hospital. Ken declined, knowing that his and Hannah's survival depended on more than IV drips and blood transfusions. Instead, he asked about home care. Glinski recommended raising the thermostat and covering Hannah with blankets to keep her warm. Restoring nutrients was equally critical; plenty of fluids, electrolytes, and iron-enriched foods would help with that.

Now Ken chewed on his knuckle, wondering if he'd done the right thing. He'd made an awfully large mess in the past hour or so.

There was no telling if Hannah would survive, but for the moment he was glad she had a chance.

They lifted Hannah onto the living room futon and monitored her for several minutes. She lay there, pale and breathing shallowly. An occasional cough escaped her throat, but aside from that, there wasn't much action.

Glinski wiped her bloodstained hands on her bathrobe and sat on the coffee table. Her gaze darted around the room before landing on his gunhand. She opened her mouth but hesitated before asking, "Who removed the bullet?"

"Nobody," Ken said.

"Someone had to," Glinski said in a hurried tone. "It was expertly done. Was another doctor here?"

Ken shook his head. He decided to tell her about the gun. By the time he finished, the coffee table was rattling from her shaking. "Settle down. I don't intend to kill anyone until tomorrow."

"Listen," she said, pulling at her collar, "I'm sorry about your mother."

He narrowed his eyes. "So you *do* remember her. At your house you pretended otherwise."

"I was scared. I didn't know what to say." Glinski nodded toward Mom's photo on the wall. "Truth is, I'll never forget her. She haunts me everywhere I go."

"That's no way to talk about her."

"Sorry, I meant no disrespect. What I'm trying to say is that the moment your family filed that lawsuit, my life came to a hard stop. I didn't sleep for three straight nights after I found out." She grimaced. "Ever since, I've felt trapped. I can always sense these invisible walls nearby—ten, fifteen feet away. They keep squeezing inward. They get closer and closer until I feel them push against my skin, my bones. Every day is like that, and whenever I enter an exam room, I want your mother to be there. I just want another chance. At the same time, I'm terrified that it *will* be her, that I'll make the same mistake again."

Ken frowned, wondering if he would feel the same about Chrissie from now on. When he closed his eyes, he saw the deep red of her bullet wound and her blood-slick hair. He imagined he'd be replaying the scene millions of times if he lived through this mess.

"What mistake?" he asked. "What mistake did you make?"

Glinski shrank away. "I...was careless. I should've asked your mother more questions. Should've sent her for tests."

"Why didn't you?"

"We get lots of patients with back pain. Very rarely is it caused by cancer."

"Tell me something," he said, recalling his dinner conversation with Dad. "Did you get kickbacks for what you prescribed her?"

"What? No." She forcefully shook her head. "It's like I said. I was careless. I made a horrible mistake. Ever since then, I've tried to make up for it."

"You can't," he said. "My mother's gone."

"I know. But those invisible walls I mentioned—they only pull back when I'm examining patients. Nowadays I inquire about everything. If I have the slightest suspicion that cancer might be present, I send my patients for tests. I do what I should've done with your mother. I know it's too little too late for her, but it's the best I can do."

Ken stared her down. He wasn't sure he bought her change of heart. She was likely telling him what he wanted to hear. Either way, he didn't have to decide her fate until tomorrow. For now, he only needed to keep her from leaving.

"Get up," he said. "We're going downstairs."

"What? Why?"

"Because I can't trust you to sit here and behave."

"Wait. Please. Hear me out."

"I did." He gestured with the gun. "Now get up."

"Okay, but—"

The doorbell rang.

Ken froze as if he'd been hit in the neck with a tranq dart. His imagination raced straight to Officer Isaacs. A neighbor had probably notified him about the gunshot earlier tonight. Ken had been in such a hurry to save Hannah that he'd forgotten about the other consequences of firing a loaded gun in his living room.

"*Help!*" Glinski shouted. "*H-e-l-l-p-p!*"

Ken poked the gun against her cheek. That quieted her, but he needed to think fast. If Isaacs were outside, Ken needed to respond now or risk having his door beaten down. The barrel tucked under her chin, he grabbed her collar, steered her toward the front door, and whispered, "Lean against the wall and don't move. If you do, I'll shoot you and whoever's on the porch. Are we clear?"

"Mm-hmm," she murmured.

The bell rang again.

When he opened the door, it wasn't Isaacs. It was Robby. His brother's eyes, glossy and red-rimmed, peered through the two-inch gap. Chilly air trickled in, bringing his brother's unwashed odor with it. Though it was hard to tell for certain, the sleeves of Robby's hoodie appeared wet with blood.

Instead of relief, Ken felt horrorstruck. "Get in here, Rob—before anyone sees you."

Robby remained on the porch. He said nothing, just stared into the living room and sniffled.

"Hurry, get in here." Ken yanked Glinski away from the wall. "I'm moving her downstairs to tape her up. Give me a hand."

Robby entered without a word. The only sound he made was an occasional sniffle. On his way to the kitchen, he paused to look at Hannah. He blinked a few times, then approached the basement door. Downstairs he grabbed the tape. It took them two minutes to attach Glinski to the shelving rack. Once it was done, Robby stared at her for an uncomfortably long time.

"Thanks for the help," Ken said, unsure what else to say. Now that things had settled down, he realized Robby was in a fractured state. The blood on his clothes might as well have been his own. In the span of a single day, he'd endured the deaths of his father and his lover—the latter caused by his own brother. That was enough to overwhelm any man, let alone one caught in the dark cloud of addiction.

"Robby..." Ken set a hand on his brother's shoulder. The muscles underneath tensed. "Let's head upstairs. Get you a change of clothes."

Robby remained silent and still.

"Maybe we can have some coffee, talk things out." Ken squeezed his elbow. He tugged gently, fearful that his brother might collapse if he pulled too hard. "But only if you want to. If you don't want to talk, that's okay."

Robby sniffled.

Ken frowned. "Look, I'm sorry about Chrissie."

The moment her name left his tongue, Robby turned and smacked him.

Ken caught the punch square in the mouth. His neck whipped sideways; his teeth flared hot. He tasted blood. When he reached to check his lip, Robby roared and tackled him onto his back.

Fists crashed against his forehead and cheek. On instinct Ken blocked the incoming blows with his forearms. He guarded his face until he felt the sharp drop of an elbow on his stomach. More blows smashed his ribs and chest before Robby grabbed Ken's forearms and tried to pry them away from his face.

Ken held strong in his defensive pose. He didn't want to fight back. He didn't want to make things worse. He just wanted this to end.

A hard pinch along his forearm followed. Pain swept over him in a fiery rush. Ken realized Robby was biting into him like a feral dog.

That did it.

Ken slammed his fist into his brother's gut and shoved him away.

Robby rolled into a stack of cardboard boxes. The upper ones toppled down, spilling towels and dishcloths over him. Robby shoved them aside and bared his teeth, which were stained with blood. In the dim light of the basement, he resembled something subhuman. When he reset his feet, he lunged forward. Both hands reached for Ken's neck, but they never took hold.

Ken jammed his gunhand hard against his brother's forehead.

Time froze, as though a pause button had been hit. Nobody moved, not even Glinski, who'd been yelling throughout the scuffle. The brothers' eyes met, and Ken watched Robby's glare wither into fear. A man could only maintain aggression for so long with a gun against his forehead.

"I want you to leave," Ken said through gritted teeth. His forearm throbbed where he'd been bitten. "Now."

Robby backed away from the revolver. On his way up the basement steps, he cast one last glance at Ken. Tears swam in Robby's eyes. A sob escaped as he rushed upstairs. The front door soon slammed behind him.

CHAPTER 31

Sᴜɴʀɪsᴇ ᴄᴀᴍᴇ ʙᴇꜰᴏʀᴇ sʟᴇᴇᴘ ᴅɪᴅ. An orange glow burned around the edge of the front curtains, lighting the living room enough to outline Hannah's silhouette. Her chest rose and dipped beneath the blanket, a sign of life. For now, everything was peaceful—not that Ken trusted the respite to last. Any second, he expected to learn that blinking his eyes could detonate a nuke or sneezing could trigger an earthquake. He felt dangerous, and not in a sexy, exciting way.

Sinking back into Dad's recliner, he removed the icepack from his chin and took another gulp of the bottom-shelf vodka he'd found stashed in a cupboard. It tasted the way paint smelled, but he needed it. More than anything, he needed to ditch his conscious mind. Escape this nightmare. Escape himself.

As more sunlight pierced the living room, Hannah shifted beneath her quilt. Her head moved. She coughed.

He rushed to her side. "Hannah? Need anything?"

After some weak coughing, she said, "Water."

He filled a mug at the sink and stuck a bendy straw inside. He guided it to her lips, and after a harsh cough she pulled on the straw. He encouraged her to drink more, remembering what Glinski said about keeping hydrated.

After Hannah drank her fill, he touched her forehead. Hot as a lit oven.

"Kill anybody?" she asked groggily.

"Let's cool you down," he said, ignoring her question. He ran cool water over a dishcloth, wrung it out, and pressed it to her forehead. "How's that feel?"

"Grimy." She pushed the quilt down and lifted her shirt to check the wound. When her finger grazed the bandages, she grimaced.

"Does it hurt bad?"

"Try shooting yourself and find out."

"Sorry."

"Stop apologizing," she said. "It's like *sorry* is the only word you know. When I get better, I'm gonna force-feed you a dictionary."

He smiled. "Least you're in good spirits. Hungry?"

"My stomach feels like it's full of sludge."

"I'll get you something to soak it up."

In the kitchen he refilled her mug and found a box of unsalted crackers in a cupboard. Dad used to love them in his soup. If he were here now, he'd cringe at the idea of sharing them with Hannah. But after everything Ken went through to keep her breathing, he now considered her his responsibility. Maybe he had simply become accustomed to the role of caretaker, but he believed it was the right thing to do.

Back in the living room he offered her a cracker. She nibbled, following each bite with a sip of water.

"You're tougher than the doctor expected," he said.

"Doctor? How'd you get a doctor here?"

"Kidnapped her." He sat on the coffee table and hung his head. "I went from shooting you to invading her home in the span of a half hour." He rubbed his eyes. "Where the hell is my life going?"

"Wherever it has to."

"I'm so screwed."

"Then blow your brains out."

"Can you tap the brakes on the sarcasm?"

"Well, excuse me for being lippy toward my almost-assassin." She nibbled another cracker. Sipped more water. "Remember, there's a way out. We'll go to LA and hit the reset button."

"It's not that simple," he said. "I...I killed Chrissie."

"You also killed my sister." Hannah said. "Or does her death not matter?"

"It does. It's just... So much happened so fast that my head feels like a beehive. I can't even think straight. And I have four more bullets."

"Know what I'd do?" Hannah said, gingerly tilting her neck. Judging by the strain on her face, it put unwanted pressure on her side. "I'd rush the next four. Don't drag things out and torture yourself. Think—would you rather have bad things happen all week long or just have an extra-shitty Monday?"

"A bad-enough Monday can ruin the whole week."

Hannah winced. Though she spoke like her old self, her face suggested she was in agony. He brought her another cool dishcloth.

"Thanks." She rested her eyelids. "Hey, you heard what I said about the floor mat in my van, right?"

"About the note? Yeah. Haven't gotten around to it."

"Oh." She sounded disappointed.

"Do you need it now?"

"No, I'm...surprised." She blinked. "Thought I'd be expendable once you heard about the note. Instead, you kidnapped a doctor to save me. Never expected that out of a Fujima."

"Didn't want anyone to die," he said.

"You're strange. Letting me bleed out would've made your life easier."

He smiled. "Maybe next time I'll reconsider."

"Not funny."

He frowned. "You're right. Especially after what I did to Chrissie."

"Don't say that. You didn't kill Chrissie. The gun did."

"Hannah, that's not true. Every choice I made led me to that point. I knew about the deadline. I should've acted."

Soon as the words left his mouth, he realized what must be done. He was no killer, but if he had to be one, he needed to pick his targets decisively. Chrissie died because he backed himself into a corner. He should've shot someone sooner, but instead he avoided his grim responsibility and hoped the problem would vanish.

In the end it didn't.

In the end the gun got its way. It forced his reluctant, indecisive hand.

But it won't happen again, he thought. *Next time, it's my call.*

CHAPTER 32

HOPING to clear his overburdened mind, Ken trudged outside in search of Hannah's van. From the moment his feet hit the sidewalk, his senses came under assault. Blinding sunlight crashed against his eyes; dead leaves crunched underfoot, the sound of each step irritating him toward insanity. At the street corner, his nostrils took a beating from a busted garbage bag. The fumes followed him, carried by a chilly morning breeze that seemed intent on suffocating him. He hurried down the next block before the air cleared. Suddenly he realized, to his horror, that he'd forgotten his jacket.

The snubnose was out in the open.

Right where anyone could see it.

Arrest me now, he thought.

He buried the gun in his pants pocket, obscuring it. No telling how obvious it looked, but he didn't care at this point. Running on no sleep had that effect on him.

Hannah's Ford Windstar was parked along the curb with its window open. The interior stank of buffalo sauce gone bad. A swarm of flies hovered inside. He reached in and discovered the lock was already popped. Somebody had looted the van. Although, judging by the crusty interior seats and scattered sandwich wrappers, there wasn't much worth stealing.

He opened the door. A squirrel darted out, scaring him into nearly pulling the trigger. His heart thumped erratically while he sifted through discarded fast-food bags on the floor. He stuffed them all into a single bag, which he tossed under the vehicle. He then lifted the floor mats and found a crumpled piece of paper.

He unfolded it. It read:

—need money, new IDs, or anything else, bring this weapon to the Sunrise Building on San Martin Ave. There you'll find a man who can help. His name is Takahashi. He'll take care of you.

All my love,

Your father

Ken rubbed his eyes and reread the note. He couldn't believe it. *Takahashi? Could this be the same guy who called Dad on Friday morning?* If that were the case, what did it mean? Did Takahashi want Dad dead? Most likely not, considering the warning had nearly saved Dad's life, but something was off here. Ken needed to ask Hannah.

After locking the van, he headed home. The moment he reached his front lawn, he noticed someone wearing a pink hoodie and khaki capris standing on his porch. He thought his weary mind was projecting fantasies, because the woman looked like Angela. He shut his eyes tight. When he reopened them, she was still there, thumbing his doorbell. A faint *ding-dong* echoed.

He hurriedly tucked his gunhand under the back of his shirt.

"Angela?"

At the sound of her name she twisted around. She didn't appear happy to see him. Her face was red, makeup streaked beneath her eyes. She'd been crying.

Over how I left her the other night?

"Hey," he said, "about Friday night..."

"You left your phone in my yard," she said, pulling it from her back pocket. "Thought you might stop by for it, but you never showed."

"Sorry," he said. "My hands were full."

She tossed her dark hair behind her shoulder and descended the porch steps. At the mailbox she handed him the phone. She smelled of lavender.

"I shouldn't have run off like that," he said.

"Yeah." She frowned. "Did you hear about Pete?"

"Pete?" The abrupt change in subject baffled him. "You mean Pete Chang? Our student?"

"Yeah. He...died yesterday."

Ken collapsed against the mailbox. It struck his side with a dull plastic thud. For a moment he stood there, picturing the look on Pete's face when the boy had rushed out of the custodian's office on Friday. That haggard, broken look.

"What happened?" Ken asked, his voice light years away.

"Overdose," she said, sniffling. "From pills."

He groaned, the mailbox creaking under his weight. It couldn't be true. Pete had been angsty all week, but Ken never got the impression that the boy was suicidal. "He didn't OD on purpose, did he?"

"Probably accidental, I'm not sure," she said, dabbing an eye with her sleeve. "Another teacher texted me and said the pills were counterfeit Oxycontin. Apparently they were made with fentanyl."

"Fentanyl?" He'd heard about fentanyl on the news. It was cheaper and more potent than heroin, so dealers often cut their supply with it. He always feared Robby might buy an unlucky score one day and end up dead. "How many pills did Pete take?"

"No idea. From what I heard there was a bottle on his nightstand that was practically full. Probably took only a couple."

A couple. That almost sounded harmless. Though Ken was no expert on drug addiction, he knew that typically when addicts decided to kill themselves, they went out using their entire stash. Popping a couple pills didn't sound like a suicide. Rather, it sounded like Pete had developed a tolerance and tried chasing a high, only to ingest more than he'd bargained for.

If his death were accidental, the blame was on whoever laced the pills. Ken envisioned some greedy, soulless asshole mixing fentanyl into a powdery solution. It sent his blood into a blaze. Surprisingly, his newfound fury arose from within his heart, not his gunhand.

"Who the fuck gave him those drugs?" he snapped.

She winced. "I have no idea. Why?"

"Just curious," he said, realizing his tone must've startled her. To be safe, he added, "My brother's a user."

"God, this is awful." She sobbed. "Pete's gone. How can this happen?"

She leaned forward to hug him. It wasn't until her arm brushed his that he remembered he had a loaded gun attached to him. On reflex, he hopped away from her.

"What's wrong?" she asked.

"Nothing. I need to process this."

"Oh." She looked away, embarrassed, and he felt shitty about rejecting her. "Ken, want to get coffee somewhere? Talk about this?"

"Now's a bad time."

"Oh."

"How about later?"

"Sure," she said, retreating down the sidewalk. Her Jeep was parked beside the next driveway. "We'll chat another time, I guess."

When she turned her back, a void expanded within his chest. For all he knew, this might be the last time he'd ever see her. It wasn't right to leave things like this.

"Angela, wait," he said. "Tonight we should do something."

She frowned. "There's a memorial event for Pete tonight."

"In that case, I'll be there. Text me the details."

"Sure. See you then."

She climbed into her Jeep and drove off.

Ken wandered into the house, struck numb by the news of his student's death. He realized he'd never get to change Pete's attitude or see how the boy developed as an artist. Ken became so preoccupied that he accidentally poured vodka into Hopper's bowl. He couldn't focus. Not with this tragedy swirling around his brain.

To think Pete would be alive if some asshole dealer hadn't sold him fentanyl.

It left Ken with a heavy heart and a clenched fist.

When he checked the stove clock, it read 8:23.

That gave him plenty of time to find and kill the bastard.

CHAPTER 33

BLACK COFFEE BURNED Ken's tongue but otherwise did little to wake him. The local news stations reported nothing about Pete Chang, but they did cover the late-night shooting at Dr. Glinski's house. Footage showed the front porch webbed with yellow tape while a voiceover explained that an unidentified woman had been shot dead inside. From the sounds of it, the police were uncertain what had happened, and the reporter mentioned that Glinski's whereabouts were unknown.

On the futon, Hannah snored. She'd been asleep since his return, and though he wanted to ask about the ripped note and Takahashi, she needed rest. Besides, he had more immediate concerns.

Hoping to learn who'd supplied Pete with fentanyl, Ken grabbed a new jacket, climbed into his Camry, and drove to his brother's place. With his gunhand tucked away, he entered the shadow-infested building. Today five people were passed out in the hallway. Some were naked, all were strung out.

He found Robby upstairs in a room that smelled of cold pizza and hairballs. Robby lay on a half-sunken air mattress, its sides squeezing in like a hot dog bun. Ken shined his phone light and panicked when he spotted dried blood on the sleeves of Robby's zip hoodie.

"Wake up." Ken shook him. "C'mon, get out of those clothes."

"Unngh? Who's there?"

"Robby, you're covered in blood."

"Man, let me sleep."

Ken opened the nearest set of curtains. Behind them, the window was covered with towels pinned to the wall. He ripped them down and sunlight poured in, exposing the room's gray walls, the crushed pizza boxes, and the scuttling roaches. He grabbed the new shirt and pants Robby had bought for his interview.

"Get dressed. Now."

"I don't care, man."

"You can't lie around in those clothes. We'll both get busted."

Ken kicked the air mattress. It shifted Robby off balance, dropping his elbow against the floor with a thud. He sat up, squinting.

"Need your expertise," Ken said. "Know any drug dealers who lace their product with fentanyl?"

Robby shrank away from the sunlight. "Shut those curtains."

"Not until you get dressed and answer my question."

Robby struggled to his feet, clearly burdened by whatever substances had helped him achieve sleep. He peeled his hoodie and t-shirt off with the hesitance of a man removing his own flesh. The pants were even more of an adventure, and he stumbled into a wall before shrugging them off his ankles.

"Fentanyl," Ken said, helping Robby into his new shirt. "Who around here deals to high schoolers?"

"How should I know?" Robby said. "Do I look sixteen to you?"

"This is serious. A student in my class OD'd yesterday. He took counterfeit Oxycontin."

"Ugh." Robby paused while sliding into his khakis. "Wish I could help, but my guy doesn't deal to kids."

"Can you ask him who does?"

"What time is it?"

"Almost nine."

"I'll ask when I see him later."

"Ask now. I need a target. Otherwise someone might die, like—" Ken stopped before mentioning Chrissie. It seemed Robby wasn't clear-headed enough to remember last night. Best to keep it that way. "Please, Rob. Contact your dealer before someone else ODs."

Robby mumbled something, then got on the phone.

"Hog? Yeah, I know it's early, but can you hurry over?" A moment later Robby shook his head and whispered, "My guy's busy."

"Where is he?" Ken said. "Can we visit him?"

Robby asked his dealer about meeting ASAP. He paused before saying, "Can it be somewhere more discreet?"

Ken whispered, "Anywhere. We'll meet him anywhere."

Robby nodded. "Cool, Hog. I'll text you once I'm there."

"Where to?" Ken said after he hung up.

"Weirdest place," he said. "He wants to meet at a baseball field."

CHAPTER 34

KEN PARKED at the edge of Broad Street Field, right outside the surrounding chain-link fence. His brother sniffled in the passenger seat. Hard to tell if the sniffling had to do with Chrissie or heroin. Either way, Robby looked like dog shit. Every aspect, from his sunken eyes to his droopy posture, screamed defeat. His lips were badly chapped, and skin was peeling from both cheeks, as though he'd used a cheese grater for a pillow last night.

After cutting the motor, Ken surveyed the ball field. A father and daughter were playing catch while the mother filmed everything on her phone, cheering each time the little girl caught the ball in her glove. Along the diamond, little boys ran the bases while another kid swung behind home plate, whacking imaginary pitches until his sister —or maybe a girl who thought him cute—shoved him to the dirt and ran off laughing.

Ken turned to his brother. "Isn't this spot a little too wholesome?"

"It's where Hog said to meet."

Ken didn't like this. Too many people around. Too many children. "Shouldn't these deals go down in an alleyway somewhere?"

"They go down where they go down," Robby said.

"Where're we supposed to meet him?" Ken said, swiveling his

172 / BRANDON MCNULTY

head. There was a boarded-up concession stand at the edge of the
parking lot, not far from the fence. A six-foot menu hung from the
side wall. The options were hot dogs, cheese dogs, and something
called "fun dogs." The rest of the menu was covered in graffiti. "That
concession stand looks shady."

"Chill, Ken." Robby rubbed his wrist under his nose. "I know
you're Mr. Clean and this is outside your comfort zone, but Hog's
picky about how he does business. Usually he delivers to the house.
We shook up his schedule, so he needed to find a spot he's comfortable with."

"I don't like the location. Doesn't make sense."

"Neither does Chrissie being dead."

Ken's stomach dropped. Looking away, he said, "About
Chrissie..."

"No. Get her name out of your mouth. I don't want a stupid-ass
apology."

"Then what do you want?"

"Hannah and Glinski dead, for starters." When Ken frowned,
Robby slapped the dashboard. "Why the fuck couldn't you shoot
them? They killed Mom and Dad. Or are you forgiving them because
you're a killer too?"

Ken's throat went dry.

"Worst part of losing Chrissie," Robby said, "is that you took
away the only person on earth who liked me."

"That's not true," Ken said. "You're my brother. I love you."

"Yeah, but you don't *like* me. Dad didn't like me either. Sometimes being liked is better than being loved. When you're liked,
people *want* to see you. When you're loved, people see you because
they have to." Robby scratched anxiously at his cheek. "Want to hear
something scary? I'm not sure I like or love anyone. My girlfriend and
my dad both died yesterday, and all I can think about is dope. I can't
wait to get more. I'm craving it so bad that their deaths barely matter.
How fucked is that?"

Ken didn't know what to say. This was as honest as Robby had

ENTRY WOUNDS / 173

ever been about the subject. If Ken patronized his brother about getting clean, he might end up pushing him away. Best to let him talk.

"I hate this," Robby continued. "Hate it so much. I just want my life back. Even just a little piece of it. Anything."

His phone buzzed. He checked it.

"Hog wants us to walk the bases."

"Us?"

"Must've seen you."

"Great." Ken exited the Camry. Though he told himself to act casual, his head swiveled, anxious to spot someone. He joined Robby inside the fence. They approached the sandy diamond with their hands in their pockets. Ken nodded as they passed the parents, who smiled uncomfortably. The kids running the bases shied away as the Fujima brothers rounded first together.

After they reached home plate, they made another round.

And another.

"Remember in high school when I blew that game against Hanover?" Robby asked. "Struck out four times. Never got a piece of the ball. Feels like my life story."

"You had some hits in life."

"Like what? I whiff on everything. Even last night with Glinski. Should've cut her throat."

"Don't say that."

"I mean it, Ken. I wanted to avenge Mom and do you a favor—slice Glinski up, get things started for you. Instead I whiffed." Robby swung an imaginary bat. "Next thing I knew my girlfriend was dead in my arms, all because I hesitated."

"Be thankful you hesitated," Ken said, studying the parking lot. "You don't want that on your conscience. Better to grieve your loved ones than your victims."

"What're you, a fucking poet now?"

As they reached home plate, Ken noticed movement near the concession stand. Someone ducked behind it.

Ken gave chase, his legs gathering speed until he was behind the shack.

Nobody here. He hurried along the back wall, squinting into the adjacent woods. They were sparse, thin white birches leaning over leafy trails. There were no shrubs or thick tree trunks to hide behind. If someone were in the woods, he'd have seen them.

Somebody's gotta be nearby.

"Nice going," Robby said. "You scared him off."

"Where do you think he went?"

"Who knows?" Robby hung his head. "Fuck. Now he's not gonna trust me."

Ken eyed the concession stand. He circled it twice. Spotted no one. On a whim, he checked the back door. It was locked, but as he tried turning the knob, he realized it was sweaty.

And fresh sweat could mean only one thing.

CHAPTER 35

KEN LOST his patience after two minutes of knocking. There was no telling how long it would take to track down Pete Chang's dealer, and every second that Hogwild played dead inside the concession stand was a second that brought Ken closer to his kill deadline. As it stood now, he had roughly fifteen hours to locate a target. After what happened last night, he wanted to unload his next bullet long before then.

"Wait here," he told Robby. "I'll be back."

"Where you going?"

"Just guard the door."

Ken hurried over to his car and grabbed Dad's folding wheelchair out of the trunk. He lugged it over to the shack and jammed it under the doorknob, locking Hogwild inside. Ignoring Robby's gripes, Ken approached the baseball diamond. He took out his wallet and held up his ID to the adults present. Heads turned as he said, "Everyone, this area is under police investigation. Return to your cars and leave immediately. It's not safe here."

By some miracle the parents bought his *Law & Order* routine. They gathered their kids and left. He watched them drive off before returning to the shack.

"Ready to come out now?"

No answer.

"Hog doesn't operate like this," Robby whispered. "He comes and goes on his own terms. He has schedules, man. He sees *who* he wants *when* he wants."

"Believe me, he'll want to see me if he knows what's good for him."

Robby squinted in disbelief. "Ken, this tough-guy act isn't gonna work."

"Who said it was an act?" Ken knocked again. "Ballpark's empty. Let's talk."

When he heard no response, he checked the front of the shack. The boards covering the order window lay horizontal, paper-thin gaps between them. One gap was wide enough to welcome sunlight. He peeked inside and saw stacks of cardboard boxes but little else.

"Back door's blocked," he said. "There's no getting out."

A shuffling sounded. Hogwild stifled his movements, but the noise was plain even to Ken's faintly ringing ears. The dealer tried the doorknob. A thud followed as he shouldered the blocked door.

Robby raced around to the front. "Ken, you're pissing him off. Don't do this. You keep this up, he'll stop delivering to me."

As if I needed more motivation to keep this up.

"Hog," Ken said, "let's quit wasting each other's time."

The man finally spoke. "Fuck off."

Time to get justice for Pete.

"A high school student died yesterday," Ken said. "He OD'd on pills."

"Sucks to be him. Now unblock the door and leave before I call my boys."

"Any of your boys deal counterfeit Oxycontin?"

"How the fuck should I know? It's not like we sample the shit together."

"Who deals to high schoolers around here?"

"Man, I don't know."

"You're not in contact with other dealers?"

"I don't ask questions. I just sell whatever shit I get from my distributor."

"Then call your distributor and ask him."

Hog laughed. "If I do that, he'll come down here and cut both our throats."

"Ken, don't push it," Robby urged.

"Right," Hog said. "You're pissed at the wrong dude. Remember, I deliver to older crowds, not kids. I'm not the bad guy here."

No, not you. Ken glanced at his sunken, shriveled brother. *You, Mr. Dealer, deserve a gold star.*

"I got standards," Hog continued. "If you wanna know who's dealing to kids, ask some kids. Don't ask me."

"Told you," Robby said. "Hog's got standards."

Ken rolled his eyes.

Robby knocked on the boarded-up window. "Yo, Hog, since we're already here, can you hook me up like we discussed?"

"Only if you pay double like we discussed."

"Great. Meet you out back."

Ken glared at his brother. *Unbelievable.* They hadn't come here to score. And where did Robby get money? Two days ago he couldn't afford a shirt and pants. That meant he'd probably stolen from Dad's upstairs dresser. To think Robby could go from crying over Dad's corpse to raiding his bedroom for drug money... It made Ken's finger curl around the trigger.

"Tell your tight-assed brother to wait in the parking lot," Hog said.

"You heard him," Robby said, his eyes pleading. "Come on, Ken. If you want my help today, I need to buy my shit now."

"Fine," Ken said through gritted teeth. "But this is the last time you spend money on a fix. Hear me?"

Robby said nothing.

Ken carried the collapsible wheelchair back to the Camry, stashed it in the trunk, and got behind the wheel. He parked where he had a clear view of the shack's rear door. Robby was there, giddy as a boy about to order candy and soda. He dug his pockets, counted out Dad's money, and handed it over. Hogwild collected it, then rubbed his thumb and forefinger together, gesturing for a little extra.

Robby ran over to the car.

Ken lowered the window. "You're not getting a penny from me."

"It's not that," Robby said. "Mind waiting five minutes?"

"For what?" Ken asked.

"Negotiating." Robby wet his lip. "Won't take long."

"How about I negotiate for you?"

"Stay outta this, Ken. I need five minutes—maybe ten. I'll try to hurry."

Robby headed for the shack. He ducked inside and shut the door behind him.

While Ken waited, a nervous cloud expanded within his chest. Without thinking, he tightened his seatbelt, afraid he might otherwise float away.

Minutes passed.

He grew weary of sitting around. He wanted answers. All he needed to do was rip open the door, point the gun, and demand names of dealers and distributors. The only thing stopping him was the consequences. He didn't know how drug dealers reacted after they had a gun pulled on them. Hogwild might harm Robby or mobilize his boys and send them to the Fujima house tonight.

More minutes dragged by.

This is taking too long, Ken thought. *I can't keep sitting around. Not while the answers to my problems wait inside that concession stand.*

With a hammering heart, he got out of the Camry. Birds cawed and motors hummed in the distance. He worried a family might pull into the parking lot at any moment. He double-checked the ballpark, making sure there were no stragglers playing catch in the outfield. Aside from oak trees trembling in the September breeze, nothing moved.

This time, when Ken tried the shack's doorknob, it spun easily. He opened the door and heard a slick popping noise coming from inside.

Sunlight leaked in and shined off Hogwild's belt buckle. It lay on the concrete floor, next to Robby's bent knee. A little higher up, Robby had his face where the belt buckle should've been. Two plump hands clutched his head, maneuvering it back and forth in a steady rhythm.

The rhythm cut to a stop as they both noticed the room had gotten brighter.

Robby leaned back to relieve his mouth of its five-inch burden. His eyes went wide, his cheeks deep red. He wiped his lips with the back of his hand and said something.

Whatever he said, it never reached Ken's ears.

All he heard was the gunshot.

CHAPTER 36

KEN WELCOMED the icy shock of the bathroom shower spray. It roused his skin to life, for better or worse. Since leaving the ballpark, he'd been numb in both body and mind. He hadn't yet processed his third murder, and he wasn't sure he wanted to.

Details trickled into his mind's eye—blood leaping from Hogwild's wounds, Robby scrambling out of the shack, their hasty drive home—but the memories hardly impacted him. Of his three murders, this one bothered him the least, despite being the freshest and most calculated. Maybe he was too exhausted to care, maybe he was growing desensitized, or maybe his conscience approved of him eliminating his brother's chief heroin source. The only downside was that Ken hadn't learned who'd sold fentanyl to Pete.

Now, as the warm water kicked in, Ken allowed the sweat, oil, and blood to roll off him and trickle down the drain.

Afterward, he toweled off and patted his gunhand dry. A fresh kill meant he could relax. Maybe even sleep tonight. All things considered, he felt great. Sure, he'd taken another life, but that particular life had tormented many others.

Not that Robby agreed.

"How could you be so stupid?" He pounded the bathroom door.

"Hog has friends, you know? Once they realize I was the last one he saw, I'm fucked."

"How would they know it was you?" Ken said, gelling his hair back—a clumsy task for a one-handed man. "We stomped his phone and dropped it down a sewer grate. Nobody will see the texts."

"Doesn't matter. He could've told someone he was meeting me."

Ken paused as he fixed his hair. "Will they come after us?"

"Probably not, but when I reach out, they might sell me some tainted product. That's how they retaliate."

"Then don't buy anything."

"You don't get it!" Robby struck the door. "I have to!"

"Calm down," Ken said.

"Calm down? You killed my dealer!"

"Relax. Before long we'll be on the road. I'll take care of you."

Ken stepped into a fresh pair of boxer shorts. They felt good against his cool, clean skin. He donned a short-sleeve button-down, khakis, and his favorite pair of argyle socks. The bathroom fan hummed above, and he focused on the sound, relegating his brother's yapping to background noise. Studying himself in the mirror, Ken didn't exactly love who he saw, but it was an improvement. Last night he'd slaughtered his brother's girlfriend while under duress. This morning, however, was different. He'd killed Hogwild without any gun-induced pressure. For the first time since Friday, he felt like he was in control.

When he opened the bathroom door, he found Robby leaning against the wall, clutching anxiously at his head. Tiny dots of blood covered Robby's cheeks and his hair looked greasy. He reeked of spearmint mouthwash.

Ken squeezed his brother's shoulder. "We'll get through this."

"You don't understand. I don't just 'get through' things. I'm a mess. Dad's dead, Chrissie's dead, you're killing people, and I don't know how long I can stretch the dope I have left."

Ken pulled him close. The spearmint gave way to an underlying sweaty odor. "We'll get through this. Once the revolver's empty and

Hannah's good enough to walk, we'll hit the road. Till then, why not grab a shower? You'd be amazed what a shower can do."

Downstairs on the futon Hannah lay flat, her arms at her sides, palms up. He'd offered her the TV remote earlier, but she declined, opting for a yoga pose instead. Her deep breaths brought peace to the living room. Ken warmed two slices of toast and carried them in on a plate.

"Hungry?" he asked, sitting on the armrest. "You look it."

She opened her eyes. "Way to disrupt a girl's zen."

He laughed. "You should see how I wake students who fall asleep in class."

"You're in a good mood. You should shoot heroin dealers more often." She tried to sit up. He set the plate down and helped her. Once she was upright, he offered her the toast. She refused. "Better wait till my stomach settles."

"How's the wound?"

"When I lie flat, it's bad. Sitting up, it's hell."

"Once you're better, we'll hit the road, the four of us."

"Four of us? Me, you, Robby, and...?"

"Hopper."

"Oh, right." She smiled at Hopper, who was snoozing on the recliner. "The only redeeming member of your family."

"Hey, I saved your life last night, remember?"

"Save Michelle's life. Then we'll talk."

"That's not fair," he said. "We both lost a loved one."

"Correction. I lost *three* loved ones thanks to your family."

"Maybe it's time to stop keeping score."

"Those points don't erase from the board." Her eyes fell on the revolver. She didn't look away as she said, "Anyway, I'm in no condition to be agitated. Let's drop the subject."

"In that case, let me ask you something," he said, pulling the ripped note from his pocket. "The buyer you met with. His name was Takahashi?"

"Yep. Total creepo. Guy kept hitting on me and Michelle."

"What else do you know about him?"

"Not much." She winced. "He can offer a lot for the gun. Seems he's well connected."

"Did you get his first name?"

She squinted. "Hmm. It was something generic like John or Jim."

"John or Jim..." Ken ran to the kitchen phone and dialed the number on the caller ID.

Takahashi picked up on the first ring. "Hello? Goro?"

"Actually, it's Ken. I have a ques—"

"I must speak with your father. It's important."

Ken hesitated. "Sure, I'll ask if he's ready to come off the toilet. What's your name again?"

"Takahashi."

"What about your first name?"

"He'll know who it is. Besides, you're the one who called me."

"True, but I don't know your name."

"It's David."

Ken held his breath. "Do you have a brother named John or Jim?"

"I'm an only child. Now put your father on the phone."

Ken set the phone down, counted to ten, then picked it back up. "Dad says he'll call you when he's feeling better. He's been sick all weekend."

"Tell him it's urgent."

"I can take a message."

"Tell him that if I don't hear from him by tonight, I'll assume he's dead."

Before Ken could respond, Takahashi broke the connection. The dial tone thrummed in his ear, and Ken wondered what that last statement meant. It was an odd thing to say. In any case, he was relieved to know that this Takahashi bore a different first name from the buyer.

He returned to the living room.

"What was that about?" Hannah asked.

"My father had a buddy named Takahashi. Not the same guy, though."

"It's a pretty common last name. Can I have some toast?"

He broke a slice in half and handed it to her.

"So, three more kills..." She nibbled her toast. "Who's next? Stalin? Hitler? Genghis Khan?"

"If only." He wondered if he'd be able to teach World History once they reached LA. Hopefully the buyer could provide fake teaching degrees in addition to fake IDs. "Tonight there's a vigil for a student of mine who OD'd on fentanyl. When I go, I'll see if I can learn anything about who supplied him."

"You're going to a *vigil?*" she asked, appalled. "Are you insane?"

"Why?" He grabbed a piece of toast. "What's wrong?"

"Idiot, you have a loaded revolver attached to you. At an event like that, you'll be expected to shake hands, give hugs, and blow your nose. You can't hide your hand in your pocket the whole time."

He bit into the toast. Its rough texture scraped the roof of his mouth as he pictured himself being offered a handshake, followed by baffled looks from Pete's family when he refused. That would put a dent in his plan to obtain info.

There had to be another way.

Studying his gunhand, he pictured different methods of concealing it—bags, sleeves, anything that offered coverage. None, however, seemed appropriate enough for an event as reverent as a teen's memorial vigil.

While he brainstormed, he grabbed his mother's quilt and wrapped it around his gunhand. The odd bulge at the end was too obvious.

But as he continued wrapping over it, he got an idea.

CHAPTER 37

THE VIGIL SPREAD eerie silence throughout Kirby Park. An evening drizzle fell without a sound, and though the breeze was constant, nearby trees dared not shake their branches. None of the gathered students, teachers, or family members spoke a word. Everyone stood in a half circle beneath the park pavilion roof. Ken and Robby faced a plastic table decorated with photos and trophies from Pete Chang's past. From his life that was no more.

Ken's free hand clutched the fiberglass cast that Dr. Glinski had wrapped for him just hours ago. After he had gathered the necessary supplies at CVS, Glinski taped him up at gunpoint, stuffing the cast full of crumpled newspaper in order to obscure the revolver's shape. The finished product looked like a shrunken boxing glove and offered no ventilation. Heat smothered his fist; sweat tickled incessantly between his knuckles.

To his left, the scent of burning candles spread through the air. A sobbing woman—Pete's mother—passed them out, and her husband followed and lit them.

Among the mourners stood Officer Isaacs and his daughter Lexi, whose all-black gothic attire couldn't have been more appropriate. Beside her stood Principal Soward, wearing a charcoal gray business suit and her trademark scowl. She was accompanied by her two teenage kids, both of whom were students at Morgan High. Soward cupped a hand around her candle's flame and glanced in Ken's direction. The moment she spotted him, her eyes narrowed.

Mrs. Chang handed candles to Ken and Robby. Once Ken's was lit, his throat went tight. He wanted to cough but didn't dare disturb the silence.

To his right he spotted Angela with several other teachers. Once her candle was lit, the flame reflected off her tear-soaked cheeks. She pressed a hand over her mouth to stifle a sob. Ken wanted to curl an arm around her but could only stare into the dancing flame before him.

Pete's parents approached the table-shrine and set three candles among the photo frames and art awards. When Mrs. Chang faced the crowd, she opened her mouth to say something and broke down crying. She slid to her knees with a hard, deafening thud. Her husband behind her held her torso upright while she moaned, and the gathered crowd joined her with harsh, heartbroken sobs of their own.

"This is too much," Robby whispered. "I'm heading back to the car."

"Stay," Ken said, blinking back tears. "I'll need you here when I talk to Pete's friends."

Mr. Chang announced that if anyone wanted to speak, they were welcome to. At first nobody volunteered. Then a kid from Morgan High stepped forward. Eddie Alvarez. The boy had goofed off in Ken's classes last year, but now he reverently marched toward the table and set something down on it. A PlayStation controller.

"Me and Pete used to play *Fortnite* together," Eddie said in a subdued tone. "It's weird saying 'used to' because we just played online three nights ago. Yesterday I texted him to see if he was down for another game, but..." Eddie paused. It was long and uncomfortable. "I-I moved here last December. Didn't know nobody. One day I'm sitting in class struggling through a pop quiz and Pete holds up his test sheet all casual, like he was double-checking it. He held it at a funny angle so I could copy his answers. I ended up passing because of him. He'd do chill things like that, y'know? He'd...he'd..."

Eddie covered his face and turned away.

Ken's eyes watered. That speech reminded him of all the little things you lost when someone died. You lost more than a living, breathing human being. You lost someone to play videogames with. You lost someone who had your back when you didn't study. You lost a part of yourself.

Two nights ago, Ken lost more than a father. He lost a source of laughter, warmth, and guidance. He lost someone who understood him, cared about him, and told him when to man up. He lost a food critic, a support pillar, a best friend.

The gathered mourners dispersed after Eddie's speech. Some broke off into small groups and traded stories about Pete. Others cried over photos and artwork. Officer Isaacs glanced in Ken's direction and offered a strange, almost neighborly, smile. Seemed this vigil could soften anyone.

Once Ken set his candle aside, he grabbed Robby and sought out Eddie, who had taken a seat under a dripping oak tree.

As they approached the boy, someone grabbed Ken's elbow.

It was Angela. She was crying, her eyeshadow in raccoon-like smears. Her chin fell against his shoulder as she wrapped her arms tight around him.

"Ken," she said, her voice muffled. "This is the worst."

He slid his left arm around her back. As her sobbing escalated, he lifted his cast to pull her into a full hug. Staring past her shoulder at the table, he noticed a photo of Angela with her students on a field trip. They were inside an underground crystal cave, one that resembled what Pete had drawn in his notebook last week. Ken could only imagine what she was going through, losing one of the many students she inspired.

Another teacher came over to hug Angela, and Ken released her.

He and Robby headed for the tree where Eddie sat, hanging his head, oblivious to the evening drizzle.

Ken squatted beside the boy. "Great speech, Eddie."

"Yeah," Robby said. "Powerful stuff."

Eddie shrugged. "Doesn't matter. Nothing I say will bring him back."

"In a way you did," Ken said. "He's back in our minds."

"Eh. Wish he was just plain here."

"We all do." Ken twitched when a raindrop struck his neck. "It's frustrating because it never should've happened. Not sure if you heard, but he OD'd on pills laced with fentanyl."

"Yeah. Fake Oxys. Makes no sense."

"Why's that?"

"Pete was no pillhead." Eddie lowered his voice. "Don't tell nobody, Mr. Fuj, but we smoked weed together all summer. Sometimes we'd have a beer, and one time Pete tried shrooms so he could draw something trippy. No pills though."

Ken frowned. "Any idea where he might've gotten them?"

Eddie shrugged. "We knew a guy, but the guy only deals weed."

"Who's your guy?"

Eddie clammed up.

"Eddie?" Ken leaned closer. "C'mon, I need to know."

"Lay off him, Ken," Robby said. "If he says his guy only deals weed, that's probably the case. Pete might've hooked up with another dealer."

"Who else might Pete have known?" Ken asked.

"No idea." Eddie turned to Robby. "Funny you said 'hooked up.' Pete was bragging all month about some girl he was with. Thought he was bullshitting, but what if he wasn't? What if his girl got him pills?"

"Who's the girl?" Ken asked.

"Didn't say." Eddie shrugged. "Eh, he was probably lying. We'd always trash-talk about that stuff—he'd joke about banging my sister, I'd joke about banging his, that sorta shit."

"The other day Pete was upset over a girl," Ken said, scanning the crowd. Through the drizzle, he spotted Lexi Isaacs by the memorial table. She had tears in her eyes and one of Pete's framed drawings in hand. Her father was nowhere in sight, presenting a great opportunity to speak with her. "Thanks for the help, Eddie. Hang in there."

"I'll try."

Rain patted Ken's shoulders as he returned to the pavilion. When he approached Lexi, she didn't react. Her attention was absorbed by the drawing she held. It depicted a floating castle comprised of human skulls. Her finger traced the structure's walls. Ken had to call her name twice before she heard him.

"What? Oh, Mr. Fujima. Hi. Did you want to see this?" She offered him the picture, and he remarked how eye-catching it was. She smiled. "I gave Pete the idea at lunch last year."

"Turned out great," he said, noticing the meticulous detail that went into each skull. "It's nice that you helped inspire him."

"Yep. Anytime I thought of something, I'd tell him."

"Didn't realize you two were so close."

"We weren't." Her shoulders sank. She sounded frustrated. "We only hung out at lunch. I invited him to the movies sometimes, but he always said no. Guess I was too weird for him."

"Don't beat yourself up." He chose his next words carefully. "Pete might've just been interested in someone else."

"Oh, he was," she said bitterly.

"Sorry to hear," he said. "Listen, when he stormed out of my class the other day, he mumbled something about girl trouble. Any idea who the girl was?"

"Does it matter?"

"It might. I'm trying to figure out why he OD'd. Don't want other students stumbling down that path."

Lexi chewed her lip. "When school started, I asked him to the movies, but he said he was seeing someone. He never mentioned her name though. Said it had to remain private till they were Facebook official. Now that I think of it, maybe he was making excuses—lying because he was too embarrassed to be seen with me."

"Did he mention—"

"What's going on here?" That voice. Soward. Ken turned and caught her glare. There were no tears in the principal's eyes. Nor was there any strain on her face, only the usual scowl. "Mr. Fujima, what's with the cast?"

"Cast?" he said, tucking it into his pocket. "We're at a vigil and that's all you're concerned about?"

"Anytime you're around my students, I have concerns." Her eyes darted to Lexi. "Miss Isaacs, would you give us a moment?"

Lexi backed away.

Once the girl was gone, Soward closed in until all Ken could see was her wrinkled face. "Don't think I've forgotten about Friday."

"Friday?" he asked.

"Yes, Friday. Specifically your extended trip to the bathroom with Peter. In retrospect, I find it interesting. It doesn't strike me as coincidence that the boy overdosed a day after I caught you in the bathroom with him."

"Caught me? I did nothing wrong. He stormed out of class, and I went to help him."

"So you say."

"It's the truth."

"I'm warning you." She poked his sternum, tapping like an ice pick. "If I find any reason to report you to the authorities, I won't hesitate."

"You won't have to hesitate, because you won't find a reason. I've never mistreated a student in my entire career. The rumors were never true, and you know it. You're not afraid of me corrupting students, you're afraid of me calling out your hiring practices."

"How dare you."

"I could say the same to you." He lifted his cast and pointed the unseen gun at her. Not only did he want to shoot her dead, but he also wanted to revive her twice so he could unload his remaining bullets. "You never gave me a chance. The job was guaranteed to your eldest daughter's boytoy."

Soward crossed her arms. "I hope you don't plan on teaching in this area much longer, Mr. Fujima. Believe me, word gets around."

His cast shook with indignation. Inside, his hand swam with sweat. His finger greased along the trigger guard before sliding through. It was so satisfying, having her one pull away from landing on her back and never getting up.

Even with dozens of people present, he wanted it. Not for the gun's sake, but for his own. Objectively speaking, there were count-less monsters who deserved a bullet more than Helen Soward, but on a personal level, there was nobody he'd rather empty his cylinder on.

"Ken," Robby said, breaking his trance. "Getting late. We should head home, man."

Ken knew his brother was right. This trip hadn't garnered any solid info on Pete's dealer, so it was time to regroup.

However, he wasn't ready to leave. He wanted to savor this, savor every second. After years of floundering in Soward's presence and feeling like she was pointing some unseen weapon at him, now the situation was reversed. It felt great, being on the other side of the gun for once. Even better, she would never know how close she came tonight.

He held his aim until she backed away.

CHAPTER 38

Two hours after the vigil, Ken's mind kept replaying his latest encounter with Soward. Something about her aggressive demeanor bothered him. As he sat in the living room recliner watching the Dodgers game with Robby and Hannah, he wondered what drew such venom from the principal. Was it the bathroom incident with Pete? The nepotism accusations? Or something else entirely?

During the bottom of the third inning, Robby called up Rodano's and ordered a large pepperoni pizza with sweet sauce. Ken's mouth watered. Hopper must've sensed it too, because he hobbled in from the kitchen. The dog loved their crust.

"Order a second pie," Ken said. An extra pie would mean hot food for Glinski downstairs. He had promised her a decent meal after she wrapped his cast earlier today.

"Can you order a plain?" Hannah asked from the futon. "I don't eat meat."

"Then take the pepperoni off," Robby said.

"It's not the same," she said.

"Order a plain," Ken said. "I don't think I can stomach anything spicy."

Robby nodded, doubled the order, and hung up. "Can't wait. I'm gonna miss all the pizza places around here. Best thing about the area."

"The local shit is that good?" Hannah asked.

"Hell yeah," Robby said, lying back on the couch. "Nothing out in LA can compare. When we moved here, pizza went from my fifth-favorite food to the undisputed champ."

"It's both cute and sad that you rank your foods."

"I meant when I was a kid," Robby said. "That's when we moved here."

"Believe me," she said, her tone sharp, "I know when you moved here. It was when I moved into an orphanage."

"Poor you," he said, sitting up. "Like that makes it okay to kill my father."

"Where were you the other night?" she snapped. "You could've saved him. Oh, wait, you were busy with a thick, juicy needle."

Robby launched from his seat. "How about I stick a thick, juicy fist in your gunshot wound?"

"How about you both shut up?" Ken said, scrolling through local news on his phone. Their bickering was starting to agitate him. "Robby, take Hopper outside so he can do his business."

"We should let him piss on the futon," Robby said.

"Enough. Go. And both of you, stop acting like first-graders."

After Robby took the dog outside, Ken turned to Hannah. Her face was red, her cheeks wrinkled. She looked like one of the mourners at the vigil.

"You okay?" he asked. "Your side bothering you?"

"I'm good."

"You don't look good."

"That's flattering."

"Seriously, you okay?"

"It's nothing." She shifted, wincing as she did. "Just that comment about acting like a first-grader."

"I didn't mean anything by it. It's just a saying."

"Ken, I was in first grade when my parents died."

Harsh silence hung between them. His instinct was to apologize, but he knew she hated the word *sorry*, especially when it came from a Fujima. "Want to vent about it?"

She shook her head. "It's complicated."

"Can't be more complicated than my situation," he said, patting his cast. "Tonight I pointed a hidden gun at my boss while attending a vigil for a student whose murder I'm trying to solve so I don't have to shoot innocent people. Top that, Miss Complicated."

She smiled. For a moment she shut her eyes, then said, "Want to know why I'm a vegetarian? See, when I was little, Michelle and I were eating ham sandwiches on the Saturday afternoon my parents died. Mom made them for us—ham with cheese and a little mustard. Michelle was a faster eater than me, so she finished hers quick and went outside to play.

"I was still eating when Dad got home. Usually when he came home, he'd chase after us and give us big hugs. That day, though, he walked past me in the kitchen as if I didn't exist. By the time I followed him into his bedroom, he'd already gotten into the shower. I noticed his nightstand drawer was open. Inside was a big silver handgun.

"That was the first time I'd seen a real gun. I thought it'd be cool to run around chasing bad guys, so I stuffed the rest of my sandwich in my mouth and grabbed the pistol. It was huge and heavy in my little hands, so I held it like a shotgun. Once I got a grip, I stuck two fingers inside the trigger guard and squeezed as hard as I could.

"Then it happened. *Boom.* Loudest thing I've ever heard. The noise damaged my right eardrum and sent me to the hospital. I still remember the inside of my head throbbing like hell and the lingering taste of that ham sandwich. I never ate ham again and eventually lost interest in all meat.

"At the hospital a doctor wrote a prescription for the pain. Dad visited the hospital pharmacy while Mom took Michelle and me back to the parking garage. Soon as we got in the car, I started crying because I realized I'd left my favorite stuffed giraffe in the doctor's

ENTRY WOUNDS / 195

office. I begged Mom to go back and get it. When she finally caved, she told Michelle and me to wait in the car.

"We waited.

"And waited.

"In the meantime, this ugly green car kept roaming around like it was looking for a parking space. The guy in the passenger seat stared at us. We got scared and thought we were gonna get kidnapped. Then Michelle spotted our parents. Dad had a little white pharmacy bag. Mom had my giraffe. They were arguing about something.

"Then came the sound again. *Boom*.

"Next thing I knew, Mom screamed. She fell, and the booming sounded again and again until Dad fell next to her." Hannah sniffled and shook her head. "They never got up."

Ken felt himself sinking into the recliner. Twenty years ago in LA his father drove an ugly green Chevy. He sold it right before they moved to Pennsylvania.

"Hannah, I—"

"Don't." She held up a hand. "It wasn't your fault. But me—if I hadn't fired that stupid gun, we would've stayed home that afternoon, and maybe things would've been different."

Ken pushed himself up by the armrests. Rather than burdening her damaged eardrum with an apology, he knelt beside the futon and patted her hand.

After a moment she sighed. "Know what I hate most about that day? I hate how normally on Saturdays we had what Mom called play day. We would visit the Griffith Observatory with our dog or drive outside the city to fly kites. I always looked forward to it, and we should've had it one last time." She met his eyes. "If there's anything you want to do before we leave here, you should do it. Whatever you love about this town, enjoy it while you can."

Ken glanced at his elbow, at the edge of his cast. Right where Angela had grabbed him tonight before they shared a teary hug. Perhaps there was still time for a goodbye. After he killed another dealer tomorrow, maybe he could ask her out to breakfast or something.

The doorbell rang. He got his money ready for the pizza. When he opened the door, it wasn't a delivery boy.

There on his doorstep stood Officer Isaacs.

In his hand was a black-and-white printout of Hogwild lying dead inside the concession stand.

CHAPTER 39

IN THE PAST forty-eight hours Ken had experienced many things that struck him as bizarre. If he'd been told last week that he would soon witness his father's execution, grab an undroppable revolver, and shoot three people dead, he wouldn't have believed a word. Now, however, his attitude toward reality had shifted. He'd developed a tolerance to the absurd. He could believe almost anything.

For that reason, he didn't even blink when Officer Isaacs flashed the photo of Hogwild's corpse. Didn't faze him one bit. Ken was honestly more surprised that the pizza wasn't here yet.

When the delivery boy arrived moments later with a short stack of cardboard boxes, Officer Isaacs pulled out his wallet and paid for the food. Now *that* was surprising. He grabbed the boxes and took a whiff of the rising steam. After a satisfied sigh, Isaacs asked, "What'd you order?"

"One plain, one pepperoni," Ken said flatly. "Both with sweet sauce."

"Nothing beats sweet sauce," Isaacs said. "Funny how we agree on certain things. Like that, and how the world is better off without Mr. Hogwild."

Ken's pulse beat within his neck. He said nothing. Chances were,

Isaacs suspected him but didn't have hard evidence. Keeping calm was critical.

"Relax, Fujima. I'm not here to arrest you. Can't blame you for shooting the bastard after his slimy cock left your brother's mouth."

Ken froze. Had Isaacs witnessed the whole thing? Or was he guessing based on evidence?

"In fact," Isaacs continued, "I'm glad you did it."

"You're...what?"

"I said I'm glad you did it." Sincerity radiated from Isaacs' steel-blue eyes. "People like Hogwild add nothing but misery to this world."

Ken suspected he was being lured into a trap. Continuing this conversation was too risky. He slid his sweaty index finger through the trigger guard and nodded at the pizza boxes. "I'll take those, thanks."

Isaacs frowned. "Can I come in?"

"No."

"Not as a cop. As a neighbor."

"Some other time."

"You know, last night a couple neighbors bothered me about another noise complaint. Said they heard a loud bang coming from your house. At the time I had my hands full with Lexi. She cried all night over her buddy Pete, so I didn't have time to pay you a visit. Then this morning I decided to follow you around. Hoped you might lead me to something good—and you did—but I never pegged you as the type to whack your brother's dealer. I was impressed."

Ken cleared his throat. "Impressed?"

Isaacs glanced up the street. "I ever tell you about my daughter?"

"You said she thinks I'm a great teacher."

"Not Lexi." Isaacs swallowed hard. "Talking about my older daughter Jess. Years back, she was in a situation like your brother's. Now she's in long-term rehab up in Shickshinny. If you want to share a couple slices together, I can tell you more. If not, that's fine. But

Lexi mentioned you were trying to figure out who's responsible for Pete's overdose. If you ever need to pick my brain, give me a holler."

A thread of unease lifted within Ken's chest. He wasn't sure how to play this. Obviously, it could be a trap. Isaacs might be wearing a wire and fishing for an admission of guilt. But if the man had witnessed the shooting—and judging by the grisly details he mentioned, he likely had—why would he need such an admission? He could've snapped a picture of Ken at the crime scene.

That meant the offer to track down Pete's dealer might be legit. Isaacs had never mentioned his older daughter before, but if narcotics had ruined her, that would explain why he gave Ken a pass. Seeing Hogwild eat a bullet must've been cathartic for Isaacs; he probably fantasized about doing the same to his daughter's dealer.

Ken knew one thing: he had to kill someone tomorrow. With that in mind, he might as well find a meaningful target.

Meeting the cop's eyes, he said, "Mind if we eat out back?"

"Not at all," Isaacs said.

A tennis ball bounced across the shadow-streaked backyard. The ball rolled from dark to light to dark again. Hopper gimped through wet grass and snatched the dirty yellow ball between his jaws. He must've smelled the pizza, because instead of returning the ball to Robby over by the picnic table, he dashed straight for Isaacs.

"The fuck?" Robby yelled. "What's *he* doing here?"

"Bought your dinner," Isaacs said, setting the boxes on the table. "Least I could do after what went down at the ballpark earlier."

Robby froze. "I don't know what you're talking about."

"Relax," Ken said. "I think he's on our side."

Robby stood, his expression horrorstruck.

"Have a seat," Isaacs said. "Enjoy the pizza while it's hot."

"Lost my appetite," Robby said, his eyes lingering on Issacs. With a nervous twitch, he headed for the house. "Watch yourself, Ken."

Ken sat and flipped open a pizza box. Steam rose toward the night sky. He wolfed down the first gooey slice he grabbed. Any meal might be his last, so he made each bite count. Across the table Isaacs chewed at a leisurely pace.

"So," Ken said, reaching for another slice, "who around here deals fake Oxy?"

"Tough question." The bench beneath Issacs creaked as he shifted his weight. "If you're intent on tracking down the exact supplier, you'll likely end up dead before you get concrete answers."

"But you said you knew who was behind Pete's death."

"Wrong. I said I knew who was *responsible*."

"What's the difference?"

Isaacs blew out a heavy breath. He dropped his crust into Hopper's mouth and faced Ken. "There's a narc in my department who took the midnight shift back in January. The only guys who willingly take that shift are ones who can't sleep or got a good reason to be on duty at that hour. This one—Jim Tormon's his name—has botched two drug busts since taking the job. Drug trafficking is a pet peeve of mine, so after the second failed bust, I started following Tormon around, the same way I followed you today. One night last month I caught him responding to a complaint about suspicious activity. He arrived on the scene and let a dealer walk right past him. Didn't stop him for questions or nothing. Just radioed dispatch and said nobody was there."

"You sure it was a dealer?"

"Positive. We have pictures of the asshole at the station. No reason a narc like Tormon wouldn't have recognized him."

Ken wiped his greasy fingers on a napkin. "Why didn't you report Tormon?"

"Report him?" Isaacs laughed. "I'd be pegged as a rat. I got enough problems, Fujima. Last thing I need is to stink like a rat. Hell, even if I'd caught the whole thing on video, there's no guarantee it would sink him. He's got connections—you know how it is."

Ken did know. But he also knew he couldn't go around shooting cops based on circumstantial evidence. There was a chance Isaacs had misinterpreted the situation that night. Or he might have a grudge against Tormon for reasons unrelated to drug trafficking.

"Is that the only time you caught Tormon helping a dealer?"

"Yeah, but I can't follow him at all hours. Usually I tail him on my days off. I realize it's a small sample size, but I'm telling you, Tormon's dirty."

"So you say," Ken said.

"It's your call," Isaacs said, rising from the bench. "If you want to keep shooting two-bit dealers, be my guest. Just remember that shooting one dealer creates a job for another. On the other hand, if you want to make shockwaves around town, go after Tormon. That's what I'd do if I didn't have two daughters it could blow back on."

"Hold on. Why are you encouraging me?"

"You asked my daughter for info, remember?"

"Right, but what do you get out of this?"

Isaacs glared, like he'd never been more insulted. "Weren't you listening? Jess hasn't been home for years because of people like Hogwild and Tormon. There's only so much I can do to clean up the streets and alleyways, but you...if you're game enough to blow away a dealer in broad daylight, you might just be the sick solution this city needs. Now, I'm not necessarily *encouraging* you to repeat today's act, but if you're hungry for more, I'll feed you whatever info you need."

Ken shut the pizza box. His stomach hissed with heartburn as he glanced down at his cast. Thankfully, Isaacs didn't know about the weapon's curse. He probably wasn't even aware there was a gun lurking inside the cast. That needed to remain secret, but he saw no reason to hide his interest in Tormon.

"Tell me," he said. "Where can I talk to Tormon?"

"You going after him?"

"Just want to ask him some questions."

"He'll be at a fundraiser next weekend."

Ken shook his head. "I need to see him by tomorrow morning."

"That soon? What's the rush?"

"Can I see him by then or not?"

Isaacs checked his watch. "Tormon starts his shift soon. I wouldn't recommend approaching him while he's on duty. If you want to catch him at a casual spot, he usually stops for coffee after his shift."

"Where at?"

"Place called the Cabin Café. It's a sit-down restaurant. He likes to read the paper at the back booth while he drinks his coffee. Guy's got a thick goatee and an ugly scar on his cheek. You can't miss him."

"What time will he show up?"

"Most days he pops in after 8 a.m."

The timing made Ken uneasy. He shot Hogwild around 9:40 this morning—there was no telling how soon the gun-induced cravings would kick in. Though he liked to believe he could stave off the urge to shoot for at least twenty-four hours, an 8 a.m. meeting with Tormon might be pushing it. And that was *if* the man showed up promptly. If Tormon didn't show—or if he proved innocent—Ken would need a fallback plan.

Perhaps Isaacs could help with that.

"Need one more thing," Ken said. "Local dealers."

"What do you mean?"

"Any of them operate near the Cabin Café?"

Isaacs nodded slowly. "If you promise to be careful, I can jot down some names and addresses. Why, what's your plan? Trying to lead Tormon into a trap?"

"No," Ken said, "just trying to schedule my morning."

CHAPTER 40

NEVER DID Ken expect to drive into a high school parking lot with a gun, but this morning was special, and if all went smoothly, he wouldn't be here long. He claimed parking spot number twenty-seven—Angela's spot—and turned on the country music station. Luke Bryan sang an uplifting tune, but Ken couldn't register the lyrics. All he heard was the sound of his own huffing breath. He shuddered in the driver's seat. Sweat evacuated his pores, and he began to stink like a pile of old gym socks. The inside of his cast felt so clammy he wondered if his skin had liquefied.

Shortly after seven o'clock, buses and cars trickled into the lot. Pontiacs claimed spots while more expensive vehicles from well-to-do families caught the shine of the morning sun. Teachers also parked. Mrs. Mathis, the art teacher, gave Ken a puzzled look as she passed him in her Saab. Then finally, dead ahead, Angela's silver Jeep swung into the lot. Upon reaching her spot, she braked and lowered her window. Her hair was in a high, tight ponytail that tugged on her hairline and left her looking agitated. When she lifted her Holly-wood-style sunglasses, she didn't appear thrilled to see him.

Ken exited his car; he had roughly two hours till kill time. Earlier, while fine-tuning his plan to interrogate Officer Tormon, he remembered what Hannah said about enjoying his remaining time in Pennsylvania. That got him thinking about Angela, and before he could talk himself out of it, he'd driven to Morgan High. Showing up here was risky, but he promised himself that he'd leave immediately if struck by any homicidal urges.

"You're in my spot," she said.

"You won't need it today."

"Oh really?"

"Remember what you said the other night?" He leaned his forearm against her door. "About how our lives are like the same old movie on repeat?"

She nodded tiredly.

He smiled. "How about calling off and joining me for breakfast?"

"Thanks for the offer, but I should be here for the students." She picked at the sleeve of her floral sundress. "It'll be a rough day for everyone."

"It'll be rough whether you're here or not." He shuffled in place. "Last night I realized how short life can be. For all we know, I could be gone tomorrow."

"Oh, I'm sure you'll be around."

"Why risk it? Let's grab breakfast while we can. I know a place you'll love."

"Let's try this weekend instead."

"Won't work." Sweat crawled along his gunhand. "Has to be today."

"Has to?" She raised an eyebrow. "Why, is the world ending and nobody told me?"

"Yep. The Pentagon sent me to warn you."

"So you're in charge of national security now?"

"Right. I'll brief you on the situation over breakfast."

"Hmm..." An amused smile crossed her lips. "Given the urgency, I suppose I should join you."

"Great. Ever heard of the Cabin Café? Haven't been there

myself, but I think you'll love it. It's off the beaten path, surrounded by woods. They've got a pond in the back and—"

"A pond? Funny... The other night this rude guy left me to drown in my own backyard pond."

"Lucky you didn't," he said, cheeks burning. "Otherwise, the world would end without you."

Grinning, she put her Jeep in drive. "Guess we should enjoy it while it lasts."

CHAPTER 41

THOUGH THE RESTAURANT promised an elegant cabin atmosphere, it was the furthest thing from romantic. The wallpaper depicted cartoonishly fake wood, the mahogany bar was covered in ketchup bottles, and the back booth they occupied faced a gravel parking lot. The duck pond was caked with algae, and many surrounding evergreens were brown with disease. As if that didn't ruin the mood enough, the temperature outside topped seventy, and an A/C unit wheezed uselessly above their table. Ken sweltered inside his jacket, desperate to keep his cast tucked away.

Across the table Angela fanned herself with a greasy menu. "I know what I'm getting."

"That was quick."

"Spoiler alert. I've been here before."

"Any recommendations?"

"To be honest," she said with a mischievous smile, "I haven't tried much of the food. This was a prime drinking spot back in college."

"When was that? Last week?"

She threw a sugar packet at him. "No jokes about my age! Do you realize I'll be *twenty-six* in a couple months?"

"Ouch. Good thing you look twenty-two."

"I do not," she said, blushing.

"Sure you do," he said. "Although maybe not after your one o'clock class."

"That one *does* take years off my life." She rubbed her temples. "Way to remind me. Might as well order off the senior menu. Or pick out a casket."

The mention of a casket sent his focus out the window. Other than his Camry and her Jeep, only three other vehicles were in the lot. None belonged to Officer Tormon, which left Ken both relieved and anxious. It was nearly eight o'clock; Tormon could show up at any moment. Once he arrived, Ken would pretend to receive an emergency call and say goodbye to Angela. Then he would follow Tormon, interrogate him, and do whatever was necessary.

A waitress came and took their orders. Angela requested the mushroom omelet and Ken ordered the same, despite his deep-seated hatred for fungi. Before handing his menu to the waitress, he asked, "Excuse me, can you serve wine this early?"

The waitress nodded. "What can I get you?"

Ken looked to Angela.

She shook her head. "None for me, thanks. New diet. You enjoy yourself though."

He ordered a glass of pinot noir. The waitress collected their menus and left them to stare at the drab vista beyond the back window. Robins fluttered from the trees, settling in the mud along the grimy pond. Their beaks poked at the soil until they lifted morning worms. The pond itself remained motionless.

He turned to Angela. "Bring your swimsuit?"

"Yeah, that and a tetanus booster."

He laughed. "After breakfast I should throw you in."

"Good luck getting a grip on me with that cast. Which reminds me, what'd you do to your hand? Schoolyard brawl?"

"How'd you guess?"

She snorted. "Seriously, what happened?"

"Can't say. It involves national security."

"Oh, come on."

The waitress brought his wine glass on a serving tray and set it in front of him.

He raised the glass. "To the end of the world."

Bemused, Angela lifted her water glass. "To the end of the world."

They drank. Beyond the cheap medicinal taste, the wine's sweetness smoothed him over. Though his mind was swamped with murder deadlines and a downpour of other worries, he savored the moment.

Sadly, the moment didn't last. His gaze kept targeting the parking lot.

"Let's play a game." She clapped her hands. "Tell me a secret you've never told anyone before. It can be serious or stupid, but it has to be something you've never told anyone before."

"You must really want to know what happened to my hand."

"Got that right."

"Too bad I already told someone else."

"You jerk. Let's play anyway. It'll be fun. Tell me something you never told another soul. That way it'll be completely between us."

"Hmm..." Thankfully Hannah and Robby knew everything that happened over the weekend, so he could disqualify his gunhand. *Might as well have fun then.* "Okay. In sixth grade I used to shave my toes."

She burst out laughing. "Whaaat?"

"Never told anyone. Your turn."

"Wait, wait. Why'd you shave your toes?"

"Because I was twelve, they were hairy, and I worried people in my Shotokan class would call me a hobbit." He clinked her glass. "Your turn."

"Okay." She narrowed her eyes. "I've never had a man walk away from my naked body until Friday night."

His cheeks warmed. "Bet it won't happen twice."

"We'll see." She clinked his glass. "Next secret."

Ken swilled his wine. He eyed its cherry-red tint and wondered how much he would have to drink before he could permit himself to talk about Olivia. Probably enough to induce alcohol poisoning. Looking across the table, he wanted to confide in Angela, but it hurt to talk about Olivia. About what happened.

"I..." He stopped himself. Tried to think of something to say. "I'm a coward."

Angela blinked. "That's your secret?"

"Yeah."

She tilted her head. "You gotta give me more than that. I mean, we're all cowards to some extent. If we always did the hardest, scariest thing, we'd be dead."

He squirmed in his seat. The vinyl cushioning emitted a fart-like sound that added to his embarrassment. He hurriedly clinked her glass and said, "Next secret."

"Fine, we'll play it your way," she said. "My secret is that I'm a coward too."

He snorted.

"See? Not so fun, is it?" She clinked his glass. "What's your secret, fellow coward?"

Ken pinched his glass by the stem and slid it back and forth across the table. He'd rather be shooting someone than having this conversation. "Can I ask you something? How much do you know about me and my ex-fiancée?"

"Not much. Somebody at school said she ditched you on your wedding day, which is horrible."

"Yeah." He gulped the last of the wine. Like a man stepping off a diving board, he felt a rush as he said, "She was cheating on me."

Angela frowned. "Ugh."

"It had been going on for three years, long before I proposed. Back then I taught full-time at a private school in Scranton, and I always invited her to the faculty events—dinners, fundraisers, everything. There was one *Dancing with the Stars*–themed event. Couples entered to win Keurig machines and other prizes. Olivia loved to dance. I didn't. She paired up with a drama teacher, and they won a Red Lobster gift card. He told her to keep it.

"One thing about Olivia is that she was organized when it came to finances. She had a drawer in our kitchen where she arranged our cash, credit cards, gift cards, everything. About a month after the competition, I was craving seafood. I wanted to take her to Red Lobster when she got home from work. I checked the drawer but found no gift card. When she got home, I suggested Red Lobster. She flinched like she'd been hit by a sniper."

Angela cringed. "That must've been an ugly fight."

"There was no fight."

"You mean she apologized?"

"No. See, I never actually confronted her." Ken wished there were more wine in his glass. He wanted to flag down the waitress, but instead he continued. "We both pretended nothing had happened. After the gift card incident, she started coming home super late. Claimed it was mandatory overtime. One night, I decided to surprise her with her favorite ice cream sundae. I went to the office at six o'clock and found it closed. When she got home hours later, I asked how work had been. She said they were swamped, that she had just left the office."

"Lied right to your face?"

"Yeah. Could've exposed her then, but I didn't. Anyway, this whole song and dance went on for three years. After a while I started rationalizing it. I thought maybe she needed a break from me since we'd been dating since high school. Then I convinced myself she wasn't actually cheating on me, that she had a 'private friendship' or something like that. I was a fool. I kept pretending the floor wasn't crumbling beneath me.

"Eventually I proposed. We scheduled the wedding for the first week after school let out. We wanted to get married in the basin under our favorite waterfall. I wore a tuxedo-themed wetsuit and treaded water while our families and friends waited on dry land. We waited. And waited. And waited."

Angela slumped in her seat. "So that's why you freaked out in my pool..."

He nodded. A lump formed in his throat. He coughed three times before finding his voice. "Olivia agreed to meet me at a park the next day. When I got there, she and the drama teacher were sitting on a bench, holding hands. She told me she couldn't go through with the marriage. Said she'd been seeing him for years. I told her I knew.

"Then she said something I'll never forget.

"She said if I had called her out on her cheating at any point, she would've been swimming with me on our wedding day." He swallowed hard. "But she couldn't marry a pushover."

Silence hung between them. The breakfast table became a conversational no man's land. He wanted to say something to kill the awkwardness, but nothing sprang to mind. He hoped Angela might respond—rescue him—but her lips remained motionless.

She pressed her thumbnail to the table and picked at a smudge near her napkin. The scratching went on, back and forth, until he could take it no more.

"Angela—"

"I'm no better," she said.

"What?"

"I'm no better." She glanced up. He recognized the vulnerability in her eyes—something he'd never seen in them before. Usually she carried herself with bubbly confidence. Seeing her like this both startled and comforted him. "My story isn't as dramatic as yours. Right now my husband, as you know, is away on business. He's probably snuggled up next to some underwear model. The usual. Honestly, it doesn't even bug me anymore. And yet, here I am, too afraid to walk away."

Ken's heart pounded. "You afraid he'll hurt you if you do?"

"No, Dom's not violent."

"Then what's stopping you from starting over?"

"That's just it." She squirmed against her seat. "I'm afraid to."

"Afraid? Why?"

"Ken, I grew up in South Wilkes-Barre, crammed into a house with three siblings and two parents who could barely carry us above the poverty line. This is gonna sound super shallow, but I hated never getting what I wanted when I was growing up. It made high school a nightmare. I couldn't express myself with the right clothes or makeup or anything. I always felt like an outcast, and some extra money could've changed that.

"Fast-forward to college when I met Dom, this hotshot graduate making big money out in Philly. When I saw him, I saw an escape. Not only that, I saw an opportunity to be a teacher—my biggest dream growing up—without having to scrape by like my parents. I mean, you know how it is, Ken. Us educators get paid peanuts."

He nodded.

"When I met Dom, I knew I could have it both ways. What I didn't realize was that having it both ways doesn't mean you can have it *every* way. Money and job satisfaction came at a cost." She fingered her necklace. "It cost me a part of myself, the part that wanted to be truly seen, understood, loved."

Ken felt his gunhand growing itchy inside the cast. The way she spoke about Dom made him wonder. "You said Dom isn't violent. Is he...emotionally abusive?"

She shook her head, dismayed. "Aside from the cheating, no. But I can't knock him for the cheating. Not after the other night in the pool." She avoided his eyes. "Dom's decent to me. He listens. Supports my career. Buys me anything I want."

"Sounds like that's the problem," he said. "Dom keeps you content."

"God, I feel so pathetic." She frowned. "I want to leave, but it's hard to walk away from a nice house, a home gym, and all that financial security. I'm addicted to it. Dom must've known because he made me sign a prenup before we got married. That stupid document is what scared me into staying with him this long." She met his eyes. "I know I can start over and support myself and be happy, but... Well, I guess we're all cowards."

"We don't have to be," Ken said. "I mean, look at me. This morning I asked you to breakfast. That terrified me."

She smiled. "Hope your bravery is contagious." She clinked his empty glass. "Enough about me. Let's hear another secret. What about 'Ken the Eraser'?"

"Thankfully, that's not a secret."

"Aw, please?"

"Maybe later."

"Fine. Back to the game. Tell me something you've never told anyone."

He stared at the tiny red puddle left in his glass. Then he looked at her, meeting her eyes. "Sitting across from you makes me glad Olivia left."

She turned away, blushing. "That's heavy for a first date, don't you think?"

But not for a last date, he thought.

He clinked her glass. "Your move."

Before she could respond, breakfast arrived. The waitress set their plates down. Steam rose, carrying the scent of egg, butter, and mushroom sauce. Though he loathed mushrooms, it made his mouth water. His eyes also watered—the last time he'd eaten an omelet was with Dad on Friday morning, which felt like eons ago.

"You okay?" she asked.

"Yeah," he said, grabbing his fork. "And you still owe me a secret."

"Next time," she said.

They devoured their meals. Ken finished a second glass of wine. He repeatedly glanced out the window, but Officer Tormon never arrived. Ken couldn't have been happier; the meal was too perfect to be ruined by an abrupt departure to commit homicide. Better yet, he hadn't felt any murderous urges, even with the deadline creeping closer.

After paying the check, he stood and felt the alcohol swishing through his brain. He welcomed the lightheadedness as they left the restaurant together, hand in hand. He couldn't remember taking her hand, but here he was, approaching their cars and wishing this morning didn't have to end.

"You know," he said, eyeing the trail behind the pond, "we shouldn't leave yet."

"Really? Why's that?"

Because I don't have to waste a drug dealer till around ten, and I have the sucker's address.

"Because," he said, "I'm not sober enough to drive. Know how many glasses of wine I had? *Two.*"

"*Two?* My God!" she said, her tone scandalous. "Can't drive around like *that.*"

"Think I'll walk that trail over there." He gestured to the woods. "You don't mind joining me, do you? I mean, you're in heels."

"Oh, please. Jeep girls come prepared." She popped her Jeep's rear hatch. Within seconds she'd slid her feet into a pair of hiking boots and tied them expertly. Any other woman might've looked silly standing there in a floral sundress and hiking boots, but Angela made it look chic. Made it look special.

He took her hand and headed for the trail.

CHAPTER 42

"TELL ME ABOUT KEN THE ERASER," she said as they ducked beneath a low-hanging oak branch.

The moment she mentioned it, he stumbled, and his head crashed through a cluster of bug-eaten leaves. One branch caught his eyeglasses and tore them from his face. They clattered to the dirt, where she scooped them up. Though his vision was blurry, he saw her grinning as she backpedaled up the trail, twirling the glasses in her fingers. "Tell me the story. It's the least you could do after I recovered your glasses."

"You know, you shouldn't pick on the visually impaired."

"Hey, I wear contacts. It's a fair fight."

He extended his hand. "C'mon, give them back."

"Not until I hear this story."

"Another time," he said. With everything going so well, he didn't want to sour what was likely to be his final morning with her. He wanted to go out on a high note. "Besides, you owe *me* a secret."

"True," she said and handed him his glasses.

They headed down the trail. At some point her arm slid around his back, and his arm curled around her shoulders. They strolled along the path together, sides brushing, hips bumping. He promised himself that if a murderous urge struck, he would turn back. None came.

She squeezed him closer. Her hair tickled his ear as she leaned in. "Glad you talked me into breakfast."

"Enjoyed it?"

"Very much. Thanks for being my bright spot on a gloomy day."

Sunlight flickered through the branches above, prying at his sleep-deprived eyes. They continued through the woods; she outpaced him in those boots of hers. She promised to slow down if he explained how his hand ended up in a cast. He picked up his pace instead.

Under a shaggy canopy of half-barren oaks, the air grew cooler. The breeze tingled his skin. The trail wove through a shadowy section and dipped toward a rocky creek, which they opted to follow rather than cross. He spoke openly about subjects he never discussed: Mom's death, Robby's addiction, Dad's crippling tumble down the stairs. In avoiding the impossible subject of his gunhand, he found himself revealing nearly everything else without fear or hesitation.

Angela listened with a kind, nonjudgmental ear, waiting until he finished before she vented about the school district, her upbringing, and her home life. At one point she met his eyes with a dark, powerful gaze.

"What I said at breakfast, I take it back."

"What part?" he asked.

"The part about not wanting to leave my cushy home. I can't keep wasting my life like this." She dragged her toe through the dirt. "Still, it feels like I'm driving down an endless highway with no exits. I want to get off somewhere—anywhere—but I can't. And as I continue driving, the lane gets tighter and the guardrails get higher. There's no way out."

He shrugged. "Leave the car and climb the guardrail."

"Yeah...that could work."

They stepped out of the woods onto a rocky, dirt-covered slope. Down below was a field of tall, waist-high grass, a pond gleaming toward the center. The moment he spotted it, he wanted nothing more than to take her there. Any other day, he would've feared catching a tick, but now he squeezed her grip and ran downhill. They raced through the sprawling grass, the blades tickling through his khakis until he reached the mud surrounding the pond.

Angela laughed alongside him before tugging him to an abrupt stop. Ken, however, did not stop. The soil underfoot was slick, and his heels slid. His stomach floated while he waved his free arm to maintain balance. It was no use. He landed with a hard, soggy plop and thought, *Why must I always make an ass of myself?*

Then, to his surprise, she deliberately plopped down next to him. She showed no concern for the mud stains on her sundress. Instead she let her hair down. Dark locks spilled onto her shoulders and gleamed in the morning light. She reached over to take his hand. Their fingers interlocked. Her touch made his scalp buzz.

On a whim, he leaned in. He closed his eyes and let the warmth of her breath guide him. He met her open lips with his own. Her kiss was cool. Slick. Practiced. As if she'd been waiting all weekend for it. Her tongue made a move that knocked his brain out of his skull.

Wow.

She pushed him onto his back, her weight a welcome burden on his chest. The soil sank gently beneath them while she leaned forward. His cheeks tingled as her hair swished downward, the sensation nearly as sweet as her incoming kiss.

He wrapped his arms around her, clutching her tight, clinging to the moment.

"We should get my dress off before it gets too dirty," she said.

"Good idea." He reached under her skirt. She trembled as his fingers caressed the smoothness of her thighs. He pushed the skirt up, up, and away, marveling at the firm curve of her hips, the softness of her belly.

She lifted the dress overhead, leaving herself with nothing but a bra and panties. She then helped him remove his clothes, working around the clunky arm cast. Before he knew it, he was naked but for the cast. The moist woodland air licked him all over.

Her eyes tempted him as she continued undressing. His heart threw haymakers when she unhooked her bra and slid the straps down her shoulders. Before the cups came loose, she crossed her arms over her chest, daring him with her eyes.

Oh, did he dare.

He made a play for the bra, but she teasingly twisted away. They laughed, and when the laughter settled, he slid his hand beneath the waistband of her underwear. He worked his fingers between her thighs, mixing his movements and rhythm until her arms dropped, allowing the bra to slide away. Sunlight warmed her tan lines. He couldn't wait another second.

He flicked his tongue over a nipple, teasing it to life. Then he raised his mouth to hers. Mid-kiss, he surprised her by tipping her onto her back. She landed with a soft slap. Her breath huffed in his face as he guided her thighs apart.

Propping himself up on the cast, he shifted his weight. Mud sank beneath his knees, and before he could sink too far, he met her eyes and eased himself inside her. Delicious flames spilled down his neck. For the moment, there was no gun, no target, no remaining bullets.

Only Angela.

Beneath him she moaned, shifting her body to meet his thrusts. As clumsy as he was working one-handed, she seemed transfixed.

Before long he was panting, approaching his tipping point. Her moaning, her slick warmth, her mere *being*—he could no longer bear the intensity.

Grunting, he started to pull out when she snapped her arms around his back, squeezing tight and locking him inside her. He grunted louder, signaling that he was ready to pop, but her grip grew fervent as her nails raked the flesh along his shoulder blades. She became too much. Explosions went off, blasting him to dust, tearing him in a thousand different directions.

He was done. Spent.

Spent but *alive*.

Holding each other, they rolled onto their sides, panting as they searched each other's eyes. He brushed a mud-streaked strand of hair from her cheek and kissed her for a long, long time.

"Know what?" she said once their lips parted. "That made up for the other night."

"I'm forgiven?"

"Not yet." She reached for his shaft, then cupped the head and massaged it until it plumped up again. "Let's find this guy a home, shall we?"

He climbed over her and picked up where he left off.

"Oh God, Ken..." She propped herself up on both elbows. Her dark eyes locked with his. As he quickened his pace, her gaze drifted beyond his shoulder. Her panting stopped abruptly. Her arm darted forward, pointing behind him. "Shit!"

He turned his head.

At the bottom of the slope stood two men wearing jackets and jeans.

One held up a gold badge. He had a goatee and a scar on his left cheek.

The man was Officer Tormon.

CHAPTER 43

BOTH PLAINCLOTHES OFFICERS stared ahead and sipped their coffee. Tormon lowered a Styrofoam cup from his lips and wiped his gray-black goatee with his sleeve. Beside him his partner—a shorter, younger man wearing aviator sunglasses—shooed a mosquito away. Neither said anything. They looked exhausted, bored even. The tall grass swayed behind them.

"Morning, officers," Ken said. Though Angela was hyperventilating beneath him, he forced himself to stay calm. Public fornication wasn't a capital crime. There was no reason for the cops to march him through metal detectors at the police station. All he needed to do was act civil and send Angela away somehow. Then he could question Tormon. But he needed to move fast. "Let me say upfront that this was my idea. Not hers. If anybody's at fault, it's me."

The officers sipped their coffees.

Ken was hoping for more of a reaction. He added, "I was wrong. I got caught up in the moment. Went further than I should've."

Another sip.

Ken was losing patience. Blood boiled through his gun-fused fingers. The dormant desire to shoot flushed through him, and without thinking he swung his cast toward the cops. His sweaty index finger found the trigger.

What the hell am I doing?

He lowered his cast to the mud.

"Here's what's gonna happen," Tormon said, yawning. "You two are gonna get dressed, head back to your cars, and leave. If you do that before I finish my coffee, we'll pretend this never happened."

"Oh God, thank you," Angela said, gasping with relief. "This is so embarrassing. I don't know what came over us."

They dressed, their backs to one another. Gone was the passion and tenderness. Instead of trading quiet compliments and an occasional kiss, they said nothing until they were fully clothed and ready to leave.

"Thanks again," she said to the cops as she hurried past them and started uphill.

Ken, however, paused in front of Tormon. "Can I ask you something?"

"You can," Tormon said, lifting his cup. "Just remember what I said. You better be gone before I finish drinking this."

"A local kid died of an overdose this past weekend," Ken said, watching Tormon's eyes. "Seventeen-year-old boy. He took counterfeit Oxycontin. Tell me, are the police doing anything to prevent this?"

Tormon paused midsip. "You some kind of reporter?"

"Just a concerned citizen."

"Ken." Angela called from the hill. "We should get going."

Ken waved her off. "In a minute."

"You should listen to your woman, *Ken*," Tormon said, his tone warning. "I'm one gulp away from finishing this coffee."

"All right," Ken said, meeting Tormon's glare, "but I hope you start doing more to protect teenagers around here. Might want to target local high schools and see about keeping fentanyl out of kids' hands."

Torman lifted his cup. "We'll take that under consideration."

"Let's *go*, Ken," Angela said.

Reluctantly, he followed her.

Once they were out of earshot, she said, "What's the matter with you?"

"Nothing."

"Nothing? Those cops were super lenient with us. Why'd you act like a jerk?"

"All I did was ask a couple questions."

"There's a time and place for that. My God, do you realize what the school district could've done to us if we got arrested for having sex in public?"

"Didn't think about that."

"Of course you didn't. Because you were too busy squaring your shoulders and mouthing off to that cop. What, was that supposed to impress me?"

"No. It wasn't." A murderous urge trickled through. "Now, can we drop this?"

As they hiked the woodland trail, his mind replayed the conversation with Tormon. The look in Tormon's eyes had been difficult to read, but his defensive demeanor raised red flags. Though it was possible he simply didn't want to discuss his job with a civilian, Ken believed the man was hiding something.

He needed to go back and find out what.

But first he needed Angela gone.

Without warning he upped his pace. She hurried alongside him. She urged him to slow down so she didn't rip her dress, and he pictured her dress shredded with bullet holes. He tried suppressing the image, but it cluttered his mind until they reached the parking lot.

As they approached their cars, she squeezed his hand. "Wait."

"What?"

"Just wanted to say... All things considered, this morning was amazing."

He wasn't about to argue. "We should do it again sometime."

"The breakfast or the sex?"

"Both."

She threw her head back and laughed. It sounded forced, but under the circumstances, any laughter was welcome. "What day?"

"How about tonight?"

"Breakfast after dark?"

"I think it's called dinner."

She snorted. "Tell you what. I'll go to the grocery store and grab ingredients for one of my mom's lasagna recipes. It's heavy on the stomach, so we might have to lie down afterwards."

"Great." He unlocked his Camry and climbed inside. "See you tonight."

He shut his door, anxious for her to get into her Jeep and leave. Instead she tapped on his window. He could've killed her for wasting time like this, but he lowered the window.

"Aren't you forgetting something?" she said.

"What?" he said, agitated.

She leaned her head through the window and kissed him.

He tried to enjoy it, but all he could think about now was getting that next kill.

CHAPTER 44

Soon as Angela exited the parking lot, Ken bolted for the woods. He needed to hurry. She had wasted three precious minutes debating whether to use ricotta or cottage cheese in the lasagna. He had insisted any cheeses were welcome, but she rambled about flavors and textures until he demanded she pick her favorite. After giving him a funny look, she climbed into her Jeep and left.

Now he reentered the forest at a full sprint. His pulse drummed between his ears. Blistering heat poured through his arm. Today's local forecast suggested a high of seventy-two, but the surrounding air felt frigid compared to the mounting inferno within him that spread across his shoulders, down his chest, and into his legs. Sweat soaked his shirt and dampened his khakis. As he hurried downtrail, his sticky thighs hindered his stride.

Stop working against me, he told his gunhand. *I'm chasing down a target. Isn't that what you want?*

As he rushed through the woods, he tripped over a tree root. Momentum drove him face-first into an oak tree. He shrugged off a dizzy spell and resumed running. A hundred paces later, his ankle rolled. He tumbled into a patch of underbrush and lost his glasses.

While searching for them, he heard voices up ahead. One grew loud and unstable; another demanded quiet.

"It's Monday," the authoritative voice said. "Where's our cut?"

"You'll get your fucking cut when I get my fucking answers."

"That's not how our agreement works."

"One of my guys was killed yesterday—you think I give a wet, sloppy fuck about our agreement?"

"You should."

Ken found his glasses, settled them on his face, and crept forward. To avoid approaching the voices directly, he climbed a nearby hill, keeping low. A fallen tree lay across the hillcrest. When he peeked over it, he spotted four men below. Two were dressed in hoodies and jeans. The other two were Tormon and his partner.

Instinctively, Ken brandished the revolver. Then he stopped himself. Shooting now would interrupt the private meeting he'd stumbled upon. Perhaps this conversation was the reason Tormon had been so eager to shoo Ken away.

Below, an angry-looking brute with a web of neck tattoos stabbed a finger toward the cops. "I want to know who killed Hogwild."

Ken flinched at the mention of his latest victim. Evidently those two scumbags were connected to Hogwild and the local heroin trade. But what about the cops?

"We didn't touch Hog," Tormon said. From where Ken was perched, all he could see was the officer's bald head and blocky shoulders. "Remember, him being dead doesn't help us."

"That's bullshit—you wanted him dead."

"You're arguing out your ass. Now wise up and pay up. Otherwise you can forget about our protection going forward."

Protection? That settled it. The cops and dealers were in bed together. Now it was time for Ken to bloody the sheets. He needed to take smart shots. If he missed, the group would scatter—or worse, return fire. Both officers were packing, and he imagined the dealers concealed their weapons under their hoodies. Though Ken had infinite ammo, the gun's cylinder was now half-empty. Every three shots would be followed by three empties, meaning his targets would have time to react. When they did, he would need to take cover.

Neck Tattoo continued his tantrum. With both fists clenched, he stomped the dirt, ranting about how critical Hogwild was to his business.

"Settle down." Tormon held up a hand. "Try acting more professional."

"Tell me what happened to Hog."

"What you heard on the news is all I know."

"Who shot him?"

"It's being investigated. Probably got shot by a junkie."

"Bullshit. If a junkie offed him, they'd have taken the dope. Hog had two bags on him when he died. That means one of your pig brothers shot him."

"The bullet came from a .38-caliber revolver. No cop in my department was issued such a weapon."

"Could've been a personal weapon."

"More likely, a junkie shot Hog and panicked, then ran away."

"Any junkie would've collected before running."

"Not if they were scared out of their mind."

"Bullshit!" Neck Tattoo glanced at his buddy, who stepped forward and whispered in his ear. Still fuming, Neck Tattoo made a vague shoving motion with his hands. He looked like a moron.

A moron who deserves a bullet.

Ken swallowed his homicidal urge and glanced around for a better vantage point. Crawling sideways, he settled in behind a moss-covered oak. It was the closest he could get to the dealers without rolling downhill. Even so, he was well out of range. Tormon, meanwhile, was near enough that Ken could count the creases along the back of his scalp. Though the cops were easy targets, firing at them might send the dealers running. Ken couldn't afford that. He intended to get his final three kills and end this nightmare.

Shoot them.

Shootshootshoot.

He lifted his cast. The revolver must've understood it was feeding time, because his arm no longer trembled.

As he lined up the shot, a twig popped under his knee.

"What was that?" Tormon asked.

Ken ducked.

"If you brought anyone," Tormon said, "order them to stand down."

"We brought nobody," Neck Tattoo shouted. "What about you? You bring pig support?"

"It's only us two," Tormon said. "Tell your boys to stand down."

"We came alone, man."

"That's a goddamned lie. You've been hostile since we arrived."

"Only cause of what happened to Hog. You owe us answers."

"We don't owe you shit. You're the ones who—"

A gunshot boomed within the forest.

CHAPTER 45

GUNFIRE. Sweet, musical gunfire.

Though Ken's first instinct was to run, hide, and save himself, the thundering symphony called out to him, urging him to join. He couldn't leave, not while these men tried to kill each other. If any succeeded, he'd have fewer lives to take. Right now, there were four on the menu. He could relieve himself of his final three bullets, but only if he dug in his heels and took aim.

Snapping out from behind the mossy oak, he lifted his cast, targeted the first human being he could find, and fired.

An explosion burst within his cast. Boiling heat scalded his hand, threatening to melt his flesh. It seared through to the bone, and though his fingers couldn't move, they had no trouble registering second-degree agony. Skin cells cried out, layer after layer roaring with pain. He staggered sideways, hitting the ground as more shots roared below.

Someone screamed. It sounded like it came from behind him.

Before he could check, more gunfire erupted. A nearby tree exploded. Bits of tree bark rained down. Someone had spotted him.

Ken ducked behind the mossy oak.

More shots rang. One man howled in agony. Another moaned.

Then came a lull. Ken peeked around the edge of the trunk and spotted Neck Tattoo. He was squatting beside his partner, who lay face down and bloody.

Hold still, you prick.

Ken leveled his gunhand and pulled the trigger. The next two shots roared, followed by silent clicks as he cycled through three empties.

As Neck Tattoo rushed for cover, he slipped in his partner's blood.

Now scrambling downhill, Ken unloaded his next three rounds, hitting nothing. As he closed in on his intended target, his field of view widened enough for him to realize, to his horror, that both cops were lying motionless. That meant if Neck Tattoo escaped, Ken would be stranded in the woods at kill time. He feared the worst for those dining at the Cabin Café.

Return fire interrupted his concerns.

He ducked behind a fallen oak, heart drumming, as bark exploded and splinters flew. He stuck his arm out and blindly fired. After three blasts, the woods went quiet. He cycled through his empties and surveyed the area. The moment that tattooed bastard ventured out from behind cover, Ken unloaded.

He missed.

He needed to get closer.

Ahead lay a dirt clearing—a flat stretch with nothing to take cover behind other than the fallen dealer's corpse. If Ken wanted a clean shot, he'd have to charge ahead and pray he didn't get picked off. One thing working in his favor was his endless ammo supply. He realized he could provide his own cover fire, and that's exactly what he did as he rushed forward. The gun's recoil bucked his stride, but he closed the gap and circled the tree where Neck Tattoo was hiding.

The moment Ken spotted his target, he fired.

Neck Tattoo shifted sideways, clinging to cover. For a moment he vanished, then an arm stretched out, a black pistol in hand. The barrel gleamed in the sunlight. Its aim wobbled before it centered on Ken.

He dove for the dirt.

Four consecutive shots boomed.

Ken returned fire from the ground, then launched to his feet. He rounded the tree, twigs and leaves crunching underfoot as he dove for an angle. His elbow and hip struck the rocky soil. As he looked up, he watched the bastard cram a fresh magazine into his pistol. It clicked home just as Ken lifted his cast and pulled the trigger.

Neck Tattoo fumbled and dropped his weapon. Instead of picking it up, he reached for his side, where a stain was spreading.

Ken's next bullet knocked the asshole on his back, both feet spread apart. Clutching his chest, he moaned like a wounded animal.

Ken rose to his feet, his eyes locked on his target, and moved to stand over him.

"Tell me," he said, cycling through his empties, "do you sell to Morgan High?"

"Wh-what?" Neck Tattoo said, grimacing.

"Morgan High School," Ken said. "Do you sell to the kids there?"

"No."

"Who does?"

"I-I don't know. My guys don't go there—too risky."

Ken hung his head. What a shame. If Neck Tattoo had a connection to Pete's overdose, this next part would've been more meaningful.

"Don't kill me." Neck Tattoo panted. "C'mon, man."

Ken touched his cast to the man's chest. "You're Hogwild's boss. Hog used to sell to my brother. Big mistake."

He fired three times in rapid succession.

He didn't stop.

He didn't stop until the gun clicked four times instead of three.

A whooshing relief blew through him. Though the flesh along his gunhand was badly burned, a sweet coolness numbed him. He dropped to his knees and sucked deep breaths. Then he heard a muffled growl behind him.

Across the clearing lay Officer Tormon, blood soaked. In obvious pain, the man lifted his service pistol and steadied his aim at Ken.

A shot thundered.

Ken ducked for cover behind Neck Tattoo's tree.

After a lengthy silence, he peeked around the tree bark.

Tormon had dropped the pistol just out of reach. His index finger scratched the barrel.

Ken sped over and kicked the weapon away.

Now he had the unarmed Tormon all to himself. What a swing of fortune. Minutes ago, Ken had been crushed when he saw three men lying in their own blood. He assumed they were dead, that Neck Tattoo would be this morning's only kill. Now it appeared he would garner two from this hectic shootout.

Tormon opened his mouth to speak. Bloody strings of saliva stretched between his lips. With his hand he wiped them before he said, "Don't shoot."

"You shot at me."

"Thought you were with them... Was afraid."

Afraid of me? Ken thought. *That's a first.*

"Call...911."

"Forget it," Ken said. "You took money from those assholes. You profited off their poison. Now a seventeen-year-old kid is gone because of you."

Tormon wiped his bloody lips. "Und..."

"Don't deny it."

"Under..."

"Under?" Ken glanced at the man's body. Was he hiding something underneath him? Like a list of the criminals he worked with? Maybe he'd had a change of heart now that he'd been exposed. Perhaps he could reveal who else was responsible.

"Under what?" Ken asked. "What's under you?"

"Unh..." Tormon groaned, straining. "Under...cover."

"Under what cover?" Ken asked.

Then it hit him. Tormon was working undercover. He wasn't dirty, just pretending to be. Undercover police work explained everything—why Tormon took the late shift, why he squandered drug busts, why he negotiated with criminals in the woods. Isaacs had been so desperate to stifle local drug trafficking that he'd overlooked this possibility. And Ken had failed to properly interrogate Tormon and gather all the facts as he'd originally planned.

What have I done?

Studying the cop's body, Ken counted three gunshot wounds. One in the leg, two in the chest. Blood painted the crumpled leaves around him. Ken was no doctor, but he didn't think a 911 call could save the man. Nor did he think it was wise to waste this opportunity.

An opportunity, he thought. *What have I become now that I see a dying man as an opportunity?*

Before Tormon's breath faded, Ken added an extra wound to his forehead.

Following the loud report, he heard something from above. It sounded like a squeal, maybe from a rodent?

But when he looked up the hill, he saw it wasn't a rodent.

It was Angela.

CHAPTER 46

KEN'S BREATH caught in his throat. Without thinking, he swung his cast behind him, as if hiding it could somehow fool her. There was no telling how much she'd seen, but he recalled a scream coming from the woods when the shooting started. That meant Angela had been here the entire time. Worst of all, she'd seen him gun down a dying officer. This wasn't how he wanted her to remember him. They were supposed to have dinner tonight. Her mother's lasagna.

Ken stumbled uphill, calling out to her, "Angela, I—"

Like a frightened doe, she darted away.

"Wait!"

He topped the hill and gave chase, his burned hand welcoming the airflow through the cast. His legs pumped faster as he closed in on her, faster still as she gawked over her shoulder. The look on her face that spelled horror only lasted a moment before she tripped and went down.

"Angela!" Ken offered his hand to help her up, but she shrieked at him. He backed away, giving her space. "I promise I won't hurt you. The cast, the gun—I can explain everything."

Again, she shrieked.

"Angela, please." He reached out. "I'd never hurt you, I swear."

"Get away!" She kicked his outstretched hand. Her eyes glared in defiance. "You hid that gun while we ate breakfast—while we had sex by the pond. Was that your plan? Were you gonna shoot me if I didn't fuck you?"

The last part stung. Ken steeled himself and stretched his hand closer. "It's a long story, but three nights ago my father was shot dead and the killer left this gun behind. I picked it up, and it's been stuck to me ever since."

She shook her head, her expression incredulous.

"I know it sounds insane, but it's true. I can explain everything."

"You're *sick*—you shot that guy in the chest over a dozen times. And then that cop. You shot them and now they're dead. Dead!"

"Calm down," he said.

Surely somebody had called 911 after the gunshots. They needed to leave. "Listen, we can't have this conversation here. I can explain everything, but we need to leave now."

"What if I stay here? Will you shoot me? Make it look like a suicide? Make it look like *I* killed those people?"

"Please take my hand. I won't hurt you. If you want to turn me in later, fine. But give me a chance to explain."

He leaned in, extending his hand.

She flinched away.

Wind gusts shook the surrounding oaks, unleashing a chorus of woodland noise. Between the scraping branches, the swishing leaves, and his own ringing ears, Ken couldn't hear himself think. Nor could he determine if any sirens were approaching. Every second he spent arguing with Angela put his future in peril.

"Listen, I can't stay here," he said. "If you're coming with me, now's the time. If not, that's okay. All I'm asking for is a chance."

The woods thrashed louder.

Angela met his eyes.

She reached for him.

But instead of taking his outstretched hand, she grabbed his cast. Careful not to point it at her face, she studied it. The shattered opening transfixed her. She angled it toward the light, eyeing the snubnose inside.

Then she glared at him.

"I have to go," he said. "Please don't tell anyone."

Without a word, she shoved his cast away.

CHAPTER 47

"WHAT AN IDIOT!" Hannah exclaimed when Ken had finished recounting the morning's events. His story had injected her with energy—more accurately, fury. She sat upright on the futon without cringing for the first time since receiving her stitches. Her eyes—vacant minutes ago—narrowed in outrage. Her fist pounded the armrest. "Idiot. You should've known cops work undercover."

"I know, I know." Frustrated, Ken yanked his busted cast from his arm and flung it at the ground. He hung his head. It felt like the weight of the two dead cops was crushing down on him. "Isaacs said they were dirty. I took his word. Figured he had insider info."

"From the sounds of it, all he has is this massive grudge against anyone who *might* be involved in drug trafficking. He doesn't care whether they're genuinely guilty. Hell, he even suspected your dad. You should've caught that."

"Well, I didn't!" Ken kicked the futon. "Instead, I fucked up, caused a shitstorm, and killed two people who were trying to solve the problem. So, yeah—you're right—I should've thought twice. Thanks for the fucking tip."

"Chill, Ken."

"Chill?" He shook all over, sweating like mad. His burned fist felt like it was melting off his arm. "How am I supposed to chill?"

"Take a deep breath," she said, eyeing the gun. "We're almost out of this."

He inhaled, catching the thick scent of the aloe he had sprayed on his gunhand earlier. It had failed to mitigate the burns, same as deep breaths now failed to settle his nerves. Images and worries pinballed through his mind. Memories of the shootout clashed with potential arrest scenarios. He wasn't sure who would link him to the massacre, but at least one person could.

"Know what worries me most?" he said. "Angela."

"Why? Think she'll rat you out?"

"Hard to say." He glanced at his empty cast lying on the floor like a charred husk. "Actually, I think she'll stay quiet."

"What makes you so sure?"

"She could've called 911 from the woods, but she didn't."

"Doesn't mean shit. She can change her mind. Especially if she's afraid you'll come after her. Or she might feel obligated to report you. Is she one of those stubborn goody-goody types?"

"Not really. She's more of a rule-breaker."

"That helps us."

"Yeah." But he didn't fully believe Angela would remain quiet. He could only imagine the pressure she was under. Her conscience was probably eating her alive. He never should've involved her. She'd only witnessed the shootout because he'd forced some last-minute romance into his schedule. Now she—the lone bright spot in his life— had to carry an unbearable burden.

He doubted she could carry it for long.

"We can't stick around," he said. "Let's leave for LA."

"Now? I can barely walk to the toilet."

"Hannah, I know you're uncomfortable, but suck it up."

"I can't. Not yet."

"You seem fine."

"Oh really?" She reached beneath the armrest and lifted the

bucket she'd been puking into earlier. "Sure I'm ready for a road trip? And what about your brother? He was throwing up in the bathroom all morning before he went upstairs."

"You'll both have to tough it out," Ken said, blowing on his burned fist. "We can't stay here."

"Wait." She pointed at the muted TV. "Breaking news. Turn it up."

Ken increased the volume. The news anchor—a forty-ish blond guy—announced that two cops and two men with criminal records had been fatally shot in the woods less than a mile from the Cabin Café. "Authorities say they have no information on the suspect at this time, but they believe it's related to drug trafficking. They request that anyone with information on the shooting contact them. Our very own Kendra Johnson is live near the scene."

The screen cut to a somber young woman holding a microphone. In the background was the Cabin Café.

"I'm here live. Earlier today, four people, including two law enforcement officers, were fatally shot near this restaurant. Businesses closed following the shootings, and residents remain in their homes. Earlier I managed to speak with some of them. Their reaction? Horror."

Ken turned off the TV. He couldn't stomach any more.

"We've got time," Hannah said. "They don't have info on the suspect."

"So they say."

"If anyone saw you, they'd have a description."

"That doesn't mean I'm safe."

"I'm telling you, they—" She coughed, then grabbed her side. "Shit."

"Need anything?"

"Yeah. Need you to go back in time and not shoot me."

"Hannah, I'm in no mood for sarcasm. Do you realize my car was parked at the Cabin Café for hours? If anyone connects my Camry to the murders, they'll check the traffic cameras. Once they get my license number, I'm screwed."

"You're being paranoid."

"Am I? Do you really believe I didn't leave a single clue behind? What if the waitress gives descriptions of everyone she served this morning? She'll remember me—I was the nervous wreck who ordered two glasses of wine with breakfast. What kind of lunatic orders wine with a mushroom omelet?"

Hannah laughed.

"What? Is this funny to you?"

"It is," she said, clutching her side again. "You need to chill."

"When will you be ready to leave?"

"No idea."

"Give me an estimate."

"Well...I feel shitty, but another night's sleep should help."

Another night. Might as well be another month. Ken wondered how long he could realistically remain undetected. Minutes? Hours? Best case scenario was that the cops suspected a local dealer had done Ken's handiwork. That might throw them off, but what about Angela? Any moment now she might dial 911.

Unless he intervened.

He grabbed his keys off the coffee table.

"Where you going?" Hannah asked.

"To see Angela."

"Are you nuts? She might call the cops the moment she sees you."

"Or the moment she doesn't see me." He rose to his feet, heart thumping around his ribcage. "It's like you said. She could change her mind any second."

"Ugh. Sometimes I hate when I'm right." Hannah dropped her head against the pillow. "Be careful. If you get busted, me and your brother go down with you."

Ken paused while zipping his jacket. In his desperation to cover his tracks, he'd forgotten about Robby. Visiting Angela could trigger a series of events that would lead to Robby being arrested for home invasion, kidnapping, and enough murder-related charges to land him in prison long-term. Ken hated to risk his brother's future.

Yet if Ken backed down now, how was that any different from when he'd allowed Olivia to ruin him? Years ago, he'd been afraid to confront her about something difficult and private. Now he found himself in a similar position. This time, however, he knew better; pretending everything was okay would only make things worse.

He pocketed his gunhand and headed for the door.

CHAPTER 48

ANGELA WASN'T HOME. Nor would she answer her phone.

Ken tried the doorbell several times before entering the backyard he'd fled from three nights ago. A chilly breeze shook the arborvitaes that provided a high, leafy fence around the yard. He sat on a lawn chair beside the empty fire pit and leaned back, listening to swishing trees and the murmur of distant vehicles.

One thing bothered him from the other night: the snapping noise he'd heard while in the pool with Angela. That noise had spooked him, sent him home, and set this nightmare in motion.

He rose and moved to check around the trees, maneuvering numerous branches. He didn't know what he expected to find— maybe some rabid squirrels—but when he lifted a low branch, he noticed something odd.

In the dirt lay a broken pencil. A blue one like Pete Chang used in class. It had been snapped down the middle, although a wood sliver connected the two halves. Ken lifted it by the pointed half and stared. What was it doing here? Had someone been hiding with it in the trees? One of Angela's teacher friends? If so, why? *Who sneaks around with a sketch pencil?*

A motor rumbled and stopped nearby. The slap of a car door followed.

"Ken."

He flinched, the arborvitaes trembling in the wind beside him. He turned and saw Angela standing at the edge of her backyard. In one arm she cradled a bulging brown grocery bag. Two plastic bags dangled from her opposite elbow. She wore a burgundy long-sleeve dress with a white belt. Her expression was deathly numb as her gaze shifted between his jacket pocket and the broken pencil in his fingers. He considered asking about the pencil, but it was the least of their worries.

The moment he stepped toward her, she set her bags down and reached inside her purse.

She pulled out a gun. A snubnose revolver. She steadied it with both hands, lining the barrel up with his chest. They were separated by the width of her swimming pool and then some, meaning that if she fired, she'd likely miss. He half-wished she'd come closer and shoot him dead.

Instead they stood there wordlessly. The arborvitaes swished in the wind; her grocery bags flapped and crinkled.

Finally, he said, "Wanted to check on you."

"I'm fine." Her voice was toneless.

"Can we talk?"

"That's what we're doing, isn't it?"

"I was hoping for somewhere more private."

"And I was hoping I'd never see you again."

"If that's what you want, I'll leave. Just say the word."

The afternoon sun gleamed off her forehead. She was sweating—no doubt panicking. It must've taken all her resolve to stand her ground with that weapon. He hated himself for putting her through this.

"Angela, I'm sorry. I came here to talk, but if that's asking too much, I understand. Just tell me what you want me to do."

With each deep breath her shoulders rose and fell.

The revolver trembled in her hand.

She shook her head.

Finally, she said, "Take my groceries inside."

He put the pencil in his other pocket, walked slowly toward her, and lifted the bags. They entered through the back porch, and he set the groceries on the kitchen table. She ordered him to tuck one plastic bag in the fridge and the other in the freezer. Aiming at him from across the room, she sighed. "I must be crazy, letting you in here."

"Yeah."

She wiped her brow with her sleeve. Sweat darkened the fabric. At the kitchen table she sat, nudging away a cluttered stack of mail. When she pulled her chair in, her unwashed hair swung alongside her cheeks. It still contained flecks of dirt and leafy bits.

"You should wash your hair," he said, taking the seat across from her.

She rested both elbows on the table, now pointing the gun at his throat.

He decided to jump right in. "Angela, what happened today wasn't supposed to happen. Not like that. All I wanted was breakfast with you."

She blinked. Her face was pale, her eyes sunken. "I'm not sure how to feel. One minute we're eating omelets, then we're having sex in the mud, then we're screaming at each other about those men you shot, and now here we are. It's like emotional roulette." She blinked again. "I'm all burned out. Confused. Like, how'd it come to this? And why are you in my kitchen hiding a gun in your pocket?"

He slowly set his gunhand on the table, making sure it was pointed away from her. "I want to explain everything."

Her eyes fell on his revolver. "Let's hear it."

CHAPTER 49

ANGELA ABSORBED the news with a series of blinks, stares, and the occasional grimace. Several times she interrupted for clarification, and Ken held nothing back. He delivered the full rundown of his weekend, revealing everything, from the hard, gruesome facts to his nagging doubts about Hannah's plan to trade the cursed revolver in for a fresh start.

After a prolonged silence, Angela slowly tucked her snubnose back into her purse and zipped it shut. However, her eyes never left him as she put a teakettle on the stove. When she sat again, she said, "I need to know one thing. Did the gun kill that cop, or was it your choice?"

He opened his mouth, then paused.

"Don't sugarcoat it. Tell me."

He nodded. "My choice."

"And the others?"

Again he nodded. "The guy with the neck tattoos, definitely. Hogwild, definitely. With Chrissie, the pressure was heavy, but the ultimate choice was mine. Same as when I shot Hannah. As for Michelle, that was self-defense."

"Sounds like the gun didn't kill anyone. It was all you."

Her words struck like a fist to the windpipe. He wanted to argue that he didn't grab the revolver with malicious intentions. That he'd tried to separate the gun from his hand and tried harder to resist its haunting pressure. That he'd killed Hogwild and euthanized the cop because he wanted safe, clear-headed kills.

Clear-headed kills, he thought. *What have I become?*

Rather than arguing with her, he said, "Yeah. All me."

For a moment she said nothing. She stared at the kitchen wall, eyes lifeless, hands folded beneath her chin. He could only imagine what thoughts twisted through her mind. Undoubtedly she was worried she could be next if she upset him. He would never consider harming her, but she didn't know that. All she knew was he'd killed five people since Friday night, and he intended to kill one more.

Her eyes met his. "Have you picked your final target?"

Ken didn't mean to laugh, but he couldn't help it. The tension in his chest was unbearable, and the fact that she seemed to accept his situation was an immense, almost narcotic relief. He'd expected many different responses from her, but not this one. "You're okay with this?"

"Not one bit. It's wrong. It's disgusting. You *murdered* people."

His mouth went dry.

"But at the same time," she said, "I keep asking myself what I would've done in your position. Can't blame you for killing your father's murderer. Nor can I blame you for shooting the others once you understood the gun's curse." She smiled a sad smile. "It's an awful situation, and you did some awful things, but I'm not sure that makes you an awful person. In fact, you did some good. Saving Hannah, sparing Glinski...that's the Ken Fujima I know."

Hearing this didn't erase his guilt, but she was right. He'd shown restraint. As much as possible. If a lesser man had grabbed the gun, Hannah and Glinski would be corpses by now. Many people in this world would jump at an excuse to unleash their hatred, but Ken had battled those urges.

Not that he'd won every battle.

"Wish I'd spared Chrissie and Tormon," he said. "Those two didn't deserve it. They were innocent."

"So were you, Ken."

Angela leaned across the table and took his hands—both his empty hand and his gunhand. Her grip was warm and firm. It eased the tension in his muscles and stirred a faint hope within his chest. He never wanted her to let go.

"Thanks," he said, meeting her eyes. "Once I leave town, you should report me to the authorities. Tell them everything that happened this morning. I don't want you getting pegged as my accomplice or anything."

"I'll be fine," she said, massaging his hands. "I'm more worried about you."

"Don't be. Things will get easier once I've used my last bullet."

"Who you going after?"

He frowned. "Good question. Up till now my biggest concern was you calling the cops. Haven't had time to figure out my next target. I suppose I'll go after another drug dealer. Ideally, I'd like to eliminate someone who deals to high schoolers. I'm still pissed about what happened to Pete."

Angela released her grip on his hands. She sank back into her chair and chewed on her thumbnail as if mulling something over.

"What?" he said. "You think it's a bad idea? Too risky?"

"No, it's...fine." She glanced into the corner of the room. Something about her demeanor was defensive. Like she was hiding something. After she'd been so candid about his situation with the gun, this came as a surprise.

"Angela? Something on your mind?"

"Just thinking."

"About what? Do you know something that can help me?"

Her chair creaked as she shifted in her seat.

"If you know anything about the person who dealt those fake Oxys to Pete, you need to tell me. Is there someone who can identify the dealer? A student? A teacher? Anyone?"

Her eyes locked with his. "I...I don't want to say it."

"It's okay. You can tell me. I just want to protect our students."

"I know you do." Reaching up, she pushed her hair back and took a deep breath. Then another.

He leaned in. "Do you know who sold Pete those drugs?"

"No," she said, "but I know who caused him to OD."

CHAPTER 50

THE TEAKETTLE WENT off with a wail. Ken startled in his seat like a solider awakened by mortar fire. He pressed a hand against his chest; his heart tapped violently, telegraphing a distress signal to the rest of his body. By the time he'd settled, Angela had dropped chamomile tea bags into two mugs. As she attempted to add boiling water, her trembling grip caused her to miss the mugs and splash the counter. When she brought the mugs to the table, she sat and stared at the wall again.

"Well?" he said. "Who caused Pete to OD?"

She shifted awkwardly, the chair creaking underneath her. "I'm sorry, I don't think I can go through with this."

He lifted his mug to his nose. The warm scent of chamomile did nothing to ease his nerves. "I know it's hard, but you need to tell me."

"I want to. I really do." She chewed her lip. "But it's like signing a death warrant."

"Whoever it is, they did something horrible."

"Still, I don't want to order an execution." Her fingers clutched her mug. "Besides, in a way, I'm responsible. I could've stopped it. I could've done something. If I had, Pete would still be alive."

Ken slid his chair around the table until their shoulders were touching. He pried one of her hands off the mug and wrapped his own firmly, supportively around it. "Whatever happened, however you messed up...I know how you feel. On Friday night I could've stayed home, could've stayed with you, could've left here five minutes earlier or five minutes later. If I'd done anything differently, I never would've picked up this gun. But I did. I regret it, and I regret almost everything I've done since. Now I'm stuck with the consequences. All I can do is focus on the future, on making things better. Same goes for you."

As the words left his mouth, his head tingled. There was a strong intimacy in sharing their guilt, their burdens, their fears. He and Angela might as well have been the last two people on earth.

"Okay." She nodded awkwardly, as if her neck were out of alignment. "First of all, that pencil you found in my backyard—it belongs to Pete."

Though it didn't surprise Ken that Pete owned such a pencil, he couldn't understand how it ended up here. "What was it doing in your backyard?"

"Pete dropped it there. On Friday night."

"The night of your party?" But if the pencil was the source of the snapping noise, that meant... "Wait, he saw us in the pool?"

"Pete lived three blocks away," she said. "That night he came here for help."

"With what?"

She hung her head. When she looked up, her eyes were glossy. "Remember on Thursday in the lunchroom, when I said I'd talk to Pete? Well, I did. After study hall I pulled him aside. He tensed up when I mentioned the parking lot, but I reassured him that he wouldn't get in trouble, that I knew he'd bought drugs, that I just wanted to know what was bothering him.

"For a while he stood frozen beside my desk. There were tears in his eyes. He asked to talk in private, so I shut the door. Then he told me about Principal Soward."

"What about her?"

"Apparently Pete needed a scholarship recommendation for one of the local colleges. Soward is pals with someone on the admissions committee, so Pete thought a letter from her would boost his chances. Anyway, he asked her, and she scheduled an appointment for after school. When he let himself into her office, he found Soward with her leg up on the desk and an electric razor in hand. She was *shaving*."

Ken grimaced. "Ugh."

"I know." Angela stared into her mug. "Pete tried to leave, but Soward insisted he stay. She claimed she shaved her legs at work sometimes, that it was no big deal. Once he sat down, they discussed the scholarship. She promised him a glowing recommendation but wanted something in return."

Angela looked off into the corner of the room.

Ken squeezed her hand. "What'd she want?"

"She wanted him to paint her toenails."

"She—you're kidding."

Angela blew on her tea, her breath shuddering. "Pete didn't go into detail. He said he painted her toes. Then she asked him to help her finish shaving. He shaved everything. First her legs, then they... kept going."

Ken squirmed in his chair. To think his student had been coerced into something like that. And by Soward of all people—the same woman who had tried painting Ken as a pedophile the other day. *The nerve of her.* It made his blood burn.

Still, one thing bothered him.

"Angela, why didn't you do something?"

"I did," she said. "That's where I screwed up."

"How?"

"After Pete confided in me, he begged me not to tell anyone. He thought it would follow him the rest of his life, but I reassured him. I said he wouldn't have told me the story unless he wanted someone to stand up for him. I considered telling the police. I probably should've. But I was afraid they wouldn't do anything. Remember, Soward's husband is in politics. I was worried he'd cover it up."

"So what did you do?"

"I snuck into her office after school. She had a meeting downstairs, so I searched her desk for evidence. I found the nail polish and started digging through the drawers for her electric razor. One drawer was locked, and I tried prying it open with a pair of scissors, but Soward came in.

"She spotted the nail polish and stared me down. Neither of us said anything. It was like we were each waiting for the other to make the first move.

"Then I asked her why she wasn't shaving today.

"She gave me a funny look, and I accused her straight up. She denied it.

"I was so furious, I ran around her desk and got in her face. We started yelling. I told her to unlock her drawer so we could see if her razor was in there. She denied it and threatened to fire me.

"Before I could stop myself, I put my hands around her neck."

"*What?*" Ken said.

"I lost control," she said. "It was like you in the basement with your father's murderer. Except I didn't go through with it. Soon as my thumbs pushed against her throat, I stopped myself. I couldn't believe I'd gone that far.

"Soward shoved me back. She denied Pete's story. Said it was his word against hers. Then she pointed to the security camera behind her desk. She ordered me to never speak against her or else the video footage would reach the police." Angela shook her head, her mouth drooped with dismay. "I backed off. What else could I do?

"On Friday I saw Pete in the hall. I didn't want to discuss anything at school, so I asked if he wanted to regroup over the weekend. He said no, but then he showed up while you and I were in the pool.

"After you left, he ran out of the trees. I'd never seen anyone so on edge. I wrapped myself in my robe and told him about my encounter with Soward. He started freaking out, yelling at me. Said he didn't want my help—that he didn't want people knowing about what happened with Soward." She swallowed hard. "He said he was losing his mind. That he only managed to sleep the night before because of some pills he took. I thought he meant regular sleeping pills, but..."

She began to sob.

Ken wrapped his arm around her shoulders. She hunched there, lifeless. It pained him that she had to bear such a terrible secret. These past three days he'd been wishing that someone out there could understand his burden. Now he wished otherwise. Angela didn't deserve this situation. Didn't deserve Pete's death on her conscience. Didn't deserve Soward's blackmail.

None of it.

"First thing tomorrow," he said, "I'm ending this."

CHAPTER 51

LATER THAT NIGHT they showered together, washing away the dirt and woodsy debris. After soaping and rinsing, they held each other beneath the warm spray. He kept his gunhand at his side, pointed away from her; his free arm circled her securely around the shoulders. Her arms, slick against his lower back, squeezed tight. Since Friday night, he'd felt as though he'd been drifting from his own humanity, but her embrace drew him back in.

She lifted her chin off his shoulder and whispered, "You can hold me with both arms."

"But the gun—"

"You won't shoot me," she said. "We both know that."

Hesitating, he wrapped both arms around her, resting the gun's cylinder against her shoulder blade. She didn't flinch.

Later they dried off and went downstairs. She led him into the front living room, where bookshelves lined the walls and comfy furniture surrounded an ornate fireplace. She started a blaze, and they made themselves cozy on a leather couch. They spooned, her back pressed to his chest, offering as much warmth as the fire. She pulled a Pooh Bear blanket over them and leaned back against him, her weight solidly soft, her shampoo mercilessly fragrant. Her hair was damp from the shower, and he caressed it and allowed his eyelids to droop.

As sleep approached, he buried his gunhand under the couch cushion. Doing so disturbed her. When she twisted around, she noticed his arm was tucked away.

"What're you afraid of?" she asked.

"Shooting you in my sleep."

"Relax," she said and draped his arm around her. Her long, warm fingers wrapped around his gunhand, holding it securely, the barrel pointed at the carpet. They lay there listening to the crackling logs. Her thumb caressed his knuckles, back and forth. She glanced back at him, smiling. "See? You won't shoot me. You're a good man."

He kissed her.

When their lips separated, she twisted around again, her back to his front. They lay together, dozing in front of the flames. He drifted in and out of sleep until her voice startled him.

"...don't you think?"

"Hmm? What?"

"I said nothing beats a cool night in front of the fireplace."

"Can't argue there."

"Will you miss the cold weather?"

"What do you mean?"

"When you're in sunny California."

"Oh." He stared at the ceiling, wishing she hadn't mentioned it. So much for savoring the moment. Now his mind wandered into future territory. He pictured eighty-degree sunshine, air-conditioned classrooms, and the old LA apartment he grew up in. Hopper and Robby would be there, but the fantasy felt empty.

"Angela?"

"Yeah?"

"Let's go together."

She laughed. "Riiight."

"I'm serious. Being with you tonight...it's like I never picked up this gun."

She rolled toward him and traced her fingertips along his chest. They left a warm, dizzying trail. In the shadows, he noticed she was smirking. "If I say no, will you shoot me?"

He stuck his thumb and index finger out, touching the latter to her temple. He dropped his thumb. "Bang."

She smiled. "Forgot that we're outlaws."

"At the very least, I am." He brushed her cheek. "This'll sound crazy, but if you want to leave with me tomorrow, I can ask Hannah about getting an extra ID."

"I-I don't know. Can Hannah even be trusted?"

He hesitated. Ever since shooting Hannah, he'd felt obligated to take care of her. Somewhere along the way, he'd started trusting her, and he never stopped to ask himself whether that was wise. "Hard to say."

"She seems shady, is all."

"If you're concerned, let me make the trip alone. Once I get my ID, I'll see about getting yours."

Angela rolled onto her back, staring upward. "Won't it be hard to start over with a new ID?"

"Maybe you won't need one," he said. "When things cool down, divorce your husband and apply for teaching positions out west. Once you're hired, meet me there."

She said nothing. He was certain she would turn him down. Ditch him like Olivia had years ago. The thought of losing Angela made him want to shoot himself.

She rolled onto her side, her back against him.

"Let me think about it, Ken."

CHAPTER 52

THOUGH IT PAINED him to leave the cushioned warmth of Angela's couch, Ken needed to head home and start packing. When he arrived, he heard Hannah snoring. He decided to pack quietly and let her snooze. Regardless of what shape she was in after sunrise, they were hitting the road and not looking back.

Upstairs he found his brother snoring, an arm around Hopper. Robby always said he hated to sleep alone, and tonight he'd found a wholesome partner. A bottle of sleeping pills lay on the nightstand, but thankfully there were no needles in sight. The sweat-stained bedsheets indicated he was already struggling through the early stages of withdrawal. He had a rough road ahead, but a clean night's rest was a good start.

Ken tucked some t-shirts, button-downs, and pants into a suitcase. Underwear and socks followed, folded neatly on top. He scoured the hall closet for toiletries: toothbrushes, soap, shampoo, hair gel, everything he might take on vacation.

That's what this is, he told himself, *a strange vacation.*

With clothes and toiletries packed, he returned downstairs. In the kitchen he noticed the answering machine was blinking. When he played the message, he recognized Takahashi's voice, once again urging Dad to call ASAP. Ken dialed the number, but nobody answered. He returned the phone to its cradle with a feeling of unease.

He collected the scrapbook containing Mom's recipes. Inside were family photos from years ago. Back when Mom was healthy, Robby was clean, Dad walked upright, and Ken himself hadn't devolved into a cut-rate serial killer. That was the annoying thing about photos; they had a way of saying, *Look, life was good once. Too bad it didn't last.*

He bagged nonperishable snacks, along with all the dog food Hopper could handle. After loading two suitcases and three duffle bags, he parked everything by the back door. He double-checked each room, but there was nothing else in the house of significant value.

Nothing other than Dad.

Ken wrote a clumsy left-handed note, requesting that Dad's body be cremated and that his ashes be spread across Mom's garden. Tears dotted the paper as he wrote. After signing it, he hurried downstairs.

Glinski, who sat taped to a chair that was taped to the shelving rack, pleaded for a glass of water. Ken brought her one. As she sipped from a bendy straw, she glanced up. She drained half the glass, cleared her throat, and in a rough voice said, "Please let me stand up. My legs and back are sore from sitting all day."

"You're in luck," he said. "I'm about to unload my final bullet."

She gawked. "O-on me?"

"No, another target," he said and was warmed by the relief on her face. "Once the gun's empty and I'm far away, I'll send someone to cut you loose."

"Seriously? You'll let me go?"

"Yep. Just promise me you'll take better care of your patients."

"I will."

He tilted the straw toward her lips. While she sipped, he said, "Robby and I will be gone after today. The lawsuit will disappear along with us. Hopefully that'll put your conscience to rest."

"It won't," she said, talking around the straw. "Doubt I'll ever get over it."

Ken hated to think what that meant for his own conscience. If she couldn't forgive herself for one botched diagnosis, how could he possibly find peace after executing multiple people? This nightmare would soon end, but a deluge of guilt would follow. He supposed he could atone by taking care of Robby and Hannah, but then what? He needed to help others somehow. Perhaps he could start here.

"Doctor," he said, kneeling so they were at eye level, "I forgive you."

Glinski said nothing. Her shoulders relaxed a bit. He hoped the rest of her would too, but she began shaking her head like a madwoman.

"What's wrong?" he asked.

"I should've caught your mother's cancer."

"We all make mistakes."

"You don't understand," she said, her voice rising. "The prescription I wrote for your mother was one I often wrote. Too often. Whenever a patient grumbled about back pain, I couldn't wait to get my pen out. Every time I wrote that script, I made money. The drug company paid me to speak at conferences, and those speaking fees took the sting out of my student loans, my malpractice insurance, my mortgage. I used to tell myself that it made life easier for both me and my patients, so what was the harm? Then your family filed that negligence lawsuit. That changed everything."

Ken pulled the glass away. He wasn't surprised by her confession; it was something he, Robby, and Dad had suspected. But hearing it from her now made things brutally real. It sent raw heat down his forearm and into his gunhand. Part of him wanted to avenge his mother, but that part would have to go hungry.

Two nights ago, Glinski had insisted she was sorry about what happened. Ken didn't fully believe her then, but he did now. She had nothing to gain from confessing to him. Nothing other than his complete and total forgiveness.

But he could only offer true forgiveness if she understood what she'd done.

"Something you should know," he said, his throat swelling. "My mom was the heart of this family. Maybe that sounds like a silly cliché, but it's the truth. She brought strength and warmth to this house. When she passed away, everyone else crumbled. I became isolated and angry. Dad drank day and night until he fell down the stairs. And Robby, well...after Mom's death he started using the pills you prescribed her."

Glinski winced.

"I'm not telling you this to make you feel worse," he said, clearing his throat. "After what I did these past few days, I'm in no position to judge you. But I do want you to know how special my mother was. And I want you to remember her. I want you to honor her every time you step into an exam room. Can you do that?"

Glinski rolled her lips together. She nodded.

"Thank you."

After she finished the water, he approached the root cellar. Though he'd sealed the doorway, the stench of decay nonetheless permeated the air. He hurriedly bit off a piece of duct tape and fixed the funeral note to the door.

Before backing away, he patted the door. "Bye, Dad."

Then he went upstairs, sank into his recliner, and failed to fall asleep.

CHAPTER 53

MORNING CAME. At the first sliver of sunrise, Ken wanted to kill. Needed to. He grew feverish; nasty thoughts crept in. The urges felt stronger today. Hungrier. Though he intended to slay Principal Soward within the hour, part of him craved immediate destruction. Anyone was fair game. Hannah on the futon. Robby upstairs. Glinski downstairs. The neighbors across the street. Even himself.

That brief suicidal urge snapped him back to reality. He spotted the suitcases by the back door and remembered he needed to load them into his Camry.

Rising from his recliner, he groaned. Everything ached. Three straight nights of little-to-no sleep had taken their toll. Walking put strain on his knees, which could've used an injection of WD40. His lower back flared with every step, the muscles moaning from all the times he'd lifted Dad out of his wheelchair. The thought of Dad drained Ken even more as he lugged the suitcases and duffle bags outside.

Shortly after he returned, Robby wandered downstairs. He looked rough, his eyelids swollen like knife wounds. Every step was punctuated by a sharp, agonized hiss. He hugged the nearest wall as he guided himself toward the kitchen.

"You okay?" Ken said.

"My legs are fucking killing me," Robby said. "I took two gabapentin. Probably should've taken three. Everything hurts. My bones feel ready to pop out of my skin." He grimaced. "We leaving soon?"

"Just finished loading the bags," Ken said, filling a mug at the sink. All the exertion had left his throat dry. A large gulp of tap water did little to alleviate his thirst. "Our suitcases are in the trunk, along with snacks and dog food. We'll transfer everything into Hannah's van later. I'd rather take her vehicle in case cops look up my license plate."

"Who's your target?"

Ken explained his plan to kill Soward. It needed to happen at her home before she left for school. Though she lived with her husband and two teenagers, he hoped to catch her alone outside the house, maybe on her way to the mailbox. If she didn't leave the house, he would ring her doorbell, shoot her, and run.

"What if somebody else answers the door?" Robby said. "You're banking on everything going right."

"Enough has gone wrong," Ken said, ripping open a packet of instant coffee. He swallowed the crystals like sugar. "I'm due for a windfall."

Robby scratched his cheek, glancing at the basement door. "What're we doing with Glinski?"

"I've thought it over." Ken choked down the stale coffee taste. "Once we hit the road, we'll find a pay phone—if those still exist—and drop an anonymous tip."

"Fuck that," Robby said. "Go downstairs and use your last bullet. End this nightmare the easy way."

"I can't. It has to be Soward."

"Too risky, man. Glinski is a layup by comparison."

"If I let Soward live, she'll get away with something unforgivable."

Robby turned scarlet. "Wait, killing Mom was forgivable?"

"Soward is irredeemable," Ken said, feeling the coffee crystals kick in. "What she did was deliberate, and there's no telling when she'll do it again."

"No telling when Glinski will overlook someone's cancer either."

"Glinski has changed."

"People don't change, Ken."

"Then why should I believe you will?"

Robby winced. "What?"

"Why bother taking you to LA if you're only gonna shoot heroin in the slums? Someday I'll get a call about you dying in an alleyway south of Little Tokyo. Think I'll be excited to identify your body? To lose the only family I have left?"

"Fuck off!" Robby roared in his face. "Don't make this about me. Just shoot Glinski already—you should've shot her instead of Chrissie."

"I shouldn't have shot anyone."

"Yeah, but you did. You shot somebody I cared about. At least get it right this time. Here—" Robby ripped open the silverware drawer. He lifted a steak knife and approached the basement door. "I'll get you started. This time, I won't hesitate."

Ken leveled his revolver. "Stop right there."

Robby laughed. "You won't shoot me. I'm your brother."

"You are. And you're the last good thing this family has to offer," Ken said, feeling his throat turn scratchy. "Mom's gone, Dad's gone, and in a way I'm gone. But you, Rob—you're the one thing I have left to root for. Don't take that away from me."

Robby bared his gritted teeth and shook his head, fuming.

Ken gestured toward the silverware drawer. "Put the knife back."

Robby returned the knife and slammed the drawer shut. "Some brother you are."

"You'll thank me someday."

"Like hell I will." Robby shoved him square in the chest.

Ken stumbled backward. His hip struck the counter, and heat burst along his side. Dark thoughts cluttered his mind: *I should shoot*

Robby. Here and now. Peg him in the shoulder and send him spinning to the ground. Then pump lead into each needle hole along his arms, savoring every—

"No!" Ken pointed his gunhand toward the floor. When he lifted his head, Robby was looking at him funny. Hannah, now awake and upright in the kitchen doorway, was eyeing the revolver with concern. The wall clock read 7:20. Yesterday, he'd shot Officer Tormon sometime after nine. Wouldn't be long before the urges intensified.

"The gun's taking over, isn't it?" Hannah said. "With Michelle it seemed extra hungry before the last kill."

Ken shook his head. "I'm fine. But we should get moving."

Leaning against the wall, she said, "Long as someone ties my shoes, I'm ready."

"Robby?" Ken asked. "Do you mind?"

Robby said nothing. For the longest time he stared at the basement door.

CHAPTER 54

ON THE DRIVE to Soward's house, Ken noticed a black Chevy Blazer with a dented bumper in his rearview mirror. The SUV had followed him through five consecutive intersections while maintaining its distance—exactly what cops did in the movies when they were tailing someone. He told himself he was being paranoid, but a lead weight nonetheless sank through his abdomen.

Maybe I'm imagining things, he thought. *Let's see.*

Approaching the next intersection, Ken flicked his left turn signal and watched the rearview mirror. Behind him, the SUV's turn signal blinked yellow. It didn't prove anything, but his next move would.

Once he reached the intersection, he cancelled the turn signal and drove straight through. In the rearview he watched the SUV pause before making the left turn.

His lungs emptied with relief.

"Something wrong?" Hannah asked. She was riding shotgun, leaning against the door, her legs stretched out. Though earlier she'd insisted her side felt fine, the grimace on her face implied otherwise.

"Keep an eye out for a black Chevy SUV," he said. "Might be tailing us."

"Relax," she said. "If the cops suspected you of killing Tormon, they'd be slamming your face against an interrogation desk right now."

"Might not be the police," he said. "Could be Hogwild's crew."

"No way," Robby said, twitching in the backseat. From his lap, Hopper barked in agreement. "Think, Ken—if anything, they're pissed at the cops, not us."

"Hope you're right," Ken said, double-checking his rearview. "Just watch out for that Chevy. We're almost there."

Principal Helen Soward, who belonged in a damp plague-infested cell in a medieval dungeon, lived in Kingston on a suburban street overflowing with two-story homes and unrealistically green yards. The houses ranged from Victorian to colonial, some showing their age despite eye-grabbing verandas and façades. Soward called 56 Benson Street home. Though a weeping willow worked hard to hide the building, the outward decay was unmistakable.

It wasn't until Ken's third loop around the block that he was convinced he wasn't being followed. He made an extra loop to survey the neighborhood and get his bearings. There wasn't much happening except for an occasional car backing out of a driveway or someone in loungewear trotting out for the newspaper. He parked along the curb three houses down from Soward's and faced Hannah.

"I'm going for a walk. You and Robby behave while I'm gone."

"That's asking a lot," she said.

"For once I agree with her," Robby said, still twitching and bouncing in place.

Ken grabbed a hoodie and Dodgers cap from the backseat. He put them on and checked his ultra-casual disguise in the mirror. He considered removing his glasses, but if he did, he might shoot the wrong person by mistake.

"Soon as you hear gunshots, get ready," he said, pulling the hood over his cap. "Then we'll drive away, switch to Hannah's van, and argue over radio stations till we reach Ohio."

"Hope you like grunge," Hannah said.

"I don't."

"Neither do I," Robby muttered.

Ken headed up the sidewalk, his legs wobbling like cafeteria Jell-O as he passed 50, 52, and 54 Benson Street. Ahead stood Soward's weeping willow; beyond it was a porch decorated with wind chimes and a smiling scarecrow. As the chimes jingled, he decided ringing the doorbell was his best option. If Soward came to the door, he'd shoot. Trouble was, her Cadillac Escalade sat in the driveway beside her husband's Land Rover. That meant her husband and kids were home, too. If anyone else answered the door, his plan would crumble.

Ken crossed the lawn to the front porch. A flimsy storm door stood between him and the foyer. His nerves paralyzed him the moment he reached for the doorbell. He kept thinking about that black Chevy, wondering if a second vehicle was tailing him, one he hadn't recognized.

He glanced back at his Camry. Robby and Hannah appeared to be bickering. Hopper poked his snout between them. Meanwhile, cars zipped down the street. Joggers hustled. Neighbors stuffed their mailboxes. Any of them could be undercover cops waiting for him to make a guilty move.

He thumbed the doorbell.

A masculine voice yelled, "All right, Helen, I'll see who it is."

Here comes the husband. Shit.

Ken hurried down the porch steps and into the driveway. The front door opened with a squeal as he ducked alongside the house. Soward's husband called out "Hello?" a couple times, then grumbled to himself.

So much for the doorbell strategy.

Ken crept toward the backyard. It was even greener than the front, with a lavish birdbath in the center and a two-car garage nestled in the rear corner. He couldn't understand why Soward wasn't satisfied with a family and all these luxuries. Why'd she have to molest a student? The whole thing disgusted him. Infuriated him.

He darted for the back door and knocked, pounding with his fist.

Footsteps sounded inside. They grew louder until the knob twisted and the door swung inward.

A salt-and-pepper-haired man in a three-piece suit peered out with an annoyed scowl. "Listen, if you're some reporter—"

Ken lifted his revolver.

The man gasped.

Shoot him, a voice whispered. *Need to shoot. Shootshootshoot.*

Ken buried the urge. "Step outside."

Mr. Soward's eyes bugged. In a small voice, he said. "P-please don't."

"Step outside and shut the door. If you make a sound, I'll make a louder one."

Mr. Soward obeyed, his movement clunky and slow, as if controlled by a novice puppeteer. After stepping outside, he reached back for the doorknob. The moment he pulled the door shut, it made an odd, rumbling growl.

It took Ken's sleep-deprived mind another moment to realize the growl wasn't coming from the door.

It was coming from the driveway.

Principal Soward was leaving.

In a wide-eyed panic, Ken swung the revolver at the husband's head. The first blow hammered his scalp and the second struck his neck. Mr. Soward shouted for help, a request that ended abruptly when Ken whacked his temple. The man crumpled onto the door-mat, and Ken sprinted for the driveway.

By the time he rounded the corner of the house, all he saw were taillights. He raised the revolver but couldn't get a clear shot. The Escalade veered onto the street, leaving him with nothing but a lungful of acrid car exhaust.

As he coughed it out, he understood Principal Soward was heading for school.

And now, so was he.

CHAPTER 55

POSITIVE THOUGHTS. Happy thoughts. Wholesome thoughts.

Ken clung to them like sweaty hands on a greased ledge. In reality he clung to Hopper, hugging the pit bull tight. They lay tangled in the backseat of the Camry while Robby navigated Wilkes-Barre traffic. Robby had insisted on driving—he said it would distract him from his shakes—and Ken welcomed the opportunity to collect himself. The lethal urges were multiplying. In the passenger seat Hannah swiveled her head, checking for cops and casting worried glances at Ken. Whenever their eyes met, he envisioned her brains sliding down the windshield.

"Keep me sane," Ken whispered to his furry accomplice.

"You say something?" Robby asked.

"I said hurry up." Soon as the words left his mouth, his wrist bent in Robby's direction. Ken hugged Hopper close and pictured clear blue skies. He needed to be patient. Needed to end the right person's life. "We need to hit Soward before she enters the school. Hannah, is anyone following us?"

"Just regular traffic. Nothing suspicious."

"Good."

They swung into the Morgan High School parking lot on

squealing tires. A trio of students jumped as Robby nearly clipped them with the front bumper. As the Camry veered around the back of the building to the faculty parking area, Ken spotted Soward's Escalade. It slid into the number 1 spot along the sidewalk, within clear sight of a surveillance camera on the corner of the building. The SUV's taillights glowed red in warning.

"How you want me to do this?" Robby said.

"Get as close as you can," Ken said, nudging Hopper aside. Without the dog's weight across his thighs, he feared he might float away. "Try to avoid the surveillance cam."

Hannah turned around with a concerned look. "Are her kids with her?"

Ken swallowed hard. "Yeah."

The Camry inched toward the Escalade.

Ken tried for a deep breath but his nostrils were stuffed. Sucking air through his mouth did nothing but dry his throat. His lungs seemed absent, and when he forced a cough, he choked instead. Kills didn't have to be comfortable, but this was agonizing.

They rolled past two parked vehicles, coming up on the vice principal's Buick.

Ken lowered his window. It only sank partway, but it would allow a clear shot. His gunhand trembled—both with fear and the snubnose's hunger.

They passed the Buick.

It was time.

Soward's passenger door opened. Her son climbed out. If he had turned his head, he would've seen Ken. Instead, the boy pulled his backpack over one shoulder and slammed the door without looking. He sauntered toward the building.

Through the Escalade's rear windshield, Ken watched Soward's daughter exit the back door on the driver side.

"Mom," she said, "can I get an Apple Watch?"

"Absolutely," Soward said, slamming her door. "Ten Christmases from now."

"I was thinking this weekend?"

"Think again."

"Holy crap, Mom. Could you even ask me why I want one instead of assuming I don't need it? Jesus."

The Camry rolled forward, pulling Ken within range of Soward and her daughter. They stood beside the Escalade, the elder shaking her head while the younger stomped her foot to punctuate her argument. The girl was blocking Ken's shot with her tirade. When she flung her hands up in frustration, he noticed a cut on her finger. Blood had smeared the knuckle, and he yearned to spill more.

Robby pumped the brake. The Camry jerked to a complete stop.

Neither Soward noticed, still engaged in their dispute. The daughter was clearly flustered. Ken wondered if *she* wanted to shoot her mother. He sure did. If the girl would only step aside, they would both get their wish.

Then his fortunes changed. The daughter groaned and dropped her arms at her sides before she stormed past Soward up the sidewalk.

"Hold it, young lady!" Soward shouted, turning her back to Ken, gifting him with a wide target. "Don't you dare walk away."

Ken lined up the barrel with her upper back. As he curled his finger around the trigger, he remembered the look Hannah gave him moments ago.

"Is that how you act in front of your friends?" Soward snapped. "You throw tantrums when you don't get your way?"

"No!" Her daughter screamed from the sidewalk. "I don't!"

"Oh, so you treat *them* with respect?"

At ten feet away, with nobody looking, Ken couldn't have asked for a better shot. Soward's eyes were on her daughter, who was arguing from the sidewalk. Had the Escalade not been blocking the girl's view, she might've seen Ken.

Might've cried out in terror.

In warning.

But she never got the chance.

Ken reeled his gunhand back inside.

"The fuck?" Robby whispered. "You stupid? Take the shot."

"No," Ken said, glancing at Hannah. "Not while her kid is around."

Robby gawked. "But you can't hit the girl from this angle."

"He can still damage her," Hannah said. "She'll never forget this if she sees it."

She wouldn't see it.

Outside, Soward followed her daughter up the sidewalk. The moment she left the snubnose's range, Ken sank back into his seat and exhaled.

Robby pounded the dash. "Goddammit! We could be on the interstate now."

"Shut up," Hannah said, her tone thick with emotion. "He did the right thing."

"Great. Real great. *Now* what's the right thing to do? Can we go home and shoot Glinski?"

"No," Ken said. "Soward's still the target."

CHAPTER 56

NEVER IN HIS nastiest nightmares had Ken imagined becoming a school shooter. Back when Columbine struck, he was a boy living in LA, and the tragedy petrified him until summer vacation. Fast-forward to 2012, the year of the Sandy Hook massacre, when he'd been student-teaching. He'd wept openly in front of his class upon hearing the news, promising them that if such a horror were to spread through his hallways, he'd do whatever was necessary to prevent it. In the years since, he'd always hoped he'd muster the courage to stop a potential school shooting.

Now, as they parked in an unmarked faculty space, he sought the courage to start one. He only hoped his students wouldn't be forever scarred by his act of vigilantism.

"What's next?" Robby asked, rocking back and forth. "March into Soward's office and shoot her?"

"Idiot," Hannah said, "have you heard that gun go off? The whole school will hear it. If someone decides to play hero and tackle Ken, we're fucked."

"She's right," Ken said, sitting on his gunhand. The urge to shoot Robby was steadily rising with each of his brother's bad ideas. "Once I shoot, the security guards will come running. They've got two guards on staff, both armed with Tasers. If I get zapped, it's game over."

"Any way to stop the guards?" Hannah asked. "Can Angela help us?"

"She called off sick," Ken said. "Anyway, avoiding the guards will be tough. One guy patrols the first floor by the metal detectors. The other's on the third floor near Soward's office."

"Wait, metal detectors?" Robby asked. "How you getting past them?"

"Getting in is easy. See that door?" Ken pointed at the rear of the building to a black metal door with a Do Not Enter sign pasted to it. "That's an emergency exit. It's locked, but teachers sneak out before homeroom for a smoke."

"Okay, then what?" Robby asked. "March into Soward's office and shoot her?"

"Not with the guards prowling," Hannah said. "He's gotta lure them away from her office. Ken, what if Robby goes in with you?"

"Fuck that," Robby said, wiping his sweaty face. "Look at me, I'm a mess. If I set one foot in that building, everybody'll freak out and sound the alarms."

Ken slapped his thigh. "Robby, that's perfect!"

"What is?"

"Sounding the alarm. If I pull the fire alarm, that'll occupy the guards."

Except pulling the alarm without being seen would be impossible. There were only three fire alarms on the third floor—one in the east, central, and west hallways. A guard usually hovered around the west hallway, near Soward's office. Meanwhile, the other hallways were flooded with kids at this time of day. Ken could wait until homeroom started, but by then Soward would've left her office to participate in the morning broadcast. That could occupy her till classes started at 8:25. Beyond that, he wasn't sure of her schedule.

He couldn't risk waiting. He needed to shoot her in the privacy of her office before homeroom.

"Robby, I need a favor," he said. "Once I'm in Soward's office, I'll need you to pull the alarm on the first floor."

"No fucking way," Robby snapped. "I didn't come this far to get arrested."

"I can't do it myself. I need to be in Soward's office when the alarm goes off."

"Then make Hannah do it."

"She's in no condition to."

"Neither am I—I'm trying to stretch the last of my dope and it's killing me. Every cell in my body hurts like a mother, I can't sit still. I want to leap through the windshield right now and scream. I can't go in there, Ken. I fucking can't."

Ken gritted his teeth. He glanced outside, struggling to picture a scenario where he could pull the fire alarm and confront Soward in her office. It was unrealistic. If the bell rang, she would likely join the mass of students and teachers filing out. Once that happened, he'd have to shoot her in front of countless witnesses. That would ruin his chances of a clean escape. This couldn't work unless someone else pulled the alarm.

"Robby, please," Ken said.

"I'm not doing it," Robby said.

"You have to. I can't be two places at once."

"Then go home and shoot Glinski."

"Not that again!" Ken snapped. "Robby, come on. I just need you to sneak in, climb one flight of stairs, and pull the alarm next to the auditorium. If you're lucky, nobody'll even see you."

"If I'm lucky? When have I *ever* been lucky?"

"Right now," Hannah said, wincing as she sat up straight. "Because I'm gonna pull that alarm for you."

Ken was taken aback. "Hannah, you can barely walk. If you pass out or something—"

"I'm pulling that alarm," she insisted, her voice sharp with conviction. "I owe you that much."

"You don't owe me anything."

"The hell I don't." She winced again. "My whole cross-country trip with Michelle—it wasn't her idea. I lied about that. It was my idea. Michelle did the legwork, but I planned everything. I made sure we found your father's name and address. This whole vendetta was mine."

Robby pounded the dash. "You bitch!"

"Let her finish," Ken said.

"I'm the reason your father's dead, Ken," she said. "I'm the reason that gun is in your hand. If we're being honest, I deserved that bullet you put in my side. What I didn't deserve was you kidnapping a doctor to save my life. You should've let me die, but you didn't." Her eyes turned glossy. "You saved me like I was family or something. Up till now, I was too bitter about losing Michelle to realize that. Hell, I was actually planning to steal that gun from you once you dropped it. I was gonna ditch you. Can you believe that? Can you believe how low I've sunk?"

Ken rubbed his forehead. This was a lot to take in. He was too tired and anxious to process it. All he knew was that they were running out of time. He could sort things out with Hannah once Soward was dead.

"Hannah," he said, "are you strong enough to climb stairs?"

"I'll do whatever it takes to pull that stupid alarm. If I pass out or get caught, so be it. Leave town without me. Got that?"

"Yeah. Once I'm in, I'll leave the backdoor open enough so it doesn't lock." He pointed to the emergency exit. "If you climb those stairs to the second floor, on your right will be an empty hallway leading to the auditorium. Beside the auditorium doors is a fire alarm. Pull it, then hurry outside."

"When should I pull it?" she asked.

"Three minutes after I enter the building. That'll give me enough time to reach Soward's office."

Hannah checked her phone. "Three minutes. Got it."

Ken removed his hoodie and donned his jacket. The pockets offered better coverage, and he needed every advantage he could get.

Before reaching for the door, he rubbed Hopper for luck and got his palm licked. "I'm going. Robby, be ready to motor."

"Hang on," Robby said, face scrunched with thought. "If she pulls the alarm, won't everybody spill outside? We'll have trouble escaping unnoticed."

Ken hadn't considered that.

"Want me to wait elsewhere?" Robby asked.

"Tell you what," Ken said. "Once Hannah's in, drive up the street to the McDonald's we passed. We can both meet you there. Hannah, you saw that McDonald's, right?"

"Yep."

"Good." Ahead, the school's back door opened, and out stepped a teacher with an unlit cigarette. The timing couldn't have been better. "Now unless there are any other questions, I'll be reporting to the principal's office."

CHAPTER 57

KEN SHOVED the third-floor fire doors open and rushed into the central hallway. Students gossiped in every direction. Some goofed off and laughed at videos on their phones. Others gathered around a scuffle, two boys slamming each other into the lockers. Metallic thuds boomed. Ken ran straight past them. He didn't bother to break up the fight. He needed to keep moving.

Stick. It. To. Soward.

Stick! It! To! Soward!

By the time he reached the western hallway, his knees were pumping and his shoes squeaked. He yelled at people to get out of his way. "*Move!*"

Students looked at him speed past like he was crazy. A gym teacher with a pathetically fake tan raised his fist and mockingly cheered him on.

"Run, substitute, run!"

The snide remark drew Ken's glare. He pictured the man's brains —if he had any—oozing down the locker. The image tempted Ken like a T-bone steak, but he buried his gunhand deeper into his pocket. He kept yelling, picking his way through the crowd, until he collided with someone.

The impact dropped Ken on his ass. Above him towered a security guard.

"Where's the fire, Fujima?" The guard winced and rubbed his gut, which resembled a lump of snow in his white polo. The man's eyes drifted to Ken's pocket. "Whaddaya hiding in there? Brass knuckles?"

"I need to see Soward—now!" Ken shouted as he jumped to his feet. Before things could escalate, he yelled the first excuse he could think of. "It's about Pete Chang—about why he overdosed."

The guard flinched. "Jeepers. What happened?"

"I'll discuss it with Soward," Ken said. He sidestepped the guard and beelined for the principal's office with a full head of steam.

Stick. It. To. Soward.

Stick! It! To! Soward!

Students backed away, clearing a lane for him. He realized they would all remember him like this. They would forever see him as the psycho who stormed up the hall and murdered their principal.

At this point he didn't care.

At this point the gun was ravenous.

He barged into her waiting room and stopped, standing tall with his shoulders back.

"Mrs. Soward is with someone," the administrator said. "Have a seat."

"No thanks." Ken dashed for the principal's door. The admin launched up from her chair, dropping a Boston cream on her paperwork as she attempted to block him. He shoved her outstretched arm aside and jerked open the door to the torture chamber.

Dark and stuffy, the room carried a dusty odor that dried his tongue as he spoke. "Principal Soward, we need to talk. It's important."

Soward scowled behind her desk, her facial muscles fighting to maintain a professional demeanor. A gray-haired man sat with his back to Ken. Horrible history would soon be made in this room, but first the guest needed to leave.

"Sir." Ken tapped the guest's shoulder. "I need to speak with the principal."

The man turned to face him: Officer Isaacs, wearing a checkered button-down.

The moment Ken recognized him, he wanted to blow the man's forehead open. Isaacs must've intuited this somehow, because his baggy eyes stretched wide with panic. Maybe he feared Ken, or maybe he feared being associated with yesterday's tragic shootout. Either way, in all the years they had been neighbors, never had Ken seen Isaacs so shaken. Sitting there in the low chair, without his uniform or weapon, he looked like half a man—like a teenage trouble-maker desperate to avoid detention, suspension, or whatever punish-ment awaited him.

"You need to leave," Ken said, glaring him down. "Right now."

"Mr. Fujima, how dare you!" Soward snapped. "Get out of my office."

"I'm not leaving. You and I need to have a discussion."

"Forget it. Officer Isaacs and I are giving a drug awareness presentation immediately after homeroom. Your silly discussion can wait."

Ken glanced at the clock. "No, actually it can't. It's about Pete Chang."

Soward showed no reaction.

"If that's the case," Isaacs said, rising from his chair, "where might I find the nearest restroom?"

Probably shat himself the second he saw me, Ken thought.

Soward hesitated. "Try the second floor. Ask my assistant. She'll escort you."

Without making eye contact, Isaacs hurried past Ken and shut the door behind him.

"Sit, Mr. Fujima." Soward reached for her pencil jar and drew out a pair of scissors. She began cutting colored strips of plastic with words printed on them: *Peter Chang: Drawn Across Our Hearts*. "Explain why you so brazenly interrupted my meeting."

He eyed the clock. Three minutes had passed. No telling what was going on with Hannah. She could've collapsed on her way upstairs or been stopped by a teacher. The alarm might never sound.

Stay positive, he told himself. *Buy Hannah some time.*

"Answer me." Soward cracked her scissors against the desk. "If you don't, I'm calling security."

"I know."

"You know? If you know I'll call security, then talk."

"You misunderstand." He leaned closer. "I *know*."

"Know what? What aren't you telling me?"

"You already know."

Soward blinked, dumbfounded.

He held his glare. "Don't deny it."

"I've had enough of this." She reached for her phone. "Security will escort you out."

Ken thrust his gunhand across the desk.

Soward froze. Speechless. Her fingers hovered above the phone; her expression melted from snide contempt to timid hesitation.

"Hands on the desk," he said.

She obeyed, pressing her trembling fingers on the plastic clippings.

Time moved at half-speed. Maybe slower. Ken no longer had a pulse. Unlike in the parking lot, his conviction remained clear. There were no kids around to be impacted by what would come next. No reasons to reconsider. Soon as the alarm rang, he would apply a few pounds of pressure to the trigger and end this.

Soward swallowed hard. "What do you want?"

"Justice."

"For the teaching position? Fine, it was nepotism. I admit it."

"Don't play coy." He gritted his teeth. "I know what happened here in this office. I heard enough details to know you deserve what you're about to get."

"What details? What're you talking about?"

"Pete Chang."

"What about him?"

Ken sneered. "Playing innocent won't save you."

"Playing innocent?" Her voice cracked. "What am I on trial for? Can you explain before you shoot me and terrify every student, teacher, and parent in the country?"

He checked the clock.

C'mon, Hannah.

"When Pete visited your office," he said, "you crossed a line."

"How?"

"By ordering him to paint your toenails."

"Toenails?" Soward rocked nervously in her chair. "What're you talking about? I never made anyone paint my toenails. I don't know who put that idea in your head, but it's not true. As for Pete, he visited my office once since school started. It was a morning when my assistant was right outside. He wanted me to green-light a fundraiser for the art club. That was it."

"Not what I heard."

"What did you hear? Who told you?"

"Angela Marconi. Pete told her you forced him to paint your toenails, shave your legs, and...other things."

"I've never—*never*—done anything like that." Her shoulders rose and sank as she breathed. "Either Angela lied to you or Pete lied to her."

Ken scratched the trigger guard. "Did you say the same to Angela when she confronted you on Thursday?"

"Thursday?" Soward blinked. "Angela hasn't confronted me about anything since last year when I denied her a pay raise."

He launched from his seat and stretched the gun to within inches of her nose. She turned away, whimpering, but Ken ordered her to stare into the gun. When she did, he said, "Tell me the truth and I'll allow you to write a goodbye letter to your family. Or do you even care about them at all, you sick sociopath?"

"Of course I do!" she snapped. "And I would never do anything to bring harm or humiliation upon them. My two youngest kids attend this school. If you think I would ever molest someone their age, you're the sick one." Her conviction stirred a slight doubt within him. "I would never do something like that to a student. Even if I were loony enough to consider it, I still wouldn't do it because I would never—*never*—bring such shame upon my family." She took a deep, defiant breath. "That's the truth, Mr. Fujima. Now, if you still plan on shooting me, let me write that goodbye note."

The blaze in Soward's eyes could've melted a chalkboard. Her words, her sincerity... His gunhand trembled. Even as murderous urges flushed over him, he wished the alarm would never sound. He didn't want to shoot.

But he had to. Angela warned him about this. About Soward and these mind games.

He needed to hold strong.

Needed to stop being a pushover.

"You're not talking your way out of this," he said. "You may have been able to blackmail Angela with the camera footage, but I've got nothing to lose other than a bullet."

"Camera footage? What're you talking about?"

"The footage of Angela confronting you in this office." He gestured to the ceiling corners. "From the camera up...there." His voice trailed off. There were no cameras in either ceiling corner. Nor was there a hanging plant or anything that might conceal a camera. His heart went numb. He looked everywhere but found nothing. Had Soward taken the cameras down?

"Where are they?" he demanded.

"Where are what? Cameras? I don't have any in here. The only cameras inside the building are in the hallways, stairwells, and entryways."

He opened his mouth to reply, but nothing came out.

"Mr. Fujima," she said, "I swear on my children's lives there have never been any security cameras in my office."

His gunhand trembled in front of her face.

"You're making a mistake," she said.

His finger slid inside the trigger guard.

"Please stop. Look, I'm sorry about giving your job to my daughter's boyfriend. He's going to be my son-in-law and my family means—"

The alarm cut her off.

CHAPTER 58

KEN PANICKED. With the alarm ripping through his skull, he couldn't think straight, think at all. Soward flinched but remained before the barrel, the easiest target on earth. His thirsty gunhand pumped bloody fantasies through his mind. When she covered her ears with her hands, he remembered that minutes ago he'd ordered her to keep both palms on the desk. Disobedience deserved punishment.

Shootshootshoot.

The ululating siren blared as his eyes traveled throughout the room—from Soward's face to her scissors to the desk photo of her family holding hunting rifles. He worried she might have a gun hidden inside her desk—

Shootshootshoot.

—but then again this was a school. There were no guns in school. And there were no cameras in Soward's office. That discordant detail from Angela's story made him hesitate. No matter how hard he looked, he couldn't find any security cams. Not when he stared, not when he blinked, not when he wished them to appear.

Now he had an impossible decision to make. If he shot Soward, the nightmare would end. He could drop the gun, wrap his jacket around it, and leave. No more bullets, no more kills, no more deadly pressure.

But if Soward were telling the truth, Ken would be executing an innocent woman. Worse yet, it would mean Angela had manipulated him into murdering someone. He didn't want to believe that. He wanted to spend his new life with Angela, the two of them keeping each other's secrets and healing each other's wounds. But if she had lied or embellished her story, that dream would die and he would be left with the dusty taste of guilt.

Maybe Angela had lied.

Maybe she hadn't.

Maybe he was misremembering because of stress, sleep deprivation, or the gun's effect on his brain.

One thing he knew, however, was that he was sick of being everyone's doormat. Too many feet had stomped him through the years, whether Soward, Robby, Olivia, or anyone else he encountered. When people saw Ken Fujima, they saw a pushover. Even this revolver saw him as such, just another wielder who could slake its morbid thirst. It had motivated him to slaughter five people, but it had also given him the power to decide who survived.

Long as he wielded such power, he couldn't let the gun dictate who died. Especially not when his target deserved to live.

That settled it.

With his free hand he pushed the gun barrel away from Soward.

Her eyes widened. The alarm blared while she gasped soundlessly with relief. Before she could reach for her phone, he whipped the revolver alongside her temple. She dropped out of her chair to the floor, unconscious.

Homicidal urges swallowed him, but he fled the room and hurried down the hall. Emergency lights flickered as he descended the stairs and joined a line of students filing out of the building. Nobody made a fuss as he exited the parking lot and headed up the street. The golden arches of McDonald's beckoned. The parking lot smelled of cheap sausage, greasy hash browns, and car exhaust. He found Hannah sitting on a bench near the entrance, breathing heavy and holding her wounded side.

"Hannah!"

She looked up. "Is it over?"

"Where's Robby?"

She gestured to the parking lot. "You tell me."

Of the half-dozen cars in the lot, none were Ken's nicked-up Toyota Camry. He ran to check the drive-thru without success. Robby was nowhere in sight. Ken checked his phone. No messages. He texted Robby and got no reply.

"What do we do?" Hannah said, wincing. "Call an Uber?"

Ken saw no other option. A driver picked them up within minutes. When they returned home, he spotted his Camry parked in the driveway, the lights on and the motor running.

He couldn't believe it. Robby had ditched them.

The Uber driver let them out. Ken helped Hannah into the Camry's passenger seat. Hopper woofed in the back.

"Once I get back," he said, "we'll switch cars and head out in your van."

"But you didn't shoot Soward," she said, glancing at his pocket.

"Didn't need to," he said and slammed the door.

The moment he entered the house, his nostrils caught a stench like decayed meat mixed with cheap perfume. He buried his nose in his elbow and staggered across the living room. He knew the basement door would be open. What he didn't expect were the footfalls pounding the concrete steps.

He and Robby met at the cellar doorway.

"K-Ken?" Robby jumped. He grabbed the railing to keep from falling downstairs. Beneath him his legs trembled horribly. "You're here?"

"No thanks to you."

"My bad." Robby moved to exit the basement but Ken barred him. "Ken, what gives? We gotta move."

"You ditched us."

"I was gonna hurry back."

"Why are you here?" Ken had a bad feeling he knew the answer.

"Because," Robby said, his eyes hidden behind unruly hair. "I wanted a moment with Dad, okay?"

Ken didn't believe him. Robby had an opportunity this morning to visit Dad. Him sneaking off to the basement had to involve another motive.

Glinski.

"Let's head downstairs," Ken said. "Say goodbye together."

"Shouldn't we leave? I mean, if you shot Soward..."

"I didn't." Ken lifted his gunhand from his pocket. "Now let's say goodbye."

"B-but the gun—"

"Downstairs. Now."

As they descended, a killer instinct slithered through Ken's brain. With each step his world got smaller and smaller while the gun invited him to shoot his way out. At point-blank, Robby was an easy target. If Ken's suspicions about what happened to Glinski proved real, he would surrender to the gun's thirst. It didn't matter that Robby was the only family Ken had left. After everything that transpired these past four days, Robby should've known better than to commit a selfish, senseless murder.

The stench grew thicker as they reached the bottom. It seemed Robby had indeed opened the root cellar to say goodbye. He hadn't entirely lied.

But as Ken stepped onto the concrete floor, he noticed Glinski. She drooped lifelessly in her chair, her chin touching her upper chest while a line of drool trailed from her lips. The smell from the root cellar should've awakened her but didn't.

That could only mean one thing.

His brother had crossed the line.

"Robby." Ken leveled the barrel with his brother's back. "I warned you."

"Ken?" Robby turned around. Fear filled his eyes, even before he noticed the revolver was aimed at him. When he finally registered it, he jumped backward, waving both hands in front of him. "Fuck, Ken —what're you doing?"

"Soward's innocent, and time's running out." Ken curled the trigger. "Might as well execute a murderer."

"Wait—I never murdered anybody."

"Don't insult my intelligence."

"I didn't."

"Glinski's dead. It's plain as the answers in the back of a textbook."

Robby coughed, then started laughing.

"How can you laugh right now?"

"Because she's not dead." He pointed at the floor near Glinski's feet. "Look."

On the ground lay a syringe next to a crumpled plastic baggie. The sight of it baffled Ken like a snowball in July. Before he could piece everything together, Robby said, "Couldn't do it, man. That's why I wanted you to kill her—because I couldn't do it myself. But letting her off easy wasn't my style. That's why I shot her up with the last of my stash. Figured I'd punish her the way I've been punishing myself since Mom died."

Ken touched Glinski's neck. When he found a pulse, he turned to his brother. "I almost killed you."

Robby shrugged. "Almost doesn't count."

Ken glanced at the crumpled baggie. "Last of your stash, huh?"

"Yeah. No more. Never again." He winced. "Next few days'll be hell, though."

Ken threw his arms around his brother. Robby twitched within his embrace. Ken hugged him hard, sending a wordless promise that they would get through this mess. He wished they could've hugged it out for hours, but Robby complained of back pain and, besides, they couldn't stick around. It was only a matter of time before Soward woke and alerted the police.

Worse yet, the gun was starving.

And it wasn't happy about being denied two easy meals.

"Let's switch cars," Ken said, leading the way upstairs. "Then we're going after Angela."

CHAPTER 59

TARGETS. The moment Ken buckled himself into the backseat, he saw targets. They were everywhere. Left and right. Near and far. Across the street. Atop a motorcycle. Behind the wheel of a mail truck. There was no shortage of people to shoot. Everyone who breathed wore a bullseye.

He wanted Hannah's skull.

Robby's neck.

The biker's knees.

The mailman's chest.

Nothing was off limits. Everyone was invited to the slaughter.

By the time the Camry reached Hannah's van, desperation had overtaken him. Heat clogged his pores. Numbness claimed his arm. His wrist bent as if pulled by a puppeteer's string. It struck him as ironic that while his hand held the gun, he was the one being operated. That realization left a minty, moldy taste in his mouth. He wanted to vomit, but not as much as he wanted to piss. And by piss he meant shoot—treat anyone nearby as a potential urinal. Crude as his thoughts had become, he couldn't shake them any longer.

One pull of the trigger, he promised himself. *Just one. Not gonna hurt anybody. Only shooting to relieve some pressure.*

They parked. He climbed outside. Staggered across the street toward the van. Buried the gun deeper into his pocket.

Hannah slid open the rear door. Gestured for him to get in.

On three, he told himself. *Just to relieve some pressure.*

One.

Two.

Trigger.

The blast thundered. Recoil spun him sideways. His ankle bent and he tumbled. Elbow smacked blacktop. Head bounced off the yellow line.

The pain barely registered.

People were screaming somewhere. Where, exactly? He didn't know. He didn't care. All he knew was that shooting and missing didn't make things better. All it did was put a conspicuous hole in his pocket. Shame he ruined another of Dad's jackets.

Should've ruined flesh.

Should've taken life.

Should've—

"Tie me up!" Ken yelled, remembering Michelle's wrists from the other night. "Tie me up before it's too late!"

Dark thoughts swept over him as Robby and Hannah grabbed his arms.

Ken blinked and found himself in the van's trunk. He didn't remember being carried there, but he was inside. He thought he might be dreaming. Robby kept him pinned down while Hannah tied his wrists behind his back. Hopper woofed until it was done.

It all made Ken furious. Furious enough to shoot.

But when he tried aiming, his wrist was met with sharp resistance. When he pulled the trigger, it didn't move. Something was blocking the trigger. He wanted to scream.

The hatchback thudded shut.

Ken felt trapped in a coffin. A coffin with windows. Outside, the world moved. He was going places. Places with people he could shoot. Shoot to thrill, baby.

"Shoot to Thrill"—was that a Guns N' Roses song? Or AC/DC? Or Van Halen? He hated 80s music, so how should he know?

Then he remembered. Van Halen sang the song playing at the Backfield Bar the other night. That song "Hot for Teacher." There was one teacher Ken was hot for, and that was Angela Marconi. But she had lied to him about the cameras in Soward's office. That wasn't so hot of her.

Why would she lie?

"Why, Angela?" Ken said. "Why? I need to know!"

"We're almost there," Robby said. "Keep your head screwed on."

"Breathe, Ken," Hannah said. "You won't get answers from Angela if you keep spazzing like that."

Ken knew she was right. He needed to focus. Straighten himself out.

If he could hang on a bit longer, he could get his answers.

Until he did, the gun would have to go hungry.

CHAPTER 60

RAIN PATTERED the van's roof. First came an erratic series of drops, like Mother Nature laying out blind fire. Then the heavens improved their accuracy, unloading steady bursts of rain. Wind whipped through the vehicle, chilling Ken in the trunk. The incoming air tasted of blood, and no matter how many times he spat, he couldn't rid himself of the flavor.

The van stopped. The hatchback opened. Two potential targets —Robby and Hannah—helped Ken get on his feet in the middle of the downpour. The deluge made the world around him resemble television static. When he turned his head, blinking against the rain, he saw Angela's two-story home. The sight both thrilled and gutted him.

Ken staggered in that direction, his wrists battling their shoelace restraints. "She keeps the back door unlocked. Let's go."

Robby and Hannah hurried him to the backyard. Their feet slid in the slick grass. Ken, unbalanced, landed on his chest and flopped like a flounder before they hauled him upright. It dawned on him that three nights ago he'd left this house soaking wet and gone home to accept the gun's burden. Now he was revisiting the house—soaking wet again—with the intent of finally dropping the same weapon.

They entered the backyard patio. Wet shoes squeaked against

granite tiles. At the back door, he shook free of Robby and Hannah's supportive hands.

"Drive to the next street," Ken said, straining against his bindings. "If the cops come, I don't want you parked right outside."

"Good call," Robby said. "Hold your fire till we undo these shoelaces."

"No, leave them," Ken said. "You saw what happened to Chrissie."

Robby fell silent.

Hannah stepped forward. "I'll do it."

Ken shook his head. "You take them off, I might take your head off."

"Pfft. You act like I've never survived a gunshot before."

"Don't push your luck."

She whispered in his ear. "The other night I left Michelle at your door with her hands tied. She died because of it. Won't let the same thing happen to you."

"Fair enough." The temptation of shooting Hannah made his mouth water, but he shook it off. "Free my left hand. But leave some laces blocking the trigger. Buy yourself time to run back to the van."

Her hands tugged at the bindings. They stretched tight, then coolly slackened along his left wrist.

"You're on your own now," she said.

"Careful, Ken," Robby said.

Through a haze of violent urges, Ken watched them rush away through the downpour. They disappeared around the side of the house, leaving him alone.

Just a man, his gunhand, and the final bullet.

He unraveled the lace from the revolver and opened the back door. It was chilly inside. Dark too. A fluorescent light thrummed above the sink, casting a sickly glow over the kitchen table. Yesterday that table had been his haven. Now it repulsed him like a crime scene. All evidence remained—their tea mugs, her purse, the unopened mail, even the arrangement of the chairs.

As his wet clothes dripped on the floor, he recalled how Angela savored cold days beside the fireplace. Sure enough, he heard popping logs when he entered the foyer. In the living room he found the fireplace crackling between two wall-length bookcases. Flames cast an orange glow across the leather couch they had spent the night on. Her wrinkled Pooh Bear blanket lay across the seat. He noticed Pooh had his hand stuck in a honey pot. Maybe the chubby yellow bear was hiding a revolver inside.

When Ken returned to the foyer, he heard a voice coming from upstairs. Not Angela's voice but a local news broadcaster. Sounded like the same woman who'd reported the double homicide yesterday. He climbed the steps two at a time, his lungs heaving as he reached the top.

Blue light flickered from the master bedroom. The TV reporter droned on. Ken approached, his wet shoes squeaking along the hardwood. He stumbled into the wall outside the bedroom, knocking a mass-produced painting off its hook. It depicted a grassy meadow, like the one they'd had sex near yesterday.

"What was that?" Angela asked, startled. "You hear that?"

Was she talking to someone? Maybe in person, maybe over the phone? He hoped it was the latter. He wanted privacy.

"Don't worry, Angela," he said as he entered the bedroom. "It's only me."

CHAPTER 61

ANGELA WASN'T ALONE. Her husband Dom stood beside the bed digging through a suitcase. Judging from the bags under his eyes and the nasty sunburn across his cheeks, Hawaii hadn't been paradise for him. When he looked up from his wrinkled clothes, he spotted the revolver and flinched. With superhuman speed he jumped in front of his wife and lifted the hardshell suitcase like a shield.

"Y-you're the guy from Friday night," Dom said, his brow furrowed. Shirts and pants spilled from the suitcase onto the floor. The reek of the man's cologne spread across the room. "Please don't hurt us. What do you want, pal? Money? Try my office downstairs."

"I don't want money," Ken said, steadying the gun. The TV was on, a news anchor discussing yesterday's woodland shootout. "I want to talk to Angela."

She peeked past her husband's shoulder. "K-Ken? What're you doing here?"

"Why'd you send me to kill Soward?"

"Kill Soward?" Dom said. "The principal?"

"I don't know what he's talking about," she said.

"You sure do." Ken stepped forward, eyes locked on Angela. His heart rammed within his chest. "Here's what's gonna happen. You're gonna explain why you lied. Right now."

"Ken, have you gone insane?"

"Answer me."

"Please leave," she said. "You shouldn't be here."

"Where should I be?" he snapped. "Back in the principal's office? Standing over Soward's corpse with a smoking gun? That's what you wanted, right?"

"Listen, pal," Dom said in a small voice. "Let's all cool down a sec. I'm sure there's a misunderstanding."

"Oh, there is," Ken said.

"Then let's talk it out." Still clutching the suitcase, Dom slid a hand into his pocket, reaching toward a rectangular bulge. "Why don't we—"

Ken stepped closer. "Drop the phone. Now."

The phone hit the carpet with a thud.

"You too, Angela. Drop your phone next to his."

Reluctantly she obeyed.

"Now kick both phones toward me."

Dom drew his trembling leg back. As Angela whispered in his ear, he hesitated.

"I said kick them toward me," Ken snarled.

Dom kicked the phones, one after the other. They slid across the carpet, stopping within inches of Ken's foot. He stomped them both. His ears welcomed the sound of cracking screens.

Angela whimpered. "Please, Ken. You're not thinking straight."

"There are no cameras in Soward's office," Ken said, thrusting his weapon forward. Both Marconis gasped. "You lied. Admit that much, or I'll shoot."

"Okay, okay," she said, panting. "I lied about the cameras."

"Why?"

"I-I don't know."

"You knew I had to kill someone. You gave me Soward's name. You *used* me."

298 / BRANDON MCNULTY

"I didn't."

"*Bullshit!*" Ken roared. "Why did you lie?"

She whimpered behind her husband's shoulder.

"Answer me."

Sobbing, she shook her head.

"*Now*, or I'll shoot!"

Again, she shook her head.

Ken began to tug the trigger before he reconsidered. If the bullet killed her, he would never learn the truth. He wanted to believe there was a misunderstanding—that once she explained herself, they could work everything out. But he needed her to talk. If the gun couldn't coax her, he needed another approach.

"Angela," he said, stepping forward to within six feet of them. "Yesterday you asked how I got the name 'Ken the Eraser.' At the time I wasn't comfortable telling you, but now I am. It's a fun story. I think you'll enjoy it."

"That's okay," Dom said, lifting the suitcase so it hid their faces. "We don't need any stories."

"Yes, you do!" Ken snapped. "Lower that suitcase so I can look you both in the eyes."

After brief hesitation, Dom obeyed.

"Please leave," Angela whispered as her frightened face came into view. "Please, Ken."

"No. You need to hear this." His breathing accelerated. "I already told you about Olivia and the drama teacher. After they moved in together, I drove up to their house every night trying to win her back. I brought her gifts—things like her favorite dinners, hot fudge sundaes, you name it. Every night I stopped by with something new. Eventually the drama teacher ordered me to stop coming to the house. Said I would regret it if I didn't.

"But I kept showing up. Every night. I just wanted Olivia back.

"Then one day after school, a student visited my classroom. She was dressed provocatively for a role in the school play, which was based on *Titanic*. She needed my help with chemistry equations, so we sat at my desk and reviewed the material. At one point I went to the chalkboard to write an example. Then she hurried up to me holding her calculator, asking if she had the math right. The moment I glanced down to check, an odd beep sounded from the hallway. When I looked, nobody was there, so I thought nothing of it.

"Five minutes after the student left, I was erasing the chalkboard when the drama teacher stopped by. He held his phone out to me. On the screen was a picture of me and the student standing near the board. The angle made it look like I was coming on to her. The asshole said if I tried to get between him and Olivia again, he would email the photo to the entire school district.

"I snapped. I yelled at him, demanding he delete the photo. He laughed, and I tackled him to the floor and pounded his face with the eraser in my hand. Chalk dust flew everywhere. He started coughing. I kept hitting him until he cried for help, at which point I fed him the eraser like an ice cream sandwich. I stuffed it as far into his mouth as it would go. I wanted him coughing up chalk dust for weeks. Not because of Olivia, but because he'd used one of my students against me. That's a line he never should have crossed."

"Same goes for you, Angela." Ken leveled the barrel at her face. "You used Pete to send me after Soward. This is your last chance to explain why."

Her lips trembled. "Okay. But please lower that gun. I can't think straight with that thing pointed at me."

Ken lowered the weapon. "Talk."

"First of all," she said, squeezing her husband's shoulder, "you should know that yesterday I was scared. I was afraid of what you might do to me."

"Get to the point."

"Sure. But first hear me out. You should know that when I—" Angela screamed and shoved her husband forward. Dom charged after Ken, the suitcase raised high. Events happened too fast for Ken to react, and the hardshell case slammed into his torso, driving him backward. Ken stumbled, lost his balance, and reached behind himself to break his fall. The corner of a wooden dresser drilled him in the ribs. Sharp pain lanced through his side. He stiffened against the sensation and dropped to his knees.

Reflexively, his fingers clenched. Including his trigger finger.

The gun went off.

The report echoed through the bedroom.

His back turned to the Marconis, Ken pulled himself to his feet. Through his ringing ears, he heard Angela's screams. He turned toward her voice; her husband's fist found his face. It crashed into his forehead and all went dark.

White lightning burst through his mind. When Ken regained his vision, he found himself looking up at the ceiling. He didn't remember collapsing. Nor did he remember Dom dropping onto him, yet now the bigger man straddled his chest, pinning him under his bulk and the overbearing stench of his cologne.

Ken tried to shake loose, but a thick forearm barred his windpipe. His face flamed from the crushing pressure. Gasping for air, he twisted his head. Dom's free hand was tugging at the revolver, struggling in vain to rip it from his fingers.

Angela shouted, "Dom—both phones are busted!"

"Then run next door," he said. "Have someone call 911."

Shit, Ken thought. *If they call 911, it's over.*

Dom leaned forward, increasing the pressure to Ken's throat, blocking airflow. If Ken planned on remaining conscious, he needed to act fast.

He glanced at his gunhand. Dom's sturdy grip on it didn't block the trigger. Ken pulled in quick succession until it roared in response.

The blast and the recoil startled Dom. When he lost his grip on the revolver, Ken whipped the weapon against Dom's cheek. It struck bone. He swung again, this time cracking the man's nose.

Dom released a garbled moan and cupped both hands around his busted nose. Blood leaked between his fingers, dripping hot onto Ken's shirt. For a moment Ken caught his breath. Then he punched the revolver against the bloody, sunburned mess that was Dom's face. A harsh crack followed, and Dom collapsed, motionless, on his side.

Ken rolled over and spotted Angela rushing down the hall. He aimed low and pulled the trigger. *Click.*

"Angela, stop!"

Her footsteps pounded the stairs, and he rose to give chase, his lungs heavy with stagnant air. He pulled the trigger four more times, readying his next blast.

Angela reached the bottom step and lunged for the front door. She caught the knob, found it locked. She moaned and looked over her shoulder as Ken descended the staircase. Panicking, she popped the deadbolt and ripped the chain lock free. The moment she grabbed the knob, he fired at the hardwood floor.

Splinters exploded near her feet.

Screaming, she fled toward the kitchen.

He pursued, his feet pounding hardwood. The moment he reached the kitchen threshold, he watched her reach for the back doorknob.

He fired, shattering a nearby glass cabinet.

She took cover behind the kitchen table, where yesterday he had poured his soul out to and been fed lies by a woman he thought he trusted. She shoved chairs in his path and flung ceramic mugs at him. He dodged mugs and a saltshaker before he barreled ahead to cut off her rear exit.

His back to the door, they faced each other, the table between them. If he wanted her dead, he could easily land the shot. But his curiosity overpowered the urge, and he demanded she answer.

Instead she lifted her purse off the table, reached inside, and withdrew her snubnose.

A pit widened in his stomach. He ducked as the first shot boomed. Her weapon was louder than his and, he imagined, more powerful. He dropped down and returned fire from beneath the table before she retreated to the dining room.

Rather than following her in, he took position along the doorway.

The moment he poked his nose out, a shot erupted. Panic flooded his brainstem. The shot pinned him back, and he ducked for a safer vantage point. He spotted Angela's reflection in the glass of one of the curio cabinets in the dining room; she appeared to be squatting behind a chair at the far end of the mahogany dining table.

He stuck his gunhand out and fired.

Angela returned the thunder with three consecutive shots. One whizzed past Ken's ear. It dawned on him that she was willing to kill him. It also dawned on him that she had just squandered precious ammo. He calculated that they each had one bullet remaining, but his would return to the chamber over and over until it ended a life.

"It's over, Angela," he shouted. "I can keep shooting. You can't. Drop your gun and start talking."

He waited for an answer.

All he heard was the patter of footsteps. She was moving.

Then so was he. Rather than chasing her through the dining room, he returned to the foyer. He knew she sought the front door, and the moment she lunged for it, he hammered the trigger. He missed, but the booming report drove her into the living room.

The fireplace painted the room in shifting orange hues. Sweat slicked his forehead. Ken noticed shadows on the far bookcase beyond the couches. Several shadows were shaped like stretched-out furniture. One, however, was shaped like a kneeling woman with something in her hand.

"Angela," he said, readying his next shot. "Drop the gun."

Angela looked out from behind the couch. Her tousled black hair hung across half her face, leaving one frightened eye staring back at him. Moisture glowed along her exposed cheek. The collar of her gray t-shirt was dark with sweat. Her head shook from rapid breathing.

"You should leave, Ken."

"I will once you answer my question."

"You won't like the answer."

"Tell me anyway."

She didn't reply, so he snapped his arm forward and fired.

She took cover.

He rushed ahead, clicking through the empties as he passed the coffee table. Time slowed down as he rounded the couch. He found her squatting behind it, the barrel pointed toward the ceiling. By the time she reacted, he had aimed at her face.

"Drop it!"

Her revolver hit the carpet.

He kicked it away, toward the rear bookcases.

Now that he had her at point-blank range, his every thought ended in murder. He'd always found her beautiful, but ultimate beauty required a bullet in the head. His gunhand wanted it. He wanted it. But there was one thing he wanted more.

"Start talking," he said.

"Okay, okay," she said, backing toward the flames. She lunged for the steel poker beside the fireplace and held it before her like a rapier. "Please don't come any closer."

"If you want to live, tell me the truth."

"Okay, I will. Really. I still owe you a secret, remember?"

Yesterday's breakfast seemed millennia ago, but he did remember. Somehow, he moved his finger outside the trigger guard. The voices, the visions crashed in on him, begging him to splatter her brains across the leather-bound volumes on the shelves. He pictured her death in infinite ways. One vision after another, recoil and blood spatter and entry wounds.

So many entry wounds.

He blinked the visions away. In their place remained the horrorstruck face of Ms. Angela Marconi. His coworker, his lover, his one-time hope for a happy future. He wanted to believe this was all a misunderstanding—that he'd missed a beat somewhere or that the gun had loaded erroneous thoughts into his head like wrong-caliber ammo.

But she had lied. He knew she had.

"Can't hold out much longer," he said, fighting the urge to shoot. "Tell me."

"Please don't kill me, Ken." Her eyes, wide and glossy, met his. "I wanted Soward gone because she knew something that could ruin me."

"What?" When she didn't reply, he yelled, "What is it?"

"She saw me with him."

"Saw you with who?"

"Last week," she said. "She saw Pete get into my Jeep."

CHAPTER 62

"Pete and I were together," Angela said, glancing at the fireplace. "I won't even pretend otherwise. And, believe me, I know what you're thinking. I'm aware of the laws, the rules against teacher-student relationships, everything. But just because he was a student—that didn't change the way I felt."

Ken shook his head. "You can't be serious."

"I couldn't be *more* serious," she said. "We loved each other, Pete and I."

"No..." His mind swam against the bizarre current. "He was a kid, Angela. A seventeen-year-old kid."

"He was a man and I was a woman." She swiped her hair away from her face. Firelight shined off her forehead. Her eyes radiated a look of utmost sincerity. "It wasn't some silly fling. It developed naturally, meaningfully, over time. Last year in class I confiscated a drawing of his, a picture of me at my desk with a look of deep longing in my eyes. The moment I saw it, I realized how empty my life was. It was as though Pete saw right through me, saw past all my forced smiles and phony energy, all the way to the *real me*. Never had I seen myself like that before. It was a moment of clarity like I've never had.

"After I praised his work, he drew me a new portrait every week.

I started to see myself differently. Then I saw *him* differently. It made me uncomfortable at first, but soon I accepted how I felt. We both did.

"This past summer I saw him almost every day. He lived nearby and used to jog past my house. One day I was in the front yard pulling weeds, wearing my swimsuit. I caught him looking at me while he pretended to tie his shoes. It was adorable. I brought him a glass of water, we talked, and I honestly didn't think anything of it. But then he came back the next day. And the day after that. All summer long we talked—no, we *communicated*. Every conversation had meaning. Being with him—there was nothing like it. I felt so alive, so nourished. When he mentioned he'd never clicked with any girls in his class, I knew what he wanted. What *we* wanted."

Ken gritted his teeth. "We're supposed to take care of our students. What you did—you're disgusting."

"Disgusting? You're saying it's disgusting to desire someone who's complex, artistic, and driven?"

"It's sick and you know it."

"Sicker than what you did? You killed five people."

"Don't go there." His gunhand wanted to silence her on the spot. "You know I had no choice. I had to kill. Either myself or six others."

"So that made it acceptable?"

"I never said that."

"No, but you *believe* it." Her eyes burned with defiance. "One crappy Friday night Ken Fujima picks up a haunted gun, and suddenly immoral acts are justified. But what about the rest of us? What about that dealer you shot—Hogwild, was it? You killed him because he sold heroin, but maybe he didn't have a choice. Maybe he did it to keep his family from starving."

"Don't change the subject," he said. "This is about you and me."

"Okay, then. Fine. How are you and I any different, Ken? You had a gun in your hand, I had a gun in my heart. I could either shoot down my soul or point Cupid's arrow elsewhere. And that's what I did. Once I got to know Pete, I fell in love. Forbidden love, sure, but not twisted love. Not by any stretch. It was genuine. You'd be surprised by the conversations we shared. Pete is wise beyond his years."

"Pete *was*," he corrected. "Not is. *Was*. Pete's no more. All because he took those pills. All because you molested him."

"I *loved* him!" She rose to her feet, gripping the fire poker with both hands. His gun no longer seemed to faze her. "He was seventeen. The age of consent in Pennsylvania is sixteen. If I weren't his teacher, it would've been legal. I told him we should wait till he graduated, but on the first week of school he came to my classroom and spilled out his soul. He said he was tired of being afraid. Nothing scared him so long as he was with me. Then he proved it to me. It started with the purest, most beautiful kiss I've ever received. I couldn't bring myself to stop him, and I'm glad I didn't."

"You're *glad*?" Ken now fingered the trigger. "You're *glad* you wrecked his life? You're *glad* he sought refuge in drugs? You're *glad* he overdosed?"

"Of course not. I'm glad for the moments we shared. I'm glad he made love to me. And I'm *proud* to be carrying his child."

His finger slid off the trigger. "What?"

A voice boomed from the hallway. "You stupid whore!"

Ken glanced over his shoulder.

Dom Marconi limped through the threshold, the lower half of his face slathered in blood from his damaged nose. He looked grotesque, zombie-like. His eyes, however, were wide with fury. He snatched a lamp off an end table and flung it at Angela, forcing her to duck.

"*Whore!*" Dom's voice vibrated with hostility. "You weren't supposed to get knocked up! You were supposed to be careful. That was our deal."

"Wait—wait!" Ken said. "You're saying you knew about this? You knew she was with Pete?"

"I caught them upstairs," Dom said. "Almost had a goddamned aneurysm."

"Why didn't you say anything?" Ken said. "Pete was a kid."

Dom pointed a bloody finger at Ken. "Clearly you've never been married, pal. Certain secrets stay within the home."

Ken aimed at the man. "Certain secrets can push someone to overdose."

"How was I supposed to know?" Dom gestured at Angela. "She said she *loooved* him and needed him. I just let the lovers be."

"Bullshit," she said. "You only kept your mouth shut because you knew I could spill *your* secrets."

"Hey, I'm not the one who ruined some kid's life."

"Oh, you've ruined your share." She looked at Ken. "Shoot him. Get your last kill and leave."

"Don't tell me what to do," Ken said, steering the gun away from Dom.

"Well, you can't shoot *me*," she said. "Not while I'm carrying Pete's child."

"*Child?*" Dom boomed. "You *fucked* a child."

"I made love to a younger *man*, you jealous cuck."

"You're dead, woman!"

Dom stormed toward her, his blood gleaming in the light from the blaze. He chased her to the rear wall; she stood her ground and swung the fire poker at him. When she missed, he seized the business end. One harsh tug removed it from her hands. He assumed a batter's stance and swung, smashing her shoulder.

She cried out in agony and fell against the bookcase. Her eyes flicked toward the corner of the room, where her revolver lay waiting.

"Angie, you fucked a little boy!" He kicked her knee, and she dropped to the floor. "Got knocked up by a goddamned kid! The fuck is wrong with you?"

The fuck is wrong with both of you? Ken thought.

"My arm..." She sat up, whimpering, cradling her arm. "It hurts."

"Oh? Your arm hurts?" Dom readied himself for another swing. "Then let's send the pain elsewhere."

"Stop!" Ken said, lifting his gun. "Both of you, *stop!*"

Both Marconis froze as he extended the revolver toward them.

The weapon shook in his conflicted grasp. He yearned to shoot them both. What he'd seen and heard from Angela and Dom disgusted him. Ken had tried to restrain himself, while these two chose the polar opposite. Angela had tricked him into nearly murdering Soward as part of a cover-up, and now Dom was on track to cave in his wife's skull. Now they watched Ken as if each were in a trance.

The fear in their eyes moved him.

Growling, he pointed his weapon toward the floor.

A *whoosh* immediately followed. The fire poker swung toward Angela's head. When she dodged, the metal tip whacked a book spine. Dom forced her to retreat toward the corner of the room. He swung wild, catching a leather chair, gashing the material. White foam spilled like pus from an open wound. His next swing shattered a decorative urn on a bookshelf.

Angela screamed, backed toward the corner. Desperately, she threw herself on the floor and slid toward the revolver. Her hand snatched it, and she spun to turn the gun on her husband.

The blast roared through the room.

Dom flinched but remained upright. It was impossible to see where he'd been shot. If he were hurt, he didn't show it. He stood over Angela, set his feet, and raised the fire poker overhead like a warrior intent on slaying a beast.

With a gargling roar, he chopped the poker downward.

Ken fired.

The bullet struck Dom's lower back. Blood burst across his white button-down, a sight so satisfying Ken dropped to his knees. After twenty-four hours of nonviolence, he savored the release. It was as though his darkest grudges were freed through the barrel. He accelerated the satisfying process, pulling the trigger again and again, cycling madly through the near-empty cylinder until he unleashed another shot.

Dom flinched through a series of clipped, awkward dance steps. The steel poker thudded to the carpet, and he slumped forward, ready to drop. He grabbed a nearby shelf, fighting to stay upright when a bullet caught his neck. He made a sound like a wet hiccup and rocked forward, flopping onto the floor in front of his soon-to-be widow.

Ken kept shooting. Every blast diminished his hunger like biting into raw meat. He hammered the trigger repeatedly. And then the most bizarre thing happened.

The snubnose slipped from his grasp.

His hand muscles relaxed. The numbness left his fingers, and cool air brushed his tender palm. As his fingers straightened, a strange paranoia seized him. He felt abandoned. Naked. Weak.

A moment later the sensation passed.

The revolver thudded to the carpet.

His hand was empty.

Joyous shouts shook his throat. He laughed and collapsed onto his side. When he reached out to break his fall, his hand jolted with pain. After holding the gun for four straight days, his unbent fingers roared with sharp, hot electricity. His thumb was no better, and his exposed palm was as raw as an open blister.

Even so, he laughed. He laughed till he cried, then laughed some more. He might've done so for days, but Angela spoke and disturbed his reverie.

"Ken," she said. "You saved me."

He pushed himself upright and rubbed his eyes. Ahead, beyond Dom's blood-splattered corpse, sat Angela. She leaned against the bookshelf, holding her shoulder, grimacing. The strain on her face softened as they locked eyes.

"Thank you," she said, nodding at her deceased husband. "Listen, you should get out while you can. Cops'll be here soon."

That made sense. He should run. Catch up with Robby and Hannah. Get motoring before it was too late.

But, mysteriously, he found it impossible to leave. As he stared past her disheveled hair into her black eyes, a wild spectrum of emotions surged through him, from his highest hopes to his deepest regrets. He wanted to kiss her and kill her and everything in between.

Before him sat a lover who accepted him despite his highest crimes, but also a teacher who had molested their student.

That left him wondering about something.

"Angela," he said. "Why me?"

"Hmm?"

"Why me?" he said. "Why pursue me if you loved Pete? Why betray him?"

"I didn't betray anyone. I loved you both. Two amazing men. I know it's unconventional, but sometimes society's rules do more harm than good." She winced, clutching her wounded shoulder. "It's like I said in the pool the other night—I was tired of living the same movie over and over. Tired of limits, rules, repetition. Tired of being afraid." She nodded toward the doorway. "You'd better hurry."

Ken didn't like her answer, but she was right about him needing to hurry. He lumbered to his feet, cradling his sore hand. He tried to stretch his fingers, but the thunderous pain worsened. He'd have to make do. He looked around for something to safely hold the revolver with. Her Pooh Bear blanket was puddled on the couch. With his good hand, he grabbed it.

"Be safe in LA," she said. "I know you're upset with me, but if you change your mind, I'll meet you there."

From outside, he heard the faint whine of a police siren. He couldn't stay much longer. Looking at Angela, he saw someone repulsive but also someone twistedly human. Someone like him.

Once he left for LA, he would be a lost, lonely man. A man with six unbearable secrets and only Robby and Hannah to confide in. But those two couldn't understand him like Angela did. He doubted anyone else could.

As the siren's wail became louder, he pictured himself in his family's old LA apartment. Pictured himself sitting down to a plate of Mom's signature curry. He could smell the spices, taste the flavors as they danced over his tongue. When he finished chewing and looked across the table, there was Angela. And in her arms was their baby.

No. Not our baby. Pete's baby.

Then it dawned on him.

"Wait," he said, clutching the blanket. "When did you find out you were pregnant?"

"Recently. Why?"

Ken remembered Pete Chang sitting at the scuffed-up desk in his classroom. He recalled the boy's aggressive lack of eye contact. The moping face. The hostile glare. The abrupt trip to the bathroom. Flinching at the mention of girl trouble.

Now it all made sense.

"It was this week, wasn't it?" he said, struggling to control his tone. "This week you realized you were pregnant."

"Right," she said.

"And you told Pete."

"Of course I did."

"Did you tell him about your plan?"

"Plan? What plan?"

"Your plan to act like the baby was mine."

She opened her mouth but said nothing.

"When I found this yesterday," he said, pulling the broken sketch pencil from his pocket, "you said Pete had come to your house for help with Soward. Initially I thought he'd snapped the pencil because he was impatient, tired of waiting all night to hear what you had to say. But now I get it. He didn't snap the pencil out of impatience but because he couldn't stand seeing you with another man. He knew about your plan to invite me over and manipulate me."

"Manipulate you? No..."

"You used me!" With agonizing regret, he recalled the sex by the pond yesterday. Him trying to pull out. Her wrapping her arms around his back. Him with no choice but to come inside her. "You used me because you couldn't admit to the world that Pete was the father. You needed a stand-in, a *substitute*, but you couldn't blame your husband. That's why you went after me—the nearest available Asian man."

"No, that's not it at all!"

"It sure is. You didn't love me—you loved that I fit into your scheme."

"That's not it!" She eyed the fire poker on the ground between them. "I'll explain everything when we meet again. You need to leave."

Flashing blues and reds shimmered behind the window sheers.

Ken did need to leave. But if he left now, she might get away with everything. Even if he sent the police an anonymous letter, it wouldn't convince anyone. He had no concrete evidence against her. Just truth from the mouth of a liar.

With a sudden lunge, he reached for the fire poker.

So did Angela.

She snatched it from the floor with surprising speed. Then she was on her feet, swinging the weapon high and wide, daring him to get close.

Outside a car door slammed.

Time was running out.

There was only one serious choice.

Ken grabbed the gun—with his bare hand.

Her jaw fell. "Ken, are you out of your—"

He shot her before she could finish.

CHAPTER 63

KEN DOVE into the musty van, slammed the door, and crawled beneath the backseat until he was hidden. Hidden from Robby, from Hannah, from the outside world. He didn't want to be seen. Never again.

Robby raced off, tires squealing on wet pavement. Hopper woofed, limped over to Ken, and licked the stubble on his cheek. Ken, lying there uncomfortably in soaked clothes, welcomed the tickling pressure along his face. It took his mind off things, if only for a moment. He reached out and patted the pit bull's head like Dad always used to.

"You sure took your time, Ken," Robby said. "You *did* shoot her, right?"

Ken cleared his throat. "Yeah."

Robby and Hannah each sighed in relief.

"And you brought the gun?" Hannah asked.

"Yeah," Ken said.

Another double sigh.

Shutting his eyes, Ken pulled Hopper closer. The dog's unwashed fur carried the smell of their living room. It transported

Ken back to a rainy day months ago when he and Hopper had dozed on the couch while Dad snored in his recliner. There had been nothing particularly special about that day, but Ken welcomed the memory of it. He savored it. Then Hopper's snout poked against his jacket pocket. Against his gunhand.

"Almost at the highway," Robby said. "Ready to head west?"

"Yeah," Ken said, "but first do me a favor."

"What?"

"See if you can find a shooting range. An outdoor one. Somewhere we can regroup for a few minutes." Ken swallowed hard. "Gotta show you something. Something you should know about this gun."

Hannah located a place on her GPS. Twenty minutes later they arrived in a muddy parking lot somewhere out in the boonies.

Ken climbed out from under the backseat and glanced through the rain-streaked windows. Oaks and elms towered outside. Ahead, a dozen wooden tables were lined up beneath a weather-beaten roof. Target boards stood in the distance. The setup resembled a driving range at a golf course. Too bad Ken hadn't grabbed a cursed golf club that required him to win six major tournaments or something.

He exited the vehicle and pressed his feet into the mud. The soggy earth sank beneath his weight. His knees ached brutally. Without the adrenaline from earlier, he had nothing to energize him. Now he was a man at the end of his line, a line drenched in drying blood.

He approached the nearest wooden table. Posted on a nearby support beam were warnings, safety rules, and explicit reminders to "only point your gun at what you intended to shoot." An abandoned notepad lay on the ground nearby, scores jotted across the top sheet.

Hannah approached, holding her side. "What'd you want to show us?"

"Yeah, man, hurry this up," Robby said, checking over his shoulder. He bounced in place, still rattled by withdrawal. "Even if nobody's after us, I'd like to get back on the road. Driving helps me focus."

Ken saw no point in hesitating.

He removed his gunhand from his pocket.

Both of them flinched.

"What? How?" Robby said, backing away. "Thought you killed Angela."

"I killed her husband," Ken said. "Then I dropped the gun and... things got complicated. She had a weapon. The police were outside. There was no time, so I grabbed the gun again."

"Ugh." Hannah pinched the bridge of her nose. "Okay, don't panic... I'm sure we can find five scumbags to kill."

"Six," Ken said. "I'll need six."

"Six?" Robby said. "But didn't you pick it up to shoot Angela?"

"Exactly. I shot her. I didn't kill her."

"*What?*" Hannah gawked. "But she tricked you into going after Soward."

"She did. She also lied about some terrible things. But I didn't kill her."

"Why the hell not?"

"Had my reasons." Ken took a deep breath. "First was practical. There was a cop right outside. If I executed her, the cop would've chased me. But as long as she was screaming in pain, the cop had to help her."

Hannah frowned. "What other reason?"

Ken chewed his lip.

"We deserve to know," Robby said. "We're in this pretty deep with you."

Ken met his brother's eyes. "When I grabbed the gun again, I realized something. I realized that whether I killed her or not, I'd have a twenty-four-hour deadline. Killing her would lower my bullet count, but if Angela died, everyone would mourn her. They would never learn the truth."

"What do you mean?" Robby said.

"She molested a student of mine. And got pregnant by him."

"Eck," Hannah said. "Wait—then why'd she send you after Soward?"

"Soward saw Pete leave school with Angela the other day. After what happened in the principal's office this morning, I'm hoping Soward will piece everything together and notify the authorities. When that happens, things will get dark for Angela."

"Yeah." Robby itched his stomach. "I'm worried, though. She can tell the cops where we're headed. You probably should've killed her."

"I wanted to," Ken said, "but she deserves worse than death. I want her to face the guilt, the shame, the punishment. I'd rather kill six more people than give her an easy out."

Robby opened his mouth but didn't reply.

"There was one last reason," Ken said, staring at his gunhand. "Since Friday night I let this revolver push me around and dictate my actions. I killed in self-defense, in desperation, and in anger. Somewhere along the way I stopped looking for a peaceful solution. I lost myself. But when I had Angela in my sights, I had a chance to take a small piece of myself back. And so I took it."

The others waited, silent.

Then Robby stepped closer. "Think I know what you mean, man."

Tears prickled Ken's eyelids. Now that he'd brought them up to speed, it was time to head out. Once the cops ID'd him as the man who'd assaulted Soward and killed Dom Marconi, the challenge would steepen. That thought left Ken both mentally and emotionally exhausted. In his grasp the gun weighed heavy, and not from the fresh ammo supply.

"We'll fight through this," Robby said, grabbing Ken by the shoulders. "Fujimas don't give up on each other."

Ken found it hard to swallow. He was glad to have his brother back, even if there was plenty of baggage to sort out between them. He would have to make amends for Chrissie somehow. For now, the best he could do was close his eyes and wrap both arms around his brother.

Robby did the same. The hug felt good.

When Ken opened his eyes, he noticed Hannah staring at her feet. Her confession from earlier was something they needed to discuss, but that confrontation could wait.

"Hannah, come here," he said. "Group hug."

She waved it off. "I'm good."

"C'mon."

"Might rupture my stitches." She turned away, then hesitated. "All right. Fine. Wherever Michelle is, I hope she doesn't see this."

Hannah gingerly curled her arms around Ken and Robby. After a moment she grumbled about her stitches and headed back to the van.

Later, as they drove along I-80 West toward Ohio, Ken crawled out from under the backseat and looked outside. Aside from two tractor trailers, they had the rain-soaked highway to themselves. He eased his aching body onto the seat and leaned back against the head-rest. Hopper climbed up and used his thigh as a pillow.

Ken petted his furry companion and considered himself lucky, at least within the context of the past few hours. Rather than being in police custody or a body bag, he was leaving town with his dog, his brother, and his newfound sister. Somehow, they accepted him. Accepted every ugly decision he'd made, every shot he'd fired.

His thoughts were disrupted by a hard thud that shook the van.

Ken snapped to attention. He looked out the rear window to see what they'd hit. Just a pothole. It shrank into the distance as they continued on. Relieved, he turned forward, but in his peripheral vision he noticed a vehicle approaching from behind.

As it gathered speed, he recognized it.

The black Chevy Blazer. Same one from earlier this morning. He could tell by the dented front fender.

Ken braced himself for lights and sirens, but none came. Even several miles later nothing happened. The Blazer followed at an even distance, showing no intention of passing.

He could only wonder who was behind the wheel, why they were after him, what they wanted.

When the time came, he wouldn't let them push him around.

As the highway stretched ahead, a lone thought brought comfort.

Six down, six to go.

AUTHOR'S NOTE

Thank you for reading this book!

Please consider leaving a review on Amazon, Goodreads, Barnes & Noble, and Bookbub. Reviews are vital to authors like me, and your support goes a long way toward encouraging others to read my books. If you could spare a few moments to write a review, I would greatly appreciate it!

For updates on future novels and stories, join my mailing list at www.brandonmcnulty.com. It's a private list and your email address will never be shared with anyone else. You'll also receive a free gift for signing up!

Finally, be sure to connect with me on social media:

youtube.com/WriterBrandonMcNulty

twitter.com/McNultyFiction

facebook.com/McNultyFiction

amazon.com/author/brandonmcnulty

goodreads.com/brandonmcnulty

bookbub.com/authors/brandon-mcnulty

ACKNOWLEDGMENTS

Without question, the MVP of *Entry Wounds* is my longtime friend Vic Rushing. Vic dished out not one *but two* editorial ass-kickings, both of which significantly transformed this book. He has a gift for analyzing the inner workings of a novel—everything from character motivations to story themes—and not a single chapter escaped his ruthless criticism. I can't thank him enough for catching my blind spots.

Samantha Zaboski is dangerous with a red pen. Her bloodthirsty edit caught roughly fifty thousand errors and challenged me to rework character portrayals, dialogue exchanges, action sequences, and so much more. She supported me through every stage of the process, acting as my sounding board and my second set of eyes. Her fingerprints are all over this story, and I wouldn't have it any other way.

Chris Bauer has a gift for crushing egos. When I emailed him an early draft of *Entry Wounds*, I was feeling a little too satisfied with the story. Then I checked my inbox a week later and got my world rocked. Bauer pointed out glaring issues and challenged me to bolster the weaker parts of the manuscript. He's my go-to guy for a reality check, and his insight is unbeatable.

Paul Miscavage has a knack for telling me which ideas to run with. When he heard me say "undroppable haunted gun," his eyes lit up, and that was all the encouragement I needed to write this book. Paul was also the first to critique the opening chapters, and his early feedback was invaluable.

Sue Ducharme wowed me with her latest copyedit. She has a surreal talent for reworking and smoothing my unruly paragraphs, and she knows how to spice up my writing with just enough sizzle. Her turnaround time is always faster than I expect, and her insights always make me a better writer.

Major thanks to everyone who read the full manuscript and provided feedback. Gladys Quinn was the first to tackle *Entry Wounds* in its entirety, and her kind words and honest criticisms sent my revision process in the right direction. Brandon Ketchum convinced me to cut unnecessary chapters. K.R. Monin pointed out jarring character inconsistencies. Dan Volovic provided gun-related insights and helped me brainstorm several wild scenarios that made it into the final draft. Devin Olshefski suffered through an early draft but stuck with it and marked every piece of horrendous dialogue he could find. Zack Hammond and Elicia Messier read *Entry Wounds* in the late stages and challenged me to rethink the ending. Carol and Denny McNulty worked their proofreading magic and caught tons of typos and other brainless errors.

Special thanks to everyone who provided research-related input. Mike Dorbad, Steph Harkins, and Kate Lytle Rushing answered my oddball medical questions with patience and clarity. Dave Scherer, Dave DeWitt, and Richard Haas answered my legal and policework questions. Tom Meluskey did what he does best and told me what cars my characters should drive.

Thank you to everyone else who provided feedback and insight: Timothy Howard Jackson, Jessica Martin Gorbet, Kammi Lutz, Mark Lewis, and Michelle Rascon.

Finally, I'd like to thank you, the reader, for grabbing onto this book and not letting go!